Lycan
other tales of suspense

Michael WhiteBear Sims

(Magi Unega Yonv)

To: Shania
Hope you all enjoy the stories

Copyright © 2018

MICHAEL WHITEBEAR SIMS

All rights reserved.

ISBN: 9781691244744

first edition

10 August 2018

tenth revision

08 Septmber 2021

lousy amazon formatting

DEDICATION

I humbly dedicate this book to my Wife, children,
my wonderful and beloved parents, and Elisi,
(may they rest in peace)
and all my amazing friends.

I Love You Dearly!

CONTENTS

The Pevensiya Horror	*1*
This is my Hmmer	*15*
The Autumn of my 16th year	*16*
Voyage to the land of the Skrælings	*19*
Cherokee Mississippi River Magic	*30*
A Tale of True Evil	*42*
Lycanthropoi	*99*
Inner Earth Gods	*169*

ACKNOWLEDGMENTS

Patti, Gunther, Kelsey, Corin,
Wayne, Duane,
Nelli (Elisi)
Thomas (Dad), Rachel (Mom),
Ranell, Ruby, Ruth
Tom Jr.
and especially
Murphy, Franklin, Holly, and Triskell

Thank the GODS!

And thanks to my Tribe

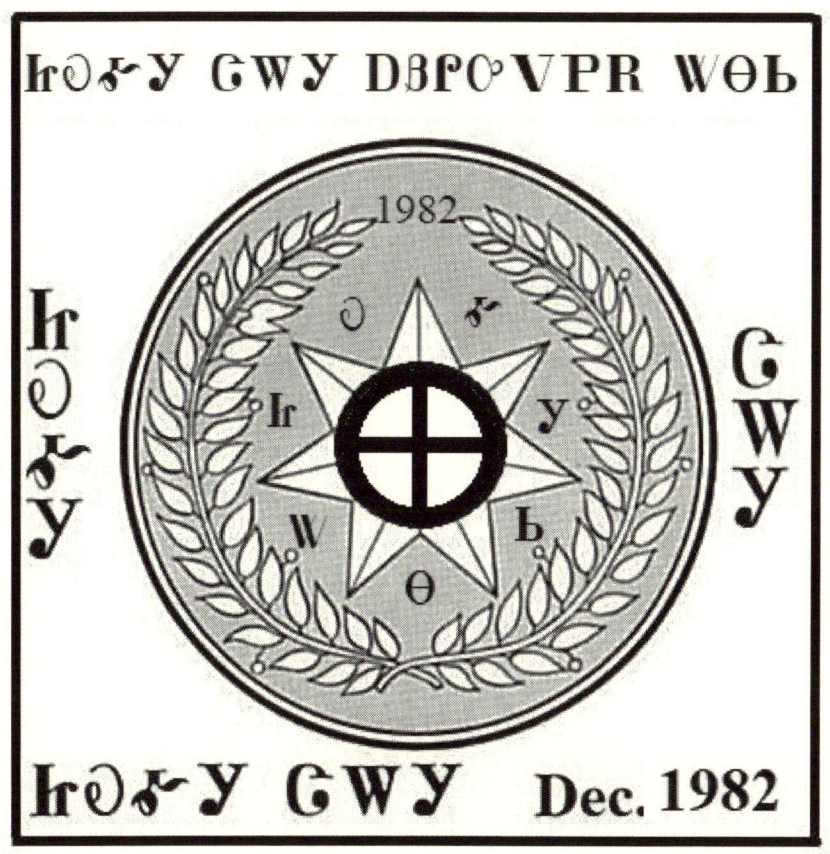

Tsikamagi Tsalagi Ayeliudotlvsv Tanasi

SGI!

1
THE PEVENSKIYA HOROR

Open report...
Pevenskiya Nuclear Enrichment Facility,
Built 1953, named for a top Nuclear Physicist, Sergei Aleksandrovich Pevenskiya
13 Sept 1970, Unknown event occurs without warning. Facility goes dark.
Military helicopters are seen flying in construction equipment and parts of prefab barricades.
More equipment and materials shipped in on the facilities rail line
Wall built all the way around the facility out to 100 meters.
Once complete all equipment and Facilities abandoned, and adjacent areas are cleared of people. Farms, Villages, towns abandoned.
Within the next five years someone or something from inside the Facility has knocked a rather large hole in the wall, roughly 5 meters in diameter.
In the early 1980's teenagers start visiting the Facilities, some never return, those that do scream about "things" in the shadows.
They report that their friends were devoured alive
Inspection by Authorities yield little to no results.
Findings include;
Trees grow thick up to the walls surrounding the Facilities
no wildlife in the area, including birds, and insects
Large portion of outer wall is toppled from within.
Large holes in wall of the Facilities, apparently made from within
Holes in Facilities are patched using steel reinforced concrete one meter thick
Hole in surrounding wall is repaired with steel reinforced concrete.
Findings one year later;
Large section of surrounding wall is toppled from within
More holes in walls of Facilities, apparently made from within
Inspectors reported missing after phoning in reports, just before the call ends screaming is heard
Military is dispatched to investigate, Military patrol is never heard from

Military vehicles found at site, but no troops
Military deems the Soldiers as deserters and closes case
anyone going near Facilities is never heard from again
Villagers from nearest town 6 kilometers away, investigate the Facilities for source of missing livestock and people
Government informed of actions of Villagers
Military arrives at Village which seems abandon, Military finds no Villagers, livestock, animals or insects, investigates the Facilities, and reports findings
On 13 Sept 1990, Military aircraft bomb area around the Facilities with napalm, entire forest around the Facilities are burned to ashes.
Attack helicopters and fighters watch for anything that might escape
Heavy bombers drop enough ordinance on Facilities to destroy a city the size of New York
Artillery rain shells on the Facilities from as far away as two miles
Arial inspection shows that the facilities and surrounding area has been turned to rubble
While being observed from air, a huge sinkhole opens under the area where Facilities were, the sinkhole is so deep that the bottom can't be seen from the air.
Aircraft flying over sinkhole disappear.
Walls fifty feet thick of stainless steel reinforced concrete made with ancient Roman formula erected around the sinkhole,
the area above the sinkhole made a "no fly" zone
All information hitherto collected by Russian Gov't is destroyed and all Official knowledge of Facilities denied, end of known data.

That is the official time line of the events, but I was there on 13 September 1970. I was a Scientist working at the Pevenskiya Facility. It was thirteen stories, eleven were underground. I worked all over the Facility and knew every inch of it. On that eventful day I was working in the Control Room of the lowest of the cooling chambers. We detected a surge of energy and we investigated. I went to look through the ten foot thick leaded glass window that looked into the chamber around the enrichment coils. There was an arc, so bright that you could not even be in the same room where it's light was. I rushed back out into the corridor and closed the door. It had been so bright that I was temporarily blinded. Victor Shenko, my dear friend and work companion was there to help me. For ten minutes I could not see at all, it was like you had looked at the sun and could see the orange after image, but many times more powerful. Victor helped me up to the Dispensary, where I was seeing much better. The Doctor examined my eyes and said that he couldn't find anything wrong, and since my eyesight was returning, said he wasn't worried. Indeed, by the end of my shift I could see as well as ever and the after image had faded altogether.

While that was happening to me, the arc in the enrichment coils had spiked and then ended. The coils were taken off line and inspected, whatever had happened, had melted the coils. The Facility shut down while new coils were being made ready. The replacement shouldn't take more than four hours. I was in the Main Control Room when the coil chamber was opened. We all heard the screams of the men as they were torn apart. We could hear their suits ripping and worst of all, we could hear the sound of the creatures that devoured them. Security had been alerted, though everyone in the control room was frozen in fear. We listened to the Security Team communicate over their radios. We heard them open fire on whatever it was they encountered, heard their screams as they too, were torn apart and devoured alive.

It was then, that all power failed at the Facility. Emergency lights came on and we all panicked. Dr. Gusarov, tried to keep everyone calm. He gave us flashlights and gas mask. Some of us were given weapons. The Tokerev pistol that I was handed felt useless. It was a 7.62 X 25 mm cartridge, and I had been well trained in it's use by the Military and Spetsnatz. I have never before in my life been truly scared, until that day. In war, I had been shot several times, stabbed with a bayonet, and been in an explosion when the armoured car I was riding in, was hit by artillery shell. I have faced the enemy many times and have been trained by Spetsnatz to fight with nothing more than my hands. Against a man, I had no worries, but now I was as scared as a baby in the night. I was physically shaking, and the Tokerev gave me no comfort. Not even an AK-47 would have made me more comfortable. We had to climb twelve stories of stairs to get out of the building. What was worse is that it wasn't just twelve flights of stairs straight up, but they were broken up and in different areas, so you could go up two flights then you had to walk across the Facility on that level to get to the next stair case which would only go up one to two flights.

   Dr. Gusarov asked if I was okay, and we led everyone out of the Main Control Room. Out in the corridor, our flashlights were useless, they no longer worked steadily. They blinked on and off erratically, which unnerved us even more There were thirty seven of us trying to move quietly through the corridors. We had to go into the Maintenance Bay on level twelve and across to the stairs on the other side. It was very cold in here, and we had to cross a huge open expanse of floor piled with equipment and parts. We could hear something moving around and our flashlight failed altogether. The emergency lights were on, but offered little help in the stacks of crates. We ran in a long line towards the door on the other side of the Maintenance Bay. We had not gotten far, when a couple of people screamed out in the rear of our line. Panic ensued and everyone made a run for the stairs. One of the Security men started shooting towards the rear of our lines and shot four of our group by accident. They fell and were dragged off into the dark screaming.

   I can never forget the sounds of those men and women, so unlike the screams you hear in war. Those screams of war are only from pain from your wounds. These screams were from the very bottom of your soul. It wasn't just pain, but sheer terror, and uttermost dread. It was if their very souls were being devoured and they being emptied of their being. I cannot adequately describe the sound or depth of the screams they made, I have never heard their likes before, and I can never forget them, for I hear them every time I close my eyes.
Rimma Lobachevsky, a beautiful Nuclear Physicist that I had been talking to since she started here, fell and cried out. I turned to help her up, when I saw it in the half light behind her.
Well I saw its form. Either it was once human, or it's form vaguely resembled human form, but much more hideous. I thank what ever god or gods for not letting me see it in its full hideousness. I aimed my pistol and shot it, in what I must assume was it's deformed head. It

turned to look at me and it's eyes glowed like an animals, but brighter. It made an indescribable noise and started for me. I pulled her up and lifted her over my shoulder, and ran for all I was worth for the stairs. My training in Spetsnatz and the Military was paying off. I passed everyone, even bearing Rimma over my shoulder. She had mercifully passed out. Several others had already made it, and the door had been slammed shut behind me. I could hear the screams of those behind me as they were taken. I knew that nothing alive was left behind. We locked and barricaded the door and started climbing up the stairs. We zigzagged through the Facility and were met by the Military when we reached the surface. We were given a medical check up and removed from the site.

I remained only long enough to give a report to the Commanding Officer. He was rude to me until I informed him of my training in Spetsnatz, at which, he took me more seriously. As I was being transported away to the Hospital, I saw the Military building walls around the Facility with a one hundred meter "no man's land" between the walls and the Facility, and I knew that nothing could stop those things that came from beyond. They had been pulled through into this world, this dimension from **between** other dimensions that exist simultaneously with ours.

What they are, is beyond our ability to understand, as the minds of mortal men cannot fully grasp what lies between this dimension and the next. Our minds were not made to understand, and I thank the gods for that! Rimma and I were married, two lost souls joined by the cosmic horror that surrounds and flows through us. We are the last of those that survived. We are aged beyond our years.

Both her and I, left that facility that night with white hair, though she was only twenty nine and I was thirty one. We both had had the black hair and Blue eyes of our Russian heritage, before that night. Rimma was still just as beautiful as she had always been, but you could tell the depth of the tragedy in her eyes, her gorgeous eyes. And we knew when something happened at the Facility. We knew and we could feel it in our souls. My Rimma died the day the sinkhole opened. I came here to die trying to return those cosmic horrors to the spaces in between the dimensions, from which they came. That's why I stole the nuclear warhead and the Neutron bomb and I know how to send them back. I am doing it so that my Rimma may rest in the peace that we could no longer find in life. I am doing it to save the world. I am not a madman.

I am Timofei Aleksandrovich Pevenskiya, son of the Great Physicist Sergei Aleksandrovich Pevenskiya, and I will save the world from what I saw that night. It was neither whole or wholesome, it's form was vaguely humanoid, but it's body twisted and mishapen. It was hideous in countenance, with a large bulbous head with horns like a rams. Tentacles where its drooling mouth should have been, and four eyes that burned with the fury of the abyss. It's arms were long and from the elbows down, were sinuous tentacles with hands, if they can be described as such, that had three boneless writing tentacle like fingers with large, round pads on the ends. Those hands that wrapped around the arms in a steely grip and held them motionless, before the tentacled mouth tore open their chest, and devoured their heart and lungs, and ripping the life from them. Those four eyes that told me that they consumed not just the life, but the soul of those that fell that day, and the weeks and months following. I will send them back to the hell from which we had brought them.

HEADLINES AROUND THE WORLD:

RUSSIANS CREATE MINI BLACK HOLE IN EXPERIMENT

13 Sept 1999

Today Russian Scientist Timofei Aleksandrovich Pevenskiya, son of the Great Physicist Sergei Aleksandrovich Pevenskiya, in a test that was deemed a success and a great tragedy, lost his life when he succeeded in creating a micro-black hole. The Top Secret Facility was destroyed immediately after the creation of the micro black hole Scientist report, Scientist from all over the world are calling it a tremendous breakthrough for Science and will be sorting through the data for the next twenty years. The Scientific community is also mourning the loss of one of it's greatest Scientist as well. The Scientist at the Large Hadron Collider in Cern, Switzerland have suspended operations for two days in remembrance of Dr. Pevenskiya. NASA released a statement saying; "His dedication will be remembered by us, as will his contributions to Physics. He was a great man and will be remembered with the greats, Newton, Einstein, Sagan, Feinstein, Oppenheimer and Fermi." More news as we receive it...

There are no records of the Pevenskiya Nuclear Enrichment Facility. All records of the Scientist and Staff are gone.
End of report...

2
THIS IS MY HAMMER

This is my Hammer.
There are many others like it, but this one is mine.
My Hammer is my best friend. It is my life.
I must master it as I must master my life.
Without my Faith, I am useless.
Without me, my Hammer is the single most powerful symbol of our Faith,
Until we rescue our Holy Symbols from the ignorance and stupidity of weak minds.
I must keep my Honour true.
I must be more Honourable than my enemy, who is trying to kill me.
I must show him Honour by example.
I WILL.
Before the Gods, I swear this creed:
My Hammer and I are defenders of our Faith, Folk, and Family,
We are the masters of our enemy,
We are the saviors of our Faith.
So be it, until there is no enemy, but peace.
WASSAIL.

Michael Sims, 2001

This is mine and mine alone!
I wrote it, accept no other claims, as they are false!

3
THE AUTUMN OF MY SIXTEENTH YEAR

I always enjoyed walking to Gene's house, although I had a car, I just preferred to walk to certain places. I guess it was just the energy of youth. Dana, the girl that I loved, had been killed over a year past now, by a drunk driver. Her family moved back to Connecticut or New England somewhere. I still missed her mightily, but had other concerns now to crowd out the loneliness. My Mother had her first heart attack and we sold our house on Yale road, one block west of the Raleigh Springs mall, and moved to Frayser, into some apartments managed by my parents friends. Thus my being only about nine blocks from Gene. It was about seven thirty and already dark. I like to walk through the woods between my apartment and his house, it added a block to the walk but I enjoyed it. In those woods had once stood a small house, gone now but for the foundations, overgrown shrubs and a low barb wire fence covered in creepers.

I was walking through the leaves, trying my best to not make any noise and was doing a superb job, when up ahead I heard a low noise past the creeper fence. I ducked down and continued over to the fence, peering over I saw two older teenagers making out on a fallen tree. I watched for only a moment, then made a slight noise. The girl straightened up and looked around, the guy was of course oblivious, and shrouded in his befuddled hormone choked cloud. They started kissing again and the guy was running his hand up her blouse and she was rubbing his crotch. Amused I made another soft sound, sort of cat like and she again jumped and looked about.

"What was that?" she asked looking around.

"Nothing, just the wind." He said and started kissing her again. They soon forgot the noise and proceeded to be horny teens, so I made another noise, not so soft and as menacing as I could muster. They both jumped and looked about. Neither spoke but tried to penetrate the darkness with their sight.

I made another low growling sound, like a cat makes when confronting another cat in his yard. You could see the relief on the boys face, even in the heavy gloom.

"J-just a cat!" he said sounding relieved. He pulled her to him and they were soon engaged in the make out session again. I waited and bided my time until he had her shirt unbuttoned and her breast exposed. She had his pants unzipped and unbuckled and had just freed his willie and was stroking it, when I gave them another dose of the cat call from Hell.

She pulled away and he stood up rebuttoning his pants. I continued to growl and hiss.

"Go check it out and shoo them away!" She whispered to him.

"Umm, sure. Okay." He said looking at her and walking very slowly towards the fence row and me. He had gotten about half way between her and I when I leapt over the low fence, screaming like the dead risen, with my arms above my head.

They both screamed, but he had turned and was running for his life, knocking her down and screaming the entire time that he ran. I jumped at her and she vaulted over the fallen tree and was soon catching up to her boyfriend, shirt still open and breast bouncing vigorously.

I didn't see how far they ran, as I was on the ground gasping for breath and crying from laughing so hard. I don't know how long I lay there struggling to breath, but at some point I was able to stumble to my feet and trudge the three blocks to Gene's house. His Mom answered the door and called her husband trying to get a coherent word from me.

I was covered in leaves and my face was beet red. My dusty face was tear streaked and I must have looked really terrible. I know they must have imagined the worst, I know that I looked like I had fallen through the woods and landed in a pile of leaves and sticks.

"Had I been hurt? Was everything okay at home? Had I been hit by a car? Did she need to call my parents?" Her and Larry looked me over, questioning me, while Gene came from the back. They got me a drink of water and I was able, with much laughter on my part to tell them what had just happened. They broke out in laughter at my telling of the story, and Gene was jealous that he wasn't present to see it all.

I still recall the scene on that long ago Autumn night, and it still makes me chuckle.

4
VOYAGE TO THE LAND OF THE SKRÆLINGS

It was late spring in Heidaby and we were preparing for the Summer voyages. The past nine voyages had been very profitable and we had become wealthy men. Bëorn had heard of stories of lands far to the west, and desired to see them. We purchased so much trade goods, more than usual, and loaded our supplies into his knarr, named the Sea Dragon. The ship had forty-four oars with a large red sail with Bëorn's personal symbol of a bright golden yellow Sun wheel with his double tines on it. It was his runar, or lucky rune that had been seen by the Godhi on the day of his birth.

The runar had been inscribed upon a piece of walrus ivory and given to his Father Sigurd for the baby Bëorn. He still carried it to this day, but now had the runar carved on to everything he owned. He had some of the finest silver and goldsmiths to make jewelry for him and his wife with his runar as the main design. The Sea Dragon had been carved over most of it's surface facing the sea with runes and his runar. The eyes of the Dragon Head on the prow had the runar carved and set with fine amber, and everyone that rode with Bëorn wore his runar, for luck. Many had voyaged with him and few had ever died upon those voyages. All became wealthy and Bëorn was a very generous man.

And so the day came to set out upon our voyage, and all our families were there. Mead horns were passed from man to man so that we could toast the voyage. When we had cleared the shore and before we dropped our oars, the Godhi blessed us and Bëorn stood at the prow and yelled at the top of his voice the name of the God of Gods, "ODIN!" He poured almost all of the mead from the great horn that he held into the sea, and then the last into the mouth of the Dragon Head prow. An enemy monk had been brought onboard, that had been captured on the last voyage, and he was sacrificed to Odin, his blood collected in a cauldron, and it too was poured into the Dragons mouth, and the sea. The body of the monk was carried out of the harbor and dumped into the sea, it too was an offering for Odin.

As soon as we were out of sight of land the sail was unfurled and set and the Sea Dragon sped through the waves as if it had grown wings. We toasted Bëorn and his great ship, and thanked the Gods for the opportunity to be here with the greatest Dane in the world. We were sailing first to Gokstad in the land of the Nords, and would take on fresh water and more provisions, as well as some of their fine trade goods. We were wealthy and purchased much trade goods, and jewelry. Bëorn purchased a piece of a star that had fallen from the sky and had been formed into an arrow hung from linen line. When held aloft, it always pointed to the North, even inside of buildings. It had cost him twenty times it's weight in gold, and he paid it gladly. We spent the night in Gokstad, and we ate and drank our fill, not knowing if there was going to be good hunting or not, of if we were going to encounter any more towns the way we were going.

Bëorn talked to many Ship owners and asked about the West. Most told him of settlements and where they were. Bëorn would mark them upon his skin maps. He had long ago gotten fine maps from mapmakers on the great lands of the Frieslanders. He had even traveled to Sikiloy and Miklagard, where the Byzantians are. He was a Jömsviking, and guarded the Emperor there for a short time. He had traveled farther than most Viking kings had travelled, and was far richer that most kings. We were all back on board before dawn, as we would leave with the tide.

There was nothing as exciting as speeding over the waves in a great ship. The sea spray was refreshing and we would cast nets out when we saw schools of fish. We ate well and gambled when we were upon the open seas. We came upon another long ship and we wagered with them as to who had the faster ship, and shouted insults back and forth. We pulled away from them until they sounded a horn in surrender. We pulled up along side them and toasted them. The Captains exchanged information about where they had been and were going. The other ship was the Jelling Dragon, and were our countrymen. They were headed to Hjaltland, which was on the way to Reykjanes.

We sailed together as far as Hjaltland, and would race there. Once again we would beat them there. We arrived an hour before they did and stood upon the piers and jeered at them and hurled insults. They would have to buy our lodging, drinks and food, and we were going to make sure that it cost them dearly. We stayed two days here in Hjaltland, and purchased some fine woolen garments and thick woolen capes, for the cooler lands farther North, we purchased extra for trade. Here we bought slaves to be sold in Reykjanes, because we were told that it would be profitable. They were monks from a place called Lindsfjarna, or something like that.

They all seemed to be loyal to one of the older monks that cursed us, and called us heathens and pagans and said that we would burn in hell. We didn't understand most of what they said, but Bëorn warned them to not invoke the name of Hel, on his ship. He told them that the Goddess Hel was often easily invoked and did not want to jeopardize this voyage. The monk stood and cursed all to burn in hell's deepest pit in the sight of Luchifern and was making some sort of hand gesture when Bëorn grabbed him and drug him to the prow, stripped him and bound him to it. Bëorn gave him one last chance to be silent, which only made the monk more vociferous. Bëorn grabbed him and ripped out his tongue with his bare hands. He then bound it in the mouth of the Dragon prow.

The other slaves were put in the rear of the ship, and kept out of sight of the prow. Bëorn had the monks legs cut off and cooked, then they were fed to the other monks. Then the arms, and then the offal of the monk was fed to them. What was left of him was thrown overboard to feed the fishes. They were fed the leftover from our scraps for the rest of the voyage and when we reached Reykjanes, they asked about the head monk, Bëorn smiled and told them that he had served a most useful purpose indeed, and that they had been eating him during the voyage. Many wretched violently and emptied their stomachs, all fell upon their knees begging for Yaysoo krisstay for forgiveness. They became so troublesome that Bëorn slaughtered them all as a sacrifice to Odin.

It seems that there were some of the Reykjanes that had converted to this Krisschin religion and they were upset about the slaying of the monks. The local Chieftain inquired as to their deaths and Bëorn said that he would explain himself only to Odin, Tyr, or Thor, and no man deserved a explanation as to what Bëorn did with his own property. The Chieftain agreed of course and explained that this Krisschin religion made men soft. We found lodging for the night and in the morning purchased as much supplies as we could carry. It seemed that there was indeed a land further West called Grœnenlandr, and that there was a land of forest beyond that. Bëorn was even more excited to get started and we set sail at once.

Out at sea, we came across some whales with long tusk and caught a few. Bëorn got first pick of the long spiral tusk, and it took one that was ten feet long, and said that he would use it for a walking stick. The meat was good and we had a nice stew from them, as well as salting the rest of the meat for the journey. Bëorn and the crew were in very high spirits and the men sang songs and had contest in which they insulted each other to see who could come up with the best insult. The weather had been fine so far, but Bëorn could tell that a storm was coming tonight. The entire Western sky was black and soon there was such lightning, that we knew that Thor was battling Storm Giants or Jormungandr, or maybe both. We all started praying to Thor, Tyr and Odin, as we stowed the sail and erected a tent to cover our supply hold and to get most of the crew out of the rain.

Jormungandr was really churning the sea with his coils in the battle with Thor. Waves were like mountains and the sea tossed us about. Bëorn, Ragnar and Olaf held the rudder in position and kept us headed into the waves. The storm moved very fast as I suspect Jormungandr wanted to get away from Thor and Mjolnir as fast as possible! Obviously Thor won this battle with Jormungandr, and the sea soon calmed again, and the clouds parted. We soon caught sight of land and knew that we had found the Green Land, though it would prove not to be that green by light of day. Normally the Sailors would find the largest mountain in Iceland and sail away from it toward the Green Land. You would lose sight of the mountain in Iceland and soon could see the highest mountain in the Green Land.

We sailed her coast until we came to the settlement called Brattahlid, and we pulled our ship up to the dock. We came ashore with gifts for the Local Chieftain, Erik the Red, and was met by him and his retinue. We gave him and his Wife fine gifts, and we were invited to feast with him as his guest. We contributed some of the whale meat and two kegs of the finest mead from home. His hall was fine and large and we feasted well, and made many toast, and when all had gotten inebriated we started with the traditional boast. They became more and more outrageous as the mead flowed, until we were all too inebriated to stand, and one by one we dropped off to sleep. All that is except for Bëorn. He kept his wits about him, being in a strange land and in a strange hall, but the old king could not keep his senses after drinking our mead and his wife had the servants took him to bed.

The servants had cleared the feast hall of food and dishes while everyone slept, and did so without waking a single person. They brought pillows, blankets and skins for those in the hall asleep. They tended the fires, and made sure that the hall was kept warm all night long. The serving girls that had been molested by the visitors were awakened and sent to their beds, and the guest were made as comfortable as possible. They were shown the very best hospitality, as should be expected of a great host.

In the morning the men were awakened gently with fresh mead, and bowls of hot water to wash the sleep from their faces. Food was brought in and soon all were awake and eager to explore the market and do some trading. They had brought much from home and from Hjaltland. We found an area at the market and set up a store and sold all of the wares that we had set out, plus bought much ivory charms and jewelry from the locals. Each man stowed his portions of the money, and paid Bëorn his share, which he stowed in a strong box aboard the Sea Dragon.

Already we had grown more wealthy and it had been exceedingly profitable. Bëorn asked the men if they wanted to go on and discover if there were truly lands in the West, or if they wanted to return home as wealthy men. But we all had the desire to go on, it having been for the most part a very easy trip so far. There were Natives here called Skrælings, and they insisted that there were indeed lands to the West and not far either. They called it the Land of Timber and said that there were Skrælings there as well, but that they spoke another language.

We purchased supplies, and as much of the ivory trade goods that we could get. We purchased beads, and mirrors, knives and hand axes to trade to the Skrælings. We were feasted again by the Chieftain Erik the Red, and sent off with his blessings and with more trade goods that he gave to us as gifts. His Son, Leif Eriksson, had sailed there already and gave us a map to the area that he had settled, and gave us much useful information. We thanked them profusely for their generosity and for the honor they had shown us.

In the morning we parted as friends and were excited by the prospects of new lands. Leif Eriksson had established a settlement called Vinland to the West and South, and we would be able to rest and make further plans before exploring further. We set out early the next morning for Vinland and the last bit of civilization we would see until we returned from the land of the Skrælings. It would prove to be a very vast land and we would only see a tiny portion, those along the great inland seas and the rivers. We loaded the supplies and set sail for Vinland.

The trip south along green coastal lands covered in ancient trees, and with many streams and rivers. We passed large bays and rivers headed into the interior lands, but first we sailed for Vinland and Leif Erickson's hospitality. We spent a week in Vinland and spoke with many that had set foot upon the coastal lands. The Skrælings they said were friendly enough and eager to trade for steel weapons and glass beads. The Skrælings also enjoyed the mead as well and were very happy to trade for it.

They would eagerly trade food and provisions for he goods that were attainable here and were considered almost the cheapest of trade goods. They would also act as guides and take you to other Skræling tribes that would be eager to trade as well. Tales of great lands and rivers and lakes were told by the Skrælings, but were considered to be lies told to impress the Danes. One of the other Jarls, Ketill Shield-breaker, would take them to the large bay and introduce them to the Skræling Chief Tall Walking Bear, whom he has had good dealings with. He advised them to give many gifts of knives, axes and beads, as well as mead. That would give them a good impression, and in return he would send warriors with them that would make introductions to other tribes, for as far on their journey as they could go.

Many more knives, axes, flint and steel fire starters, and beads were purchased, indeed much of our stock of coin and gems were exchanged for these trade goods. Our hopes is that we could make it far inland and trade with as many different tribes as we could, then return in a year or so to start our own Settlements, and become Jarls ourselves. That is where the real wealth is at, and also the real power, to become a Jarl by your own wit and prowess, is to gain fame and to win honour.

We set sail in the morning and followed Ketill Shield-breaker to the meeting place, which was the settlement of the Skrælings. Several of the Skrælings spoke a fair amount of our language which made it easy. After Ketill made the introductions we feasted and gave gifts to the Skræling Chief and to his warriors. Ketill and his men left after mid day and we talked to the Chief and made the arrangements to go farther inland through the great bay. The Skrælings said that their tribe was L'Nug which means "The People" in their language.

We traveled through the bay to a river and down the river to a very large lake. Our L'Nug interpreter, Standing Wind, introduced us to the Iracoi tribe and they took us across the great lake called Niigani-Gichigami to a river then an even bigger lake called Waabishkiigoo-gichigami. We met with several small six man boats, that had no sails but could be paddled with great speed. The tribe was call Erielhonan, and our Iracoi warriors asked if we could trade some of our iron axes for one of the kanue boats, which we did. We thanked them and they rowed back towards their lands. We were able to communicate with them through Standing Wind, and they lead us to one of their settlements called Gichi-Biitoobiigong. We were surprised at how large it was, and we marveled at the wooden palisades and long houses. They reminded us of home and some of us became homesick. They had even larger versions of the kanue boats that would hold up to twenty or thirty men.

They were armed with a variety of weapons, spears with stone or bone points, clubs of wood or stone, knives of stone or bone, spear throwers, and bows and arrows also with bone or stone points. The use of metal was totally unknown to them. The warriors showed off their new axes and introduced us to their Chief Wind Through Trees. Our interpreter was able to broker a deal to be guided to the largest of lakes where we were told was a river that flowed South and became a huge, great, fast flowing river, called the Misi-ziibi. They say that there are tribes along that river that build huge mounds and worship strange Gods.

We were asked to stay and feast with them, and we accepted happily. The Long houses were huge and could hold up to sixty people. Entire families, spanning generations would live in one. We brought out some mead to share with our host and many got so drunk they were unable to stand. We traded weapons and beads, and other trinkets with them, and many of their women were curious about us. Almost all of us found a woman to share a bed with that night. We enjoyed ourselves immensely, but never let down our guard. We were cut off from our ship, and there were few men left to guard it. However no harm came to anyone, and we gave thanks to the Gods for our luck so far.

In the morning we were given much smoked meat that would keep for a good while, as well as fruits and vegetables. We loaded sweet water from nearby springs and made ready to sail. The men said good bye to the women who seemed reluctant to let them go, but we parted and boarded our ship. Many of the men and women rowed along with us for a ways in the great kanue boats. Then waved us on as we set sail and sped over the waves of the great Waabishkiigoo-gichigami. We soon came to a river which opened into a small lake the Natives called Waawiyaataa, and sailed over it very quickly to the river on the other side.

Many Native tribesmen gathered and watched the passing of the Sea Dragon, and no doubt were in awe at it's size and sped, Mayhap they mistook it as one of the kanue boats of their Gods. We came to the great Naadwewi-gichigami, which was truly large, we could not see both shores. And though it was close to the first of Summer, the winds blew cold from the North. Because the wind was strong, the Sea Dragon cut across the waves and we were glad that we would soon be off this great water.

We came at last to a narrowing of the land and we passed through to the Ininwewi-gichigami and were speeding to the far shore of the lake. These lakes seemed to unsettle the men, who thought that evil spirits dwelt deep within the waters. We were told that there was still another large lake that we were passing on our right called the Anishinaabewi-gichigami, and we were glad to hear that we would not have to cross it as well. We came at last to the Settlement at the mouth of the river, called Gaa-zhigaagowanzigokaag. Here we met the Meshkwahkihaki tribe that would lead us to the Potawatomi tribe and we traded with all of them. The mead being the most prized of goods..

Here our interpreter would leave us to go back to his lands. We gave him much in way of trade goods to get him back to his people. We thanked him and from here on out, we were on our own, among strange wild people, who knew not metal weapons, but who would outnumber us from here to the end of our travels. We sailed down the river which widened as we went further South-West. Storms hit the Great Lakes behind us and they continued for many days. We dropped out anchor and rode out the storms. The river rose and over flowed the banks, and soon our ship drifted with the flood. We pulled up our anchor and let the ship float down river.

The sail served as shelter for the crew, except for the pilot, who stood out in the rain and guided us. We took turns until we found some trees sticking up out of the river to tie up to. We slept and rested for two more days when the storms finally ceased. The river was very wide now and had spread out over much of the land, and we could not tell where the banks of the river was. We kept the Sea Dragon in the middle of the river to avoid running aground, and set our sail. We sailed until it started getting dark and we found a place to tie up again. We kept our fire small, and used our sail to hide the light from any tribesmen that may be around. In the morning we all put out oars and rowed because Bëorn said we needed to.

We found a place where there was land close by and we sailed close to shore. We saw deer and other animals and we decided to go ashore and hunt for fresh meat. We soon had two deer for our cook pots and the men were much cheered by that. The gloom of the Great Lakes and the weather had taken it's toll upon us, and now with the setting sun and fresh meat, we were in better spirits, and even opened our last keg of mead. We had an enjoyable evening and sang songs of our heroes and the Gods.

In the morning we ate a quick meal and set our sail and soon came to the Great river, that they had called the Misi-ziibi. With the flood waters it looked more like a Great inland ocean, except here and there were islands and large areas of trees with their roots submerged. As we sailed further South, the warmer it got, and in some places the insects were so bad that we had to set the oars and row to get away from the great clouds of them. We sailed from morning til dusk and would tie up around some trees, where we would gather wood and sometimes find animals to kill and eat. From time to time we would see a bluff off to the East. Tribesmen would gather and watch us. Sometimes they were afraid and ran away when we approached, sometimes they were hostile and would attack, and we would easily defeat them.

Occasionally we would find some that were friendly and we would trade with them. Some times we would be welcomed to their Settlements and we would enjoy ourselves, and the company of the women. Once we were taken into their village and treated as guest, then when we were asleep, they attacked us. But we never slept all at the same time and would keep a watch, and give silent alarm. They did not stand a chance against our shield wall and our steel spear points and swords. Then we would slaughter them all, just as they intended to do to us. We would take the women and use them and then sell them to another tribe further down the river.

Many of us had become ill and most of us desired to return home, but no one wanted to go back the same way. We knew that all river lead to the sea, and knew that this one must do so as well, and so would set sail and sail as fast as the ship would carry us. From time to time we would stop and trade for food and fresh fruit. We were told that just a days journey down the river was the Chatah village of Chucalissa, which was a trading village and that there were old people there that said that there was a great salty water further South. We were told that we could get a large amount of provisions there for the journey. We came to a place to tie up for the night, and tried to rest. Many men were still ill, two had gotten worse and one had died. We built a pyre and burned his body, and lamented his loss. We were encouraged by stories of the sea though and determined to go further.

As always we set a watch, but even the watch could not see into the gloom of the night. A rain of arrows showered down upon us, and tribesmen swam out and around our ship and tried to climb aboard from the river side of the ship. We hauled up our anchor and pushed off with the oars. Some stood with a shield over those that rowed and we sailed out of range. We caught one of the tribesman on our ship, and we tried to communicate with him. He was a Chickashan warrior his name was Bloodglutton. We bound hid hands but when we weren't looking he sprang to his feet and kicked us.

He was nimble and could roll and spring back up somewhere else and kick. He kicked Hrafn the Black in the throat and crushed his windpipe and he died. When we caught Bloodglutton, we chopped off his legs and threw them in the river. We bound his stumps so that he would not bleed out and hung him from the Dragons mouth at the prow. This of course brought hostility from the other Chickashan warriors, and we were weakened now with fevers and chills, and still it grew hotter and more pestilential with the biting and stinging insects.

When we drifted too close to shore, the Chickashans would shower us with arrows, poisoned darts and spears, until only Bëorn was left. He spilled oil over the bodies of his crew and readied the Sea Dragon to be a funeral pyre for them all. He was ill, but still would fight until he was no longer able to use a weapon. He would not go easy and the Valkyries would take him to the Halls of Valhalla. He saw the Chickashan warriors upon the bluff and he shot his bow at them. His bow was much more powerful than those the Chickashans used and he was able to kill them at a greater range. He used his bow until he was out of arrows, then stood behind his shield with his spear ready. He had oil spilled everywhere and had a fire ready. All he would have to do is kick the remaining bucket over and the oil would flow to the fire and it would set the ship on fire.

The Sea Dragon ran aground and the Chickashans sprang aboard the ship. Bëorn had spread the oil around, so that once they were on the ship, they would not be able to get off without going through the burning oil. Many of the warriors fell before Bëorn's spear, until it was riven in twain, and he drew his sword Gunnlogi, Battle flame, and he continued to cut them down. He kicked the bucket of oil over as twenty warriors sprang aboard the ship and they slipped in the oil and caught fire. Bëorn let out a fierce battle cry and started hacking them to pieces. Their Chief was aboard and turned to flee when he came face to face with Bëorn. Bëorn swung his shield but the Chickashan stepped aside and thrust his spear at Bëorn. It sank into his throat and Bëorn swung Gunnlogi, sinking it deep into the Chickashan chiefs head. They fell together to the deck and was quickly consumed by the flames. The Sea Dragon burned to the waterline and sank, the muddy bottoms covering the wreckage and the bodies, where they would remain for a twelve hundred years.

5
CHEROKEE MISSISSIPPI RIVER MAGIC

Cherokee Mississippi River Medicine magic

My Grandmother or Elisi was Tsalagi, or Cherokee and very proud of the fact, as well as Choctaw, and Chickawsan. Which you Whites call Chickasaw. She still spoke some Cherokee, and she called me Tsuts, which is an affectionate term that means boy. It's a shortened form of the word Atsutsa, which can be used as an affectionate term for any Tsalagi man. When I was born, she said that she saw the sign of the sign of the Bear over me, and said that it was a Great White Bear, and so that is what she called me Unega Yonv, White Bear.

Grandmother, told me many things and taught me that the Tsalagi had many medicines and magics that the White men didn't have, and that one of the most powerful was the Mississippi River, which had

a great spirit, called Wailing Woman, who would help with good and bad medicine magic. Mississippi was the French rendering of the Anishinaabe words Misi-ziibi which means Great River. Tsalagi Medicine isn't some deep dark secret, it's like any form of study and you have to be dedicated to it. Unfortunately with the Removal Act, most of our Elders died on the Trail of Tears. My family stayed behind, and thereby became outcast in the Tsalagi community. But we still had our Family Bible, printed in the late 1700's and filled with Tribal, and Clan information, and I could look in there and see my Ancestors. Grandmother would explain the writing that was in there. It was Tsalagi, created by the Great Sequoia, who gave it to our Ancestors in 1825, and made sure that every Tsalagi could read and write, in our language. I tried to learn as much as I could.

Elisi would teach me about medicine and spirits, and said that everything had a spirit, and that if you could live in harmony with these spirits, you could live well. But you couldn't do it in cities. Too much motion, noise and disturbance. You had to live outside of the towns to hear the spirits. I would spend summers with her and she would teach me things. The odd thing was that her Tsalagi beliefs did not coexist with her Pentecostal beliefs, and she seemed, like many of our People, divided. My Mother and Father did not share elisi's beliefs because they were Christians. The odd thing was, no matter how devout my parents were, they left my spirituality up to me, even at three years old.

So I grew up experiencing all kinds of spiritual influences. At five, I started going to a Catholic church with my friends Pietro and Maria, or Peter and Mary as everyone else called them. Only their parents called them that in their home. Peter was an Altar boy, and I got to try that as well. The Priest was always telling me facts about Christianity like, "All the great cathedrals in Europe were built over ancient Pagan worship sites." I couldn't talk to Mother and Father about paganism, so I spoke to Elisi.

She told me that paganism is a hateful term for the beliefs of Indigenous Peoples spiritual beliefs. She told me that the Native Americans were "pagans" and that the Whites had used Christianity and their Christian doctrine of Manifest Destiny to destroy the Natives by the millions. It was a sin to kill a White man, but "Indians" had no soul and it wasn't a sin to kill them. I look around now and see that modern man, no matter what their color is, has definitely sold his soul for nothing.

Elisi would take people who were sick, or afflicted with spirits, or who needed the Mississippi River Medicine, down to the Wailing Woman. She would make offerings to the river spirit and have the person either stand in the waters or lie in them, and she would sing to Wailing Woman and the river, and they would be healed. Elisi knew the Medicine from her Elisi, and her Elisi knew it from her Elisi, and on back through the mist of time was the Medicine taught, and it was handed down from Mother to Daughter until modern times when the hold of the Christian beliefs would finally destroy the links that held together the chain of wisdom, and the Medicine would pass down no more.

It is said among the Tsalagi that we have been here for fifteen thousand years, and that once we had five dialects of our language, but the White man and his Christ destroyed our peoples to the point where on two dialects are now known, and our stories and Medicine dies with our People. Elisi tried but the Christian belief blocked the true Spirit of the Tsalagi, and it broke the unbroken chain of wisdom and Medicine passed down from the first Tsalagi.

One day we were downtown and Elisi took me to visit Wailing Woman, the Mississippi river. She handed me a bag full of tobacco and lead me to the edge of the river. We took off our shoes and socks and put our feet into Wailing woman. Elisi sang a song, but I couldn't understand the words, though I understood that she was singing to Wailing Woman. She had me throw the bag of tobacco into the river and said that it was an Offering to Wailing Woman, and that if I needed her help, to bring an offering of tobacco and to give it to her and tell her what was the matter and Wailing Woman would take care of it.

One day Elisi became ill, and went to the hospital. I couldn't get downtown to Wailing Woman, but lived close by the Wolf River, and so I took an offering to the spirit there. I took off my shoes, put my feet in the water and sang. I remembered the tune and the sounds, and maybe I didn't sing it right, because the Wolf, either did not share with the Wailing Woman, or both of them together could not stop death. Elisi died and I was left alone with my family that did not understand the spirits. Soon after Elisi's death, we were downtown, and I took my allowance and bought some tobacco for Wailing Woman, we could back then, no one even paid attention to a kid buying tobacco. I went to Wailing Woman and took off my shoes and gave her my offering and sang to her. I could feel Elisi and Wailing Woman, and they spoke to my heart, and I no longer mourned my Elisi. I knew that her spirit was always with me in my heart, and that Wailing Woman had waited to tell me that, and Elisi had taught me to listen.

At 17 my Mother died, and I went to Wailing Woman, but she told me that my Mother had gone to the Christian afterlife, and she could not help me. I became depressed. I went to see Bishop Dozier, the Arch Bishop for the Memphis Diocese. I asked him to endorse my application to become a monk at the Monastery of St. Michael, the Priest that did the exorcisms, and he told me that he couldn't. I asked if he would endorse my petition for Priesthood, again he refused. I had spoken with him from time to time in my young life, and he was a wise and caring man, often very witty. So when I asked why not, he said that he knew me to be a very "passionate" young man. I asked if it wasn't a helpful quality in a Priest to be passionate about his avocation, and he agreed that it was, but that it was the "carnal passion" that he had heard ascribed to me, and that my name was mentioned many times in the confessional. My response was simple, "They named names in the confessional?!?".

It was true, I was a very "passionate" young man and had spent many hours with older women, most married and bored. It had been the seventies and the free love was out there, and I had been drowning in it. This was the final straw. It had started when I was six, and I had been molested by an older woman. I never told anyone, especially Elisi, but continued with her and other women until I was eighteen. On my eighteenth birthday, I announced to my friends, that from that day forward, I would be celibate. That got a good laugh from them, but as the days and months wore on, they took me more and more serious. Sex had lost it's hold on me and I could focus on more important things in life.

At sixteen, I had become involved in a Coven of Witches, and my High Priestess had studied with Sybil Leek. I was thoroughly enthralled with it and told her about Elisi, and the spirits and Wailing Woman. At seventeen after my Mother died, I was introduced to another witch who had an occult shop in Frayser. I started hanging out there, since I had moved out on my own, and then started working there full time. By the time I was eighteen, I was a part owner of the business. I studied all I could about spirituality in all it's forms, and met the Drapers. They were Chickamaugan Cherokees, and my Elisi had said that we had descended from the Chickamaugans. We spoke at length and I showed them the bible and the Cherokee writings. I was still living with my Father then at seventeen. Shortly there after, my world seem to come apart at the seems. The apartment caught fire because of faulty electrical wiring in a building built in 1900. The bible was destroyed by the fire, and my Father decided to move into my Sisters house with her husband. I had to get out. The ringer in it all, was that My Ceremonial Magick teacher had fallen in love with Linda, my first High Priestess, and they were moving away!

Wailing Woman said that it was time that I be on my own. That the shop was the best place for me, so I listened to her. I took other jobs at night, and at one point was working two part time jobs and still working in the shop. But I developed a following of loyal customers, who would only come to see me and do as I instructed them to do. Through the shop I met many interesting people, who could see the spirit in me, and know that I was the "real deal" the genuine article. I wasn't there to rip people off, but to help them, to help my spirit grow and develop, and always there was the River Spirit Medicine magic. I studied Voodoo, Hoodoo, Santeria, Witchcraft, Celtic witchcraft, Norse magic, Runes, Ceremonial Magic, witchcraft from some fairly famous people in North Carolina, you name it, I was studying it. I even got initiated over the phone by Israel Regardie.

My Elisi never told me everything about medicine and magic, none of my teachers did, I had to learn on my own, and boy did I ever learn. That's when I developed "SPOT REMOVER", and had a sign there in the shop with prices, at the bottom was Spot Remover.....$10,000.00. That's right, ten thousand dollars. I know you are asking yourself, 'what the hell is spot remover', other than the obvious cleaning agent.

Well, Spot Remover was what I had to do to clean up the mess you made, when you absolutely would not listen to me, when I told you that you definitely did NOT want a love spell, or any REAL spell done. I used to do plenty, or give guidance on how to do them, and they always came back wanting me to clean up the chaos it inevitably created. They would come back and say, "Oh my god, he/she's driving me crazy! She/he destroyed my car, he/she's calling at all hours! You have GOT to help me!" I would just look board and point at Spot Remover on the sign and say "I told you so." No one ever payed the ten thousand dollars, but usually wound up in court or jail over it.

Mind you, spells don't always work the way you want them to, especially love spells. They have a bad habit of backfiring on you and you fall in love with someone else who can't stand you, while the person that you wanted is now hopelessly in love with you. For most people, magic is like firing a bullet wildly into a bunch of rocks, you may hit what you aim at, but it might ricochet as well. I charged one hundred dollars to guide you through the spell process, charged a thousand if you wanted me to do the actual spell, and people paid. I always warned them of the consequences, but no one ever listened. Magic always backfired on them, because they really didn't understand what they were doing.

When they got themselves into a mess, and weren't going to pay for the Spot Remover, I always told them about Wailing Woman and what to do. Sometimes it would work for them, kinda, sometimes it didn't. Most people don't really believe in their hearts, so the medicine doesn't work well for them, if at all. But it lives in my heart, along with Elisi and Wailing Woman. When people wanted me to do something but didn't want to pay me the price of a spell, I would charge them a nominal fee and go to Wailing Woman and sing to her, and make my offering, and she would do it. I told many people about the River and what to do, I never knew if they believed me or not, nor did I care, it was Elisi's Medicine.

Once, I took a "medicine woman" to see the Wailing Woman and show her the Tsalagi River Medicine. We took off our shoes and stepped into Wailing Woman and I sang to her. I changed the song, because the song Elisi sang was her own song.

So I told the medicine woman to find her own song to sing to Wailing Woman, but that the song was also a prayer and instructions at the same time. We gave offerings of tobacco to Wailing Woman and I sang to her to introduce the Medicine Woman, but Wailing Woman wasn't fooled by her, and she showed the medicine woman many visions that frightened her, because her heart was false and she wished only to abuse the Medicine and the people who would come to her, and she fled and became a good Christian woman. Wailing Woman knew that I wanted people of a like mind around, it makes life easier and less lonely. But those that came into my life and used the magic or medicine to abuse others and to molest them for sex or other reasons soon departed, and I knew the real reasons. Wailing Woman and Elisi would guide me, and give me visions.

That's how the medicine works, and you have to have a clean spirit to use it. Kalvlvtiahi, or The One Above, God is the Great Spirit YOWA, though there were three distinct incarnations of God. Just like in Christianity, God is a triumvirate, Unetlanvhi, or "Creator", Unahlahnauhi, or "maker of all things" and Kalvlvtiahi, or "The one who lives above", together they are YOWA. I won't bore you with the Tsalagi religion, then other spirits, but not like other Native Religions, we don't worship the lesser spirits, but honor them and ask their help. It is they who give us visions and help with the good medicine and act as intermediaries to The One Above. It is the reason that the Cherokees took to Christianity so readily, they are incredibly similar, and yet still very different.

The Mississippi River Medicine is to be respected at all times, and not to be used lightly, and if you offend the Wailing Woman she will pull you into the river to serve her until your relatives make an offering and appease her wrath. Then she will release your spirit to go join Kalvlvtiahi. There is a legend that the earthquakes of 1811 through 1812 were caused by the Wailing Woman for the many offenses caused to her by the changing Natives of the area and the newer White settlers. She grew enraged because her people had fled and let the White settlers move in and they were careless and damaged the land and river that she asked Kalvlvtiahi to intercede. So great was the damage that Wailing Woman flowed backwards for three days to fill the area affected by her wrath, and so astounded at the ferocity of Kalvlvtiahi's intervention

that she wept for the land and peoples. I tried to teach others who claimed to have Native blood, but fear was strong in their hearts and so their spirits wavered and they had not the strength to carry the Medicine. Elisi is in my heart and I do not have the fear that fills the hearts of others. The River Medicine is stronger than all the other spirits, except for those in the Great Ocean Waters. They are much larger spirits, and have much more strength.

Once, I had a friend and she said to me that her brother was afflicted with demons, and that they inhabited his body. I tried to tell her that the demons were actually unhappy spirits in torment, and that they inhabit bodies to torment others. She was so afraid and didn't know what to do. I told her to bring her brother to the Mississippi River and that the Medicine would take away the demons. She did not believe, but I made her bring him anyway. She brought him, but had to get four strong friends to help her, because the spirits fought them. He started screaming when he saw the water, because the spirits inside of him could see the Wailing Woman, and knew the Mississippi River Medicine magic.

We got him undressed, smudged him with cedar, sweetgrass and sage and put him in the waters and he made noises that I never heard before. I sang to the River and Wailing Woman drew out the spirits from his body. Soon he was at rest and his spirit was pure again. It took awhile for him to recover, but he came to the River and Wailing Woman twice to thank her. We made offerings of tobacco, sweetgrass, cedar and sage. Each time he got better and was healed in his heart and spirit, and we asked for permission to take some water for him to keep with him and bless his house, and we could feel the warmth and love of Wailing Woman.

At his house we smudged every room, then placed drops of water in each window sill, starting at the back of the house and working forward and you could feel the house getting less heavy. When we had finished and had smudged the final front room and forced the bad medicine from his house, you could feel it, you could even see it. His house was much lighter and brighter. The family believes in the Mississippi River Medicine and Wailing Woman now.

Sometimes, I go away from the city as Elisi said to do, and I lay beside the River and listen to the song of Wailing Woman and she fills my heart with her song. She sings to her lover the Wind Spirit. They sing to each other and I listen as other animals and spirits join their song. Sometimes I will take my rattle and make a pleasant accompaniment, or maybe a drum. I wish that I could play the flute, so that I could play it for Wailing Woman. Quiet is the best though, so that I can hear the song of the wild and let it fill my heart and spirit, let it clear my mind of the city, to cleanse the negativity and be a part of the spirit world.

Many times over the years I have lead groups of people to the Mississippi River, to give offerings and to feel Wailing Woman's power. So that maybe their spirit will open up, and see that there are other spirits that dwell along side them. Not to be feared but to be respected, like all life. I hear them tell me their experience with Wailing Woman, and how she spoke to them. They tell me about how they can feel her power and sometimes, when they think others can't hear, they tell me that Wailing Woman's Medicine has healed them.

They ask me how they can get to know Wailing Woman, and to seek her guidance and wisdom for themselves. Or if they can bring others back here, and if I will share with them as well. I tell them that Wailing Woman is here and all you have to do is respect her, open your heart and spirit to her, and she will sing to you, just listen to her voice. Make an offering to her, and stand or sit with your feet in the bosom of her waters. They ask me, "what do I offer her? I tell them that your spirit must be open, or no matter what the offer, it will not be accepted. So first open your heart,let your spirit be free to know the presence of Wailing Woman. Offer her tobacco and sweetgrass, cedar, sage, juniper. Bring your shell and burn these herbs to please the other spirits. Bring the Medicine Pipe and use it with Wailing Woman and the Medicine will be doubled. Sing a song to her and the other spirits listening. Ask them for wisdom and ask them to help with Medicine. Do not doubt, do not let fear enter your heart, go and be open and let your spirit give, the Medicine and wisdom will come.

Tobacco is a sacred plant, known for thousands of years to our Medicine Men and Women, it carried our prayers to Kalvlvtiahi, and the heavens. It was sacred and could heal, if you knew how.

The same with cedar, juniper, sage, and sweetgrass. We had Medicine for most ailments, and every plant had a Medicine inside it. White willow bark for pain, jimson weed for breathing troubles, garlic and onion for blood infections and to clean wounds. Some for food, sage for meat, maple for the sweet sap, and acorn for bread. Maize for all types of food, especially Frybread!

Elisi's frybread was the best! You could eat it plain, or with butter and honey, cinnamon and sugar, or molasses. Meat and gravy, chocolate gravy for a special treat. Frybread was for any time you wanted something special. Elisi would make her food in the center of the table, and never measured anything. I watched her many times make frybread, or biscuits, or cornbread, and never once did she measure anything. She said that she started cooking when she was four. She would help her Unitsi, her Mother, cook meals for the family. She had been doing it for so long, she no longer needed to measure, a skill I learned as a Sous Chef.

I will always be happy to guide a group to the waters of Wailing Woman the and the powerful Medicine she bestows, if you will be respectful, if you will make offerings, if you will cleanse yourself and listen to Wailing Woman. She is waiting for you and the Medicine waits, and Elisi waits. What are you waiting for? For me? I am here, take my hand and bring an offering, we will go to Wailing Woman.

The Mississippi River is sad because it is so polluted by chemicals now, and Wailing Woman grows weaker because man is trying so hard to destroy the earth with his poisons, and radiation so that the even the spirits die and then the Earth will perish and so will the animals, the ones that fly, the ones that walk on four legs, the ones that walk on two legs, those that crawl and those that slither, and those that swim. All will perish and so will man. The spirits will sicken and die, and Earth will be lifeless for a while.

Then Unetlanvhi, or "Creator", Unahlahnauhi, or "maker of all things" and Kalvlvtiahi, or "The one who lives above", together they are YOWA and he will remake the Earth. He will heal the spirits and raise them up again. He will make the animals again and the Earth will prosper. He will bring the spirits of our Ancestors back and they will

once again live on the Earth. Wailing Woman will again live in fresh and clean waters and the Mississippi River Medicine will again be pure and potent, and Elisi will sing her songs to Wailing Woman, and if I am worthy, I will join Elisi and sing to Wailing Woman.

I was sitting by the river one day singing softly to it, when this man and woman came along and spread out a blanket and they lay down upon it. I stopped singing and watched them, watched what they were doing. I had hid myself among some scrub nearby, where they couldn't observe me as I watched them. They spoke very little before they started kissing, their hands explored the others body, as their mouths hungrily tasted the others kiss. I grew angry for she was the woman that I loved. She was with a man that I knew not, and she was being false to me.

They began undressing each other and they kissed the areas of the others body that was now bare. How pale and flawless was her skin. No mark or blemish upon it's pale perfection. She was the most beautiful woman that I had ever seen, and I trembled in anger and pain. Her long curly hair fell like silken strands, gossamer across her shoulders and perfectly round breast. Her areole were dark brown and large as were her distended nipples. His mouth closed upon one of them and she threw her head back and a sound of pleasure and desire escaped her throat, as she arched her back and neck.

He was finely muscled and stoutly built, and his strong arms wrapped and unwrapped around her body as if they were trying to touch every part of her. She responded to him and he to her, in a way that she had never responded to me before. They continued undressing each other and kissing each others bodies as they did so. He kissed her in the most intimate of ways, in places that I had never thought of kissing, and she enjoyed it so much. She returned the kisses on various body parts of his, and there could be no doubt that he was enjoying it. While she had his manly parts in her mouth he gave a sharp cry and started shaking. She kept doing whatever it was she was doing until he stopped shaking.

She kissed her way up his body and and they made small talk. His manly part was no longer rigid but had gone flaccid. I came out of the

scrub and approached them, she tried to cover herself and he grabbed for his trousers. There was a pistol on his belt, that I had not noticed before, so distracted by my cheating love and her great beauty. He drew it and aimed it at me, while I cursed her for the feckless slut that she was. He swung the pistol and hit me in the side of my head, knocking me to the ground. My hand closed upon and large stone, as he approached me, and bent over me, I swung it at him. I felt it hit and could her a sound like the one you hear when you thump a watermelon. His head erupted in a spray of red and he fell to the wet stones, part of him in the Great River. I heard the explosion of the pistol, four times it fired.

I felt two of the bullets hit me in the chest, felt the firy hot lead as it sank deep into my chest, I felt the air rush from my lungs and the fire spread through my chest. It was so difficult to breath. I turned to her and one of the bullets had tore through her temple.

I pulled her to me and covered her face with kisses, but instead of enfolding around me, her arms were limp by her side. Instead of caressing me, her hands were like ice and her body was losing all it's warmth.and she was limp in my arms, and the feeling of her soft flesh against mine was still some how magical. I kissed her face all over and wept knowing that he had killed her, and that she had cheated on me. I sang to Wailing Woman, though it was getting more and more difficult to do so. I could hear again my Elisi's song in my ears.

I picked her up and held her to me, and then suddenly, we were in the river and Wailing Womans arms welcomed us both. I became weakened, and almost dropped her, but my hands still grasped her pale hands. The river washed over her face, and I did drop her then and saw as she slipped beneath the waves of the Mississippi, into the arms of Wailing Woman.

I stumbled back onto the banks and tripped over the mans body and fell backwards. My head struck a stone and the universe exploded in my head. There was a searing pain and I could not see for a few moments except for the stars that flew past my eyes. I could feel the gentle arms of the Wailing Woman as she reached for me. I could here her talking to me, telling me to let her heal my wounds.

I had dislodged the mans body and he was pulled into the river as well and taken away. I was getting cold and Wailing Woman said that the time was short. I crawleded into the Great Mississippi River and felt the warmth of the Wailing Woman's embrace. She held me like a lover and I could taste her kiss and she pulled me to her bosom and carried me away with her. We were one now, and she promised that she would take me to Elisi, but we were now joined forever as we should be.

I originally wrote this tory for a "writer's group" They were to publish it in an anthology. They kept telling me to change this or that, and before long, it became the story in my first book, and my original story and ending were lost. I include this latest version to right the terrible injustice those "writer's" imposed upon my beautiful story. Though not the original ending, still far better than the perversions they had me infuse into it, thus destroying the purity of all it spoke of.

6
A TALE OF
TRUE EVIL

True evil. Rarely have Americans ever encountered true terror in their every day lives. For three weeks in October 2001, the Beltway Sniper gave ordinary Americans in Washington D.C. a taste of "true terror." Seventeen people died and ten others were critically wounded. Men and Women of all ages and races were killed indiscriminately. True terror comes from the kind of a truly sick and twisted individual, who can without remorse, destroy the life of men, women and especially children. What feeds their sickness is the terror created when the life of an innocent or good person, is ended suddenly and violently. It is the connection with real evil that is born in the psyche of an individual that has created the need to destroy the good and decency that exist, and to create a world where sickness is the norm and decency is the sickness. Hollywoods agenda is to destroy decency, and spread the sickness.

Thus it was into this sick society that Tellar Monroe was born. His parents were ultra-liberals, with degrees in bullshit subjects that had nothing at all to do with the real world. Because they had no real skills, they found jobs in the corporate sector, which they claimed to despise so much. They became, at least on line, what can only be laughingly called 'social justice warriors'. Tellar was raised in this all too common form of insanity, and became the embodiment of that insanity to the point of pure evil. That same insanity ended the marriage of his parents when he was six years old.

At the age of eight years old, he climbed into the window of a dwelling of a single mother with six children, that lived next door. Three of the children were at school and the other three, triplets were sleeping peacefully in their cribs while the mother worked in the kitchen, washing clothes and dishes. Tellar looked at the babies as they slept soundly. He slipped his arm through the bars of the crib and gave the first child a sharp, swift chop to the front of the throat. The babies eyes snapped open and it kicked and flailed as it tried to breath, but couldn't. The child died fairly quickly, which did not satisfy the monster that Tellar was becoming.

Tellar walked to the next crib and placed a pillow over the babies face and pushed down until the child stopped flailing. Tellar removed the pillow and looked at it's face, and felt nothing. Neither death had satisfied Tellar, or given him a feeling that he had accomplished something. He couldn't understand what he wanted to feel, but they had not given him what he needed. Tellar carefully wrapped the other child in it's blanket and carried it over to the window and set it down. He crawled through the window and picked up the child and carried it through the back yard and through a hole in the wooden fence. He climbed up onto the railroad tracks and followed them down for a ways until he came to the overpass. He looked around and up and down the tracks and saw no one. He unwrapped the baby and threw it over the rail and watched it fall eighty feet to the pavement below.

The child literally exploded when it hit. Bright red blood splattered in all directions, and for the first time Tellar smiled. It filled him with enormous satisfaction to watch the child die so violently. He scrambled down the tracks, off the over pass and through the scrub brush that covered the side of the hill. By the time he got down to the dead child, seven people were around the child, five women and three men. One man was on the phone calling nine one one. He was two feet away looking between two of the women, who were all turned away from the poor baby.

Four Police cruisers arrived and one of the Officers immediately noticed Tellar, which no one else had. When the Officer asked Tellar what he was doing there, he said that he had seen a 'dirty woman' drop something off the bridge, and he wanted to see what it was, but couldn't figure it out. The Officer took Teller to the Detectives that had arrived, so that Tellar could describe the 'dirty woman' to them. After the Detective was finished talking to Tellar, The Lieutenant took him home to talk to his parents. Tellar's mom was now divorced, and a Medical Coder and worked from home and was shocked to see the Police bring her son home.

Two other Police cars arrived as the Lieutenant was talking to Tellar's mom. La Quisha Ford, mother of the triplets, came out of her house next door, screaming and crying incoherently. Neighbors that had gathered outside to gawk at all of the Police cruisers, started running toward her as did the Officers. Tellar looked at his mom and told her that he was hungry. She took him in and made him his lunch, while the neighborhood was eagerly watching what was going on and live messaging the events. Tellar calmly ate, disinterested in the goings on outside. After lunch Tellar went to his room and took a nap, and dreamed sweet dreams of killing the babies.

The Police scoured the rail yards and Hobo Camps for a "dirty woman" the next few weeks and checked with Tellar from time to time about what she looked like. They tried to get a sketch from Tellar, but never found the woman, of course. In the weeks that passed La Quisha Ford moved away, leaving the house abandoned. Tellar had played with the Realtor's key box until he found the combination and opened it. He took one of the keys from the box and opened the door. He explored the house. Most of the furniture was gone now, save an old recliner, which Tellar was able to push into the babies room at the back of the house.

Tellar would come here often, even telling his mother that he was spending the night at a friends house and sleeping here. He would open the windows and let the breeze blow through and think about killing people. While exploring the attic one day he found a concealed stairway that lead to a basement of the house. He walked down the stairs and looked around. There were small windows around the top of the basement walls giving only a little light. He found the light switch and turned it on, and to his surprise the light actually came on, while none of the other lights in the house worked.

There were two larger windows and when he looked out of them, they were under the back porch. The rest of the windows on the outside were covered by lattice work. There was a very good chance that no one even knew about the basement now, as the only way in was in the attic and it had been covered. He opened one of the larger windows and tried to climb out, but it was still too high. In the corner of the basement he found some wooden stairs and he moved them over to the window. Now he could easily climb out.

He looked around and started sorting through the stuff left here. Most was just garbage which he threw out of the window and towards the other end of the porch. He found some black spray paint and he painted the windows, so that no light came in, or went out. He found three boxes of chains, of varying sizes and lengths, and another box of padlocks with keys. He found some baseball and softball bats, as well as an ax and a hatchet. There was a folding card table and two chairs and set them up.

He found some old porn magazines and even a couple on BDSM. They gave him ideas about how to use the chains and padlocks. He found some old cheesy novels about crime and murder and he read them eagerly. His favourite one was about a Gangland assassin who used all kinds of methods to kill his marks. There was one story about beating his mark to death with a baseball bat and this peaked his interest.

One Saturday morning Tellar told his mother that he was going to play and he skipped off down the street and then doubled back to his secret hideout in the basement, to get his bat. He looked them over carefully and decided on the wooden baseball bat over the aluminum softball one. He climbed out the window and scooted out underneath the porch. He skipped off to try and find some one to kill. He wandered around the train yards, because sometimes they had sleeping Hobos.

He went to the Hobo camp and there he saw a homeless woman who was sitting under the viaduct and drinking a beer. He hid behind some empty crates and watched because another homeless man walked up. They talked for a bit and then the woman started trying to get the man to have sex with her.

"Hey sexy, that's a nice bulge you got in your pants, how about letting me suck it for you?" She said and then licked her lips a couple of times, smiling at him.

"Well okay, come get it. Do you swallow?" He asked her but Tellar didn't know what he meant.

"Of course, a lady never spits!" she said grinning her half toothless grin, as she knelt in front of him. He had his pants down and Tellar could see the mans very large penis and the woman started sucking it.

Tellar watched in fascination until the man started moaning and telling her that he was coming. Tellar didn't know what he meant, but the woman was humming and the man was shaking.

She got to her feet and lead him over to her filthy blanket and he sat down, back to the wall of the viaduct. She pulled up her dress and dropped her panties and sat on his lap and began moving up and down, back and forth. She was moaning and telling him that it felt great. She was kissing him and then she sat still. She was shaking and holding him. She breathed hard and couldn't speak for a few moments. The woman got off him and lay down, the man got between her legs. At first they just kissed, and then the man started moving again.

Tellar had seen enough. He knew that they were having sex, but he wasn't interested in watching any longer. He walked quietly up behind the man who said he was coming again, he took careful aim with the bat and swung it as hard as he could. There was a wet thud sound when the bat made contact with the mans head. Tellar felt the shock as it thudded up his arms. There was a spray of blood as the man's head snapped forward and he lay still upon the woman, who was oblivious to the fact that he had just been killed.

Tellar walked around to where he could get at the woman's head. Her eyes were closed as he raised the bat over his head. The woman opened her eyes and saw Tellar. She started to scream when he brought the bat down as hard as he could upon her forehead. Her scream ended abruptly and her face distorted as did the shape of her head.

Tellar looked at her, her eyes bulged from their sockets, blood was gurgling out of her mouth and nose. Her dead eyes stared in horror. Tellar was able to roll the man off of her and looked at his face, but he could see nothing except some blood dripping from the mans nose. Tellar swung the bat and hit him in the forehead and watched it cave in. He hit it again and the skin split and he could now see the mans brains. He hit the man again and watched as the head broke open and part of it fell to the ground, still connected to the skin. He hit the woman another couple of times until she was unrecognizable and her brains were scattered upon the dirt.

Tellar looked around and saw his footprints. He searched for and found a garden rake. He raked his footprints away and made sure that no trace of him had been left behind. He was walking back to his hideout and was walking behind a strip mall when he saw a drunk urinating by a dumpster. Tellar walked up to him and the drunk turned to look at him.

"You want to touch it?" The drunk smiled at him and waved his penis at him. Tellar slammed the bat into the mans crotch as hard as he could. The mans breath escaped in one massive "oof", as he dropped to the pavement.

Tellar swung the bat as fast as he could make it go, and felt the solid impact on the drunks head. The shock wave thudded up his arm more intensely this time. The drunk started screaming and Tellar started swinging the bat as fast as he could, delivering multiple blows to his head. The screaming abruptly ended after the second blow.

When Tellar had finished he looked at the mans body. He had totally destroyed the mans head, and his blood and brains were everywhere. Not far away was a trash can with a fire in it. Tellar went and threw the bat, his hat and jacket into the fire, then ran back to his hideout. Tellar had several gallons of water stored here, and poured some into a wash basin that had been left in the basement. He washed himself and his clothes as best he could, then went home. Tellar's mom met him at the door and was surprised to find him so wet. Tellar told her that he went swimming down by the river in a small pond that he had found. She told him that he needed to be careful around the river, but didn't tell him not to go back. She knew that would only make him want to do it even more. She made him change and take a bath, which he did. He lay in the tub and wondered what it would be like to bathe in a persons blood.

The police had found the bodies of the homeless people and the drunk, and put out public statements asking for any information, but no one ever came forward. Tellar was very careful and would kill only every so often. He pushed bums and homeless people in front of trains or off the overpass, but less and less frequently. Seven years passed and every day Tellar would think about killing again, but he had things he had to do now, that curtailed his desires until after his fifteenth birthday. His body count was thirteen.

By his fifteenth birthday, many things had changed. He had tunneled under the house to a culvert only thirty feet away from his hide out, since people now lived in the upper house he could no longer sneak through the yard to the porch and crawl under it. Now he had a way in that he camouflaged with junk. He had learned through an Apprentice program how to do simple carpentry work and had built a new doorway complete with a locking security door.

Tellar had a job now at Simon Fraser's Hardware store, and had saved quite a bit of money, and had two separate jars that he split his money in. One his Mother knew about, the other she didn't and he had amassed several hundred dollars between the two. He was wondering around one weekend morning and came across a family having a yard sale. They had a bow and some arrows as well as a cross bow with some bolts. He purchased both for only thirty dollars and hid them in his hide out. He spent another one hundred and ten dollars on new arrows and bolts as well as hunting tips for them, at a near by Sporting Goods store.

He read about archery and practiced with the bow and crossbow. He read books on archery at the library, and was anxious to kill someone with the new weapons. The murder rate had dropped drastically in the past seven years, but only because he had gotten involved with other activities at school, plus he had gotten a job, and had enjoyed the past few years. He had run across a few nasty people and had enjoyed thinking about killing them, and now suddenly he had the means.

One had been a particularly nasty bitch that had tried to cause a lot of trouble for him at work. He knew where she lived and he went to check out the surroundings. Her house was a large mansion with a tall wooden fence around it and a pool behind the house. The hills behind her house led up to a woods just thirty yards from her back door. Tellar watched her sunbathe and knew that he could hit her from here with an arrow. She still wore a bikini even though she had gotten fat in the past seven months.

Her breast were bigger and her belly was round. Often she would remove her bikini and sunbathe nude not caring if anyone was watching. He thought that she was even more disgusting now. He watched for several days and her routine was fairly consistent and she was always by the pool at one in the afternoon. He would be out of school on the following Friday, Good Friday and he knew exactly how to make his Friday a good Friday. He had pried loose three boards from the fence behind her house.

After breakfast Tellar kissed his mom bye and told her he was going to go hang around with some school friends and that he would be home for dinner. She was happy to see Tellar so excited about his friends and glad that high school seemed to have brought out the best in him. He made his way to the culvert and grabbed the bag containing the bow and arrows, and then careful to not be noticed, wound his way around to the bitches house.

It was only one twenty when he arrived, but she had just walked out to the pool. She removed her robe and she was wearing the bikini. She sprayed suntan lotion on herself and lay on the pool recliner and put her sun glasses on. Tellar stuck four arrows into the ground in front of him He tested the bow string and then nocked an arrow, drew it back and aimed. He raised his bow up and fired. He watched the arrow speed away and arc gracefully through the air coming to rest in the exact middle of her belly. The razor sharp broadhead sliced cleanly though her skin and muscles and the baby in her womb. She started to scream, but he had already loosed another arrow, which came to rest in her left breast. The third arrow penetrated her right eye, and killed her instantly.

Tellar looked around to see if anyone had reacted to her short scream, but he saw no one. He hid his bow and arrows under some scrub brush, then trotted down to the fence. He pulled them aside and slipped through, then looked around. He didn't see anyone around and had a kerchief around his face and a baseball cap to disguise his features, in case of cameras. He ran up to her a yanked the arrows out, causing massive amounts of damage. He looked at her wounds and smiled. He washed the arrows in the high chlorine water, and then got back through the fence and pushed the boards back into place. He used a rock to push the nails back into place.

He retrieved his bow and arrows and jogged back to his hide out. The bitches husband was away on a business trip and found her two days later. He had never called to check on her and neither had anyone else. By the time he found her she was swollen up and smelling to high heaven. The police searched everywhere and knew that the murder weapon was a bow and arrows. There were thousands of bows in the area, as it was a favored weapon for hunting deer.

Tellar phoned the tip hotline and told them it was a "hit" paid for by the husband, and hung up. The investigation got ugly after that and the news stories filled the evening news for weeks, which is where Tellar learned that he had killed the unborn child. This gave Tellar a warm feeling that he couldn't explain, but he liked it. The Police reluctantly released the husband for lack of evidence but watched him carefully for the next year.

The year wore on and when October arrived the annual Punkin' Chunkin' Festival arrived and there were catapults and air cannons everywhere. One afternoon Tellar saw a young boy playing around one of the catapults. Tellar talked to him and cranked down the catapult, then told the boy to sit on it while he got his picture. He pretended to snap pictures of the boy and then he handed him the rope release and told him to yank it. The boy was smiling and yanking on the rope, with Tellar egging him on.

When Tellar heard someone coming he changed his tone and was telling the boy to come out of the catapult, when the people came around the corner, Tellar looked as though he was trying to coax the boy from the catapult. The boy finally yanked the release hard enough to release the arm, sending the fifty pound boy two blocks through a second story window and killing an old woman watching Wheel of Fortune.

When the Police arrived Tellar told them his story of finding the boy in the catapult and trying to get him out when it launched him into the air. The other two couples were interviewed and they corroborated his story. Tellar cried when he talked to the Police and they let him go when his mother arrived to pick him up. By the time she arrived he was quiet again and seemed to be in a state of shock. She took him home and put him to bed. The next day at school, Councilors talked with him about grief mitigation. He talked to them and cried. Then became morose and wanted to go home.

The school called his mother who came and got him. She let him play video games in his room until dinner time. He told his mother that he did not want to talk about it again, and she told him that he did not have to. She let him alone for the next few days. Under the circumstances the Punkin' Chunkin' Festival was canceled. The town mourned the tragic accidental death of young Jerrold Nadler. Tellar would take his bow and arrows and go into the woods and practice his archery skills. He was very good and never seemed to miss his targets. He tried to hit his arrows like he had seen in a movie once, but only succeeded in tearing the fletchings off. It was now hunting season and Tellar got a hunting license. He was always bringing home deer meat, and his mom had actually filled the deep freeze. He started selling the extra meat and made a good bit of money doing so. He added the money to his savings, which grew rapidly.

One day he came across an unoccupied deer stand. The hunter had left several arrows there, so Tellar took them. They were very unique and had been painted red and black with the fletchings in a red/black banded design. As he sat there in the deer stand he saw two girls walking through the woods and talking about boys. One squatted and started urinating while the other kept watch for others. They were around twelve and he thought they were cute. While the one was keeping watch, Tellar nocked an arrow and shot the squatting girl. His arrow hit her at the base of the skull, severing her spinal cord and killing her instantly. She did not move nor make a sound. When the girl watching had grown impatient and turned to berate her friend, Tellar shot her in the right eye, she stumbled backwards and fell dead. Tellar climbed down and was walking over to look at the girls when he heard someone coming. He ran as quietly as he could and fled the area.

Each of the hunters in the area had distinctive markings on their arrows to identify the kill, as game animals often would run long distances before dying. Tellar was almost clear of the woods when he saw a little boy, about five years old playing nearby. He raised his bow, took careful aim and shot the boy in the back, again severing the spinal cord, penetrating the heart and sternum. The child was thrown forward by the force of the impact of the arrow, and he died quickly.

Tellar skirted the woods, staying concealed and had gotten close to the hidden entrance of his bunker, when he spotted Officer James Strickland, eating donuts from the Divine Donuts and drinking coffee. He took the last arrow and fired hitting Officer Strickland in the liver. The arrow passed through, and the Officer spouted blood, screaming into his radio. The damage to his liver was massive and he bled out out before the ambulance could arrive. The arrow was lodged in the door of his Cruiser, and was as good as a signed confession in it's uniqueness. Tellar disappeared into the hidden entrance and waited.

He crept out of the bunker, under the porch and made his way home. He had climbed through his bedroom window and came down stairs to ask his mom for a late lunch. Mrs. Mc Feeny was sitting at the dining room table with his mom and they were talking about the news of the four murders, which was being heavily broadcast over TV and radio. They stopped when he entered the kitchen. His mom was surprised to see him and asked were he had been, and he told her in his room asleep, as he was still not feeling up to getting out. She smiled at him and he said hello to Mrs. Mc Feeny who smiled back at him.

Tellar's mom made him a sandwich and got him a soda and some chips. He thanked her and said goodbye to Mrs. Mc Feeny and walked back to his room. It seemed that everyone was perplexed by all the murders, and how senseless they were. People were now becoming afraid to walk around, for fear of being murdered. Tellar ate his sandwich and then went to bed. He planned on waking early and heading for the train yard. He was going to hop a train to the next county and see what he could find at yard sales tomorrow. He had his backpack loaded with some essentials and had set aside about four hundred dollars to buy hunting equipment like arrows, crossbows, some knives, maybe even a rifle.

When he woke, he dressed quickly, and put an extra six hundred dollars in his pack, just in case he found a really good deal on a rifle. He went down stairs and made four sandwiches and put them in a plastic bag. He put four bottles of tea in the bottom of his pack, placed a cold pack on top of them and then laid the sandwiches on top of the cold pack. He put a change of clothes on top of those. He closed up the pack, slung it onto his back and left the house. He was dressed all in black and had a long black overcoat on. He walked down to the train yards, always on the watch for hobos or homeless people that might set upon him for money or mayhem. His hands in his pockets holding onto a quick opening knife.

He encountered no one on his way to the yard, and hopped the train heading out East. He could walk back from the next county from this direction or hitch a ride, either way this was the closest direction to his house. He sat back and ate a sandwich and drank one of his teas. When he saw the houses in the next county he stepped off from the rail car and made his way to the subdivision looking for yard sales. There were at least nine different ones in this neighborhood alone. It was still early, so he stopped in a convenience store and ate at the Charlie's Chicken. He talked to the girl cleaning the tables. She was cute and Tellar and her seemed to hit it off. Both were Juniors in high school, and they both seemed to dislike the same subjects. They exchanged numbers and Tellar left, walking to the closest yard sale. Here he found a bike with really solid rubber and silicone tires four inches wide, an electric motor had been attached and it had been fitted out as a "survival bike". It had a metal locking box and rifle mount on the front handle bars, a carry rack over both front and rear wheels, with two more locking boxes on each side of both wheels. The rear carry rack had a crossbow rack attached to it. It was all flat black and had various pouches here and there. There was one hundred feet of paracord attached to the front of the bike, and one pouch held a mess kit. There was a tactical tomahawk on one side and a small tactical shovel on the other and a tomahawk tactical walking staff attached to the long frame of the bike. It was quite striking to behold. The lady wanted two hundred dollars for it, which was the value of just the bike. The extras and customizations were worth at least another seven hundred dollars. He paid her without hesitation.

Teller rode from yard sale to yard sale buying arrows, crossbow bolts a couple of hunting knives, a few pocket knives, a small survival fishing kit with a small rod and reel set, and four more baseball bats. He bought a gym bag that he could bungee cord to one of the carrier racks, that was long enough to hold the arrows and bolts. He bought a pump action .22 rifle, and a Mossberg 500, 12 gauge shot gun. At the last yard sale he found two Remington 700 rifles both .308 caliber. One had a removable box magazine. The lady wanted two hundred dollars each, but he talked her into selling both for three hundred and thirty one dollars, which he showed her was all that was left of his money. He actually had a twenty that he kept in his wallet for emergencies. He carefully wrapped up the rifles and shotgun in a tarp and bungeed it to the rear rack and headed home.

It was an easy twenty mile ride on the bike down the four lane highway, and Tellar enjoyed the ride immensely. Before he knew it he was back on familiar roads and had ridden down into the wide drainage ditch where his secret door to his hideout was located. He moved the pallets and crates, pulled back the vines, and lifted his bike into the culvert, and climbed in behind it. He pushed it up to the door and unlocked the security door and the inner door and pushed his bike inside. He had insulated the ceiling with Styrofoam that was the same eighteen inch thickness as the floor joist. Then he added a wooden ceiling. It was enough to cancel any sound that he might make, and also muffled any noise from upstairs. He had made wooden pegs in the back wall, and there he stored his weapons. He had found an old wooden gun rack by the side of the road once and had installed it in his "lair". It was where he kept his baseball bats, now it would hold his rifles and shotgun. He had purchased a few rounds for his guns when he bought them, though he was not old enough to legally do so.

He started taking the extra stuff off his bike and cleaning it up. The bike was furnished for Armageddon! There was a lot more hidden in and on this bike than any but the guy who built knew of. He must have spent a fortune on the weaponry alone. All the racks and carriers were worth about two hundred, the M48 Tactical weapons were beyond belief! There was the Tactical Walking ax, the M48 Cyclone dagger on both front forks, each handlebar had an M48 stinger attached, on the left side was the M48 tactical Shovel and an M48 tactical knife. On the right side was an M48 double bladed tactical tomahawk and an M48 tactical tomahawk. Under the wide comfortable saddle were stitched four nylon sheaths, each had an eight inch polymer spike, with the words "CENTRAL INTELLIGENCE AGENCY" on one side of the triangular blade and "LANGLEY VIRGINA"on another. There were two pairs of hinged handcuffs and a pair of legcuffs, as well. All of these were hidden by velcro panels that covered a central metal panel attached above the electric battery. All other weapons were hidden as well. The boxes were sealed and had a silicone gasket to keep anything in them dry.

He hung all the weapons on the back wall and in the gun rack. He had a nice little collection going. He fixed himself a workbench and work area, where he could work on the weapons and on the arrows and bolts. He took the now much lighter bike back out the door, locked up and made his way out of the culvert, being very careful to look around first before coming out from behind the vines. It was getting dark and he made his way home. He would go out again tomorrow for more yard sales.

His mom was happy to see him and he showed her his new bike. She was happy for him and he was so proud of his bike. They ate dinner and watched the news together. There was a story about the killings with the red and black arrows. It seems that they belonged to a local Rabbi and that the Rabbi did not have an alibi for the times of the murders which happened within minutes of each other. He had been arrested and charged with the four murders. Tellar's mom shook her head and asked what this world was coming to when a Rabbi went around killing people. Tellar knew the Rabbi was innocent, knew that he had killed those people and that the Rabbi was being charged for them. He got up, took his plate and put it in the sink and ran water on it and then kissed his mom goodnight. He went to his room, and went to bed.

    The next morning Tellar got up early again, made himself some sandwiches and tea, just as he did the morning before, packed his backpack and headed out. He locked the bike outside his house and went over the back fence and headed for his lair. He retrieved his crossbow and some bolts, and carefully made his way back. He put the crossbow in the rear rack and bungeed it in, and put the bolts in one of the carriers. He rode along the highway enjoying the crisp morning air. He would take smaller roads and wound his way around the neighborhood, and seemed freer that he ever had before. He was dressed in black and gray clothing and had a hoodie on under the long jacket. Behind the bank he saw an Armored car at the drive up ATM, Two men were working at it. One would watch out, while the other typed on the screen. Tellar got closer, laid his bike down behind some bushes and got his crossbow ready. Suddenly one of the men stepped back and opened the door of the ATM and knelt down. The other looked around and then started to walk around the armored car. Tellar shot the walking guard in the back of the head, cocked it and shot the other in the left temple. Both were dead. Tellar looked, but there was no driver. He approached the ATM and there were three full bins, that they were going to replace the three empty bins with. Teller took all six, and bungeed them to the back of the bike, took his bolts and slung his crossbow over his back. He pedaled to a nearby abandoned gas station and opened the bins, two of which were filled with new twenty dollar bills, one filled with new ten dollar bills and the other three containing about twenty one hundred dollars in tens and twenties, the new bins totaled fifty thousand dollars in them. He hid the bins in an old pit filled with grease, oil and debris, put the money in his pack, racked his crossbow and sped back to his hideout. While climbing into the culvert, he could hear sirens from all directions. He locked himself in his lair and counted the money. Fifty two thousand, one hundred dollars. None of the bills serial numbers had been recorded, but that didn't matter to him. He would trade the bills here and there for coins or deposit them into his account along with his paycheck.

He had shown his mother his bank account and told her that he was trying to be responsible and save his money. She was even prouder of him. From time to time he would take a bag of loose coins into the bank and they would run it through their coin counter and then the total would be credited to his account. It was an easy way to launder small amounts of money. He would make small purchases with a twenty dollar bill and ask for coins back in change.

The Federal and Local Authorities, were concentrating on a well planned heist by professionals, instead of sheer dumb luck by a homicidal teenager. The murders and heist went unsolved as there was no witnesses and the camera only recorded one assailant making away with the canisters, to presumably, an automobile out of camera range. No one would have thought about a boy out riding his bike. He went to school and then to his job after school, did extra chores for people around the neighborhood for pay, and then take his check and money to the bank. He would do carpentry work for some of the older people around his neighborhood, for a reasonable price, if they provided the materials. He stockpiled bricks and some quickrete, in his lair and finally bricked up the windows and doorways. He reinforced his doorway and even built a cinder block wall with with a steel door to keep his weapons and money safe.

Tellar turned sixteen and his mother asked him what he wanted. He told her that he wanted to fix up his own private apartment in the cellar, she was surprised that he would want to be in a musty, dusty old cellar, but said that she would help him get it cleaned up. There wasn't much down there to begin with, as she never used it. He had made friends with several professionals down at Fraser's hardware store where he worked. He got one of the Electricians to come help install a fluorescent light fixture in his basement, while there the man ran him a couple of circuits off his electrical panel, so that Tellar could have a real workshop in his basement. He even refused to accept payment from him. Tellar asked him to stay for dinner, which he did. They talked about electrical work and maintenance and Carpentry. Tellar was fascinated with it all. Tellar found out about pre-formed galvanized steel arches and forms, and he decided that if he could get his hands on some it would help in tunneling under to the house next door, where his lair was. The house was closer to his house than to the culvert, only about twenty feet to tunnel under. He was able to get stuff from construction sites that were left over or just outright ordered for him by the Foremen. Tellar was well liked and knowledgeable, and learned very quickly.

He tunneled under the yard joining the two houses to each other with a ten foot high and ten foot wide tunnel with galvanized culvert piping cut lengthwise and used for the upper support with cinder block walls. He reconstructed the culvert entrance the same way. He also put a hatch door on the outside of where the tunnel met the culvert, with a "WARNING HIGH VOLTAGE" sign upon the door. The hatch had a key cylinder on the outside and a locking bar system on the inside. Once engaged, the door could not be opened or unlocked from outside. He put a security door on the tunnel from his house to his lair, and had changed out all of the cylinders with Schlage PEAKS cylinders which most people called "HIGH SECURITY" but were actually a key controlled system. The keys were proprietary to the Locksmith.

He reinforced the Safe rooms door and also put better locks there as well. He hid the tunnel door behind a large wall hanging that he got at the flea market. He had continued to buy guns and ammo, arrows and bolts. He had a very fine workshop set up as well as a nice little efficiency apartment in his basement. He had cut into the duct system and added a vent. He ran a string of lights through his tunnel, and added a wind turbine generator to help run the electricity that he was using. It did such a great job that he added a second, which brought his mothers utility bills down a lot. He added a door to the outside and a security door, so that he could come and go without disturbing his mother.

He had watched a show about hidden safes and safe rooms and decided to build secret compartment shelves and furniture around his mom's house and his lair, as he was calling all of it. He worked out how to conceal the tunnel door behind a sliding refrigerator and then did it. He did all this to lay low and keep out of sight. The murders and the ATM robbery had drawn too much attention to his area. He wandered around two counties buying weapons, and survival equipment. At one yard sale he was approached by an older man, and they talked about weapons and hunting. The man, who had introduced himself as Arturo, invited Tellar back to his place to see his collection of guns and antiques. Tellar accepted his invitation and put his bike in the bed of

Arturo's truck, got into the cab and they talked small talk until they arrived at Arturo's house, which was on a large wooded lot, surrounded by hedges and fences, for privacy, and pulled into the garage. They went in and down the stairs to a den that was the full size of the house.

Arturo had been a Military Sniper and had all of his awards and medals in a large shadowbox display on the wall of his huge den. His Bravo 51 Sniper Rifle with suppressor was displayed on a specially built shelf, behind it were pictures of some of the places that he had been to. Arturo asked if Tellar could spot him in any of the photos, but he couldn't. Arturo pointed out everywhere he was in each picture, he was of course camouflaged. Arturo pointed out several guns displayed on the walls of his den. They were arranged beautifully, with daggers and bayonets and swords making patterns and designs between the different guns. There were columns spaced evenly through the den to support the upper level of the house. Each of the columns were covered in knives swords and guns. Along the back wall were seventy five M1 Garand rifles lined up in a rack. Above them were thirty M1911 pistols, thirty M9 pistols, some with suppressors. Some Enfield/Webley .38 caliber revolvers and slightly larger .45 caliber revolvers. Arturo also had two WWII era M1 Thompson Submachine guns, as well as several MP40 Schmeissers.

Along another wall were his newest guns, some common ones like the Smith and Wesson revolvers of various sort. But there were some very large pistols that looked like they were straight out of a Sci-Fi movie. One was a Smith and Wesson 460XVR, a .460 Magnum revolver with fluted barrel and a huge recoil compensator. The bullet was huge! Tellar could imagine shooting people at close range with this gun and imagine the damage it would cause. All along the lower sections of two walls were shelves with boxes and cases of different types of ammo. Arturo pointed out some that was illegal to even own in the United State, because it was strictly for assassinations. Some exploded, there were mercury loads, and some that you put poison or radioactive pellets in the hollow point, then put a plastic cap to fill the gap, and if you didn't kill them out right, the poison or radiation would. There were sub-sonic rounds that when used with a suppressor equipped pistol, were practically soundless.

Tellar told Arturo how impressed he was by the collection of weapons. Arturo approached Tellar and reached out for him. Tellar put his arms around Arturo's neck and they kissed. Arturo was very aroused and ran his hands under Tellar's shirt. Arturo was kissing Tellar all over his neck and cheeks, and then back to his mouth. He reached down and Tellar was erect. He took Tellar by the hand and led him to a room that he had not seen, at the other end of the den. Inside was a large bed. Tellar and Arturo wasted no time in getting undressed Tellar was a virgin and it wasn't long before he had his first orgasm. It was an amazing feeling and was returning the favor to Arturo. They played around for another hour, both cumming two more times. Tellar asked where the bathroom was and Arturo told him. Tellar went and used the restroom and made sure that he left no fingerprints. He came back down stairs and could hear Arturo in the room.

 Tellar grabbed the 460XVR and a box of ammo and quickly loaded the five rounds, and walked to the bedroom. He leaned against the doorway and Arturo smiled at him. Tellar returned the smile. He pulled the pistol from behind his back and Arturo laughed, Tellar pulled the trigger. The gun kicked liked a mule and Tellar almost lost it as the recoil drove it back and over his head. The bullet slammed into Arturo's face and blowing his head apart. A large hole appeared on the headboard, which was covered in Arturo's brains and blood. His heart still beat and each time it did, blood would squirt from an artery. Tellar got dressed and rolled Arturo's body into the floor. He rolled up the sheet and took it with him.

 Tellar knew that Arturo lived alone and that he wasn't expecting anyone to come over anytime soon. He picked several pistols, knives and swords and took them to Arturo's truck and loaded them up. He loaded the ammo for those guns into the truck as well. After had had finished, he searched for and found the laundry room. He grabbed a full bottle of bleach and poured some over the bathroom area, to destroy any DNA that might be there. The rest he poured over Arturo and the bed. He had filled Arturo's truck with guns and ammo and decided to drive it to his house. It was getting dark and with the dark windows in Arturo's truck, no one would see who was driving it. Just as he sat in the truck about to start it, his cell phone rang. Tellar jumped, he had not been expecting it to ring. It was his Mom, she was going to go visit a sick friend and said that she would probably be home late and asked if he minded stopping on his way home and getting himself something to eat. He told her to not worry that he was just about to call her. He would get himself something on the way home. He asked if she wanted him to pick her up anything. She said that she was so proud of him and how he had grown up and become responsible, then said that she would be fine and to be careful. She said that she loved him he returned the sentiment. They hung up and Tellar knew that he would be able to unload the truck and dispose of it and move everything down into his lair, before his mother returned home.

He had taken the suppressor equipped weapons and the sub-sonic ammo as well as quite a bit of other weapons and ammo types. He smiled all the way home imagining the type of mischief he could manage with them. He made sure that the tarp was tied down as well as he could, to cover the weapons in the back along with his bike. He drove carefully and made it home without incident. He backed into his drive way and stopped when the tail of the truck was even with the door of his basement apartment. He got out and quickly unloaded the truck of the weapons and ammo. He decided to return to Arturo's for a second load of weapons.

He loaded up another load of guns and ammo and was looking around Arturo's house when he found the safe in the closet. It was six feet high and six feet wide, and had a standard electronic lock on it. Tellar had read where people often make the combinations something memorable like a date. He remembered Arturo's dogtags by where he had kept the Bravo 51. Tellar typed the first six digits into the combination lock and got a green light and heard the bolt retract. He turned the handle and opened the door. There was expensive jewelry in the safe as well as gold, silver and platinum bullion, old coins and cash, over one hundred thousand in cash. There was also several passports and documents in here. It seems that Arturo was a hit man, who got old, sloppy and horny, and it had cost him his life. Tellar got a duffle bag and loaded the valuables into it and carried it to the truck, loaded it and left. He had gotten the truck unloaded at his house, and moved the truck out to the street and down to the next house, and parked it. He was sitting on the porch, when his mom drove up a few minutes later. They talked for a few minutes and then his mom said that she had to get to work extra early tomorrow and kissed him goodnight.

Tellar had been taught how to hook-up the trailers at work and how to back them up to the loading docks to help Mr. Fraser out. He was taught how to hook them up correctly and how to guide and steer them, so he was very familiar with them and often helped others hook-up the rental trailers as well. After his mom had left for work, Tellar drove Arturo's truck up to Fraser's Hardware and asked Mr. Fraser if he could rent a trailer and a two wheeler. He told him that he was going to get paid to help a friend of his mothers move some furniture. Mr. Fraser smiled at him and told him that he could use the trailer for free as long as he brought it back swept out and clean. Tellar returned the smile and thanked him. They shook hands and Teller left to pick up a trailer. He chose one of the medium sized ones with a Tommy lift, and hooked it up and connected the brake light connector. Tellar drove to Arturo's house. It was still quite and you could not see the neighboring houses. He backed up to the garage door and got out and opened the door.

Inside the garage was a large tool chest on wheels. He released the wheel locks and pushed it into the trailer and put the wheel locks back on. He started loading the guns next and took them all. Next he loaded the ammunition on to the two wheeler and made several trips back and forth, until it was all loaded up. He searched the house again and didn't find anything else that he wanted. He locked up the house and left. He closed the garage door and locked it with the keys, got into the truck and drove out the long drive again. There were no cars this early, so no one saw him come or go. He backed carefully into his driveway and stopped just at his door. He unloaded everything into his lair. The guns and ammo were being stored under the next door house, in the safe room that he built. He stacked the guns as best he could, he was definitely going to have to build some racks for them. The ammo had to be stored in the larger room in his "original" lair because he now had so many weapons. He would purchase the lumber and materials to build the racks for the rifles. He used pegboard and hooks for the pistols. He got a dehumidifier for his gun room to keep his guns from rusting. He bought wire shelves and arranged the ammo into calibers and types of ammunition.

There were four medium sized crates and three large crates that had been painted over and Tellar had had to use the two-wheeler to move them. He opened them now. The medium sized crates contained hand grenades, and two of the large crates held Claymore mines, the last one held one hundred pounds of C4 plastic explosives with detonators. In one of the crates were the Military Manuals on each. Tellar read them and learned how to rig his Lair to self destruct. Tellar knew that one day his luck would change and he would be caught, and as long as he could get back here, he could go out like a rock star! For now, he put one of the suppressed pistols in his waistband, and drove the trailer back to Mr. Fraser's hardware store and dropped it off, he had put his bike in the back of the truck and now drove off to dispose of the truck. He found a spot behind some vacant buildings and parked it. He doused the interior with gasoline. While he was doing that a homeless woman walked up to him offering her oral services for twenty dollars. Tellar drew the pistol and turned to her and shot her four times in the chest as fast as he could pull the trigger. She collapsed at his feet. He picked her up and put her in the truck, behind the wheel, doused her with the remaining gas, tossed the can into the cab, and lit a piece of newspaper and threw it into the truck and slammed the door. He pushed his bike quickly away from the truck and before he could get too far away, the truck windows were blown out. The in rush of oxygen caused the fire to flare up and the truck was engulfed in flames. Black smoke billowed from the truck and Tellar knew that the fire would soon be discovered. He got onto his bike and pedaled away as fast as he could. It wasn't long at all before he heard the fire trucks sirens and horns sounding. He dismounted his bike and went inside Sandy's Cafe for breakfast.

Tellar had been seen fleeing the scene, but at a distance, and then only from behind. The fact remains though he had been seen, and while he wanted to use his new weapons, he knew that he had to lay low. He concentrated on work at Mr. Fraser's hardware store. Some of the local Contractors were trying to hire him away from Mr. Fraser, and had offered him a lot more than he was making, but Tellar knew that he would not have the flexibility that he had with Mr. Fraser. For now he worked as much or as little as he wanted, and could leave at any time. He wouldn't be able to do that with the Contractors, plus, he would have to join the union. Still, the contractors referred small jobs to Tellar. Mr. Fraser told him that he could get his Drivers License if he was working on jobs, and that he should do it. Tellar told him he would think about it, but that would mean that he needed a work vehicle and insurance. Mr. Fraser said that he could help with that as well.

Simon Fraser called Clarence Saunders, a local HVAC Contractor, because he knew that Clarence was replacing his work trucks, and wanted to see if Clarence had one of his older ones in very good condition and how much he could let it go for. Clarence told Simon about one of his smaller work vans that was in excellent condition and that he could let him have it at a very reasonable price, and would even leave the work benches and storage bins in it. They agreed on the price and Clarence brought it up to the hardware store and dropped it off. When Tellar got to work, Mr. Fraser had him go out to the van and clean it up. When Tellar had finished Mr. Fraser told him that he had bought it for Tellar and that Tellar could pay him back for it. Tellar was excited and thanked Mr. Fraser and even hugged him. Mr. Fraser called his insurance man and got him to come out and sign Tellar up for insurance on the vehicle. Now all Tellar had to do was get his license to drive, and Mr. Fraser even volunteered to take him to get it. He couldn't wait to get home and tell his mother.

Tellar had been laundering the money from the armored car, passing the bills here and there and getting the change back and then depositing it in his account. He would take in money at least once a week along with his paycheck and deposit it as if it were for jobs. It wasn't long before he had over ten thousand dollars in the bank, before his eighteenth birthday. Soon he was dividing the money between a checking and savings accounts and had his mother added to his accounts. If anything happened to him, she would get the money without having to go to court. Everyone was proud of Tellar, and many of the Professionals in his life referred work to him, and Mr. Fraser added him as the official handyman of Frasers Hardware. Tellar paid for a new paint job for his van, and he was hiring the Professionals to do work at his mothers house. He replaced the windows, got new insulation and new roof, all for less than what others would pay because he was always doing things for the owners of those companies. And when Mr. Fraser took him to get his license, he passed with flying colors. Mr. Fraser took him and his mother out to dinner to celebrate.

Many of the women where Tellar's mother worked would call Tellar to do work at their houses. They always tipped him, and most offered to satisfy him as well. Tellar usually took them up on their offers of sexual favors. Tellar had five, ten gallon water cooler tanks in his room, just inside his door. He would separate the pocket money into dimes, nickles, pennies, quarters and larger coins and bills in the last one. Tellar's mom would save her pocket change for a week and them hand him a Ziploc bag full of mixed change. Tellar would sort the coins, then put them in the appropriate bottle. Between Tellar and his mom it took seven months to fill those five bottles. Tellar loaded them up onto his van and took them to the bank, where they were poured onto the floor and then scooped up and into the bulk coin counter. Everyone was surprised by the amount of nine thousand seven hundred ninety four dollars and forty-four cents, which was bagged and then the amount deposited into his checking and savings accounts. The bank had to report the large sum to the Treasury Department and an Agent Malone came out and interviewed him and his mother, They also interviewed Mr. Fraser who assured them that Tellar was on the up and up and was just a hard working young man. Agent Malone smiled and said that with such large sums, that the bank had rules and regulations that forced them to report them. He was happy to hear that a modern kid was actually doing something to contribute to society as a whole and was getting ahead because of his hard work. Agent Malone finished his interviews with the Bank personnel, and that was the end of it, no one could say one bad thing about Tellar, who from all accounts was a hard working young man, set on saving his money.

Tellar had been working on his skills. He had set up a plywood training board and had been studying how to throw knives, axes and shurikin. He had even been practicing with the suppressed pistols, and shooting wooden targets. He designed hidden compartments in his van and always made sure that he had at least five guns where he could reach them. He insulated the van with special sound deadening materials and made a heavy stainless steel port that could be locked from the inside so that he could snipe from the van. He had a suppressed .22 caliber rifle and often shot squirrels and pigeons in the park, from the van. He continued looking for rifles, ammo and bows at yards sales. Usually just before hunting season started, he would find the most, as people had replaced last years model with the latest and greatest. He had widened his search to the two neighboring counties and across State lines.

It was on one of these excursions into the bordering State that he got the opportunity to kill again. He had stopped to eat a sandwich at an abandoned factory when he saw another work vehicle drive up and stop under an over hang. Tellar was parked in the dark opening of a building and couldn't be seen. He put gloves on and took the suppressed .9mm and walked carefully through the buildings, until he came to the rear of the work van that had pulled up. It was rocking back and forth and Tellar could hear the man and woman moaning while they had sex. The side door was open and he carefully peeked through the door cracks. Suddenly the man cried out as he climaxed and collapsed upon the woman who was laughing with pleasure. Tellar stepped from behind the open door and put a bullet into the man's temple. It traveled through his skull and out the other side into hers. He searched them and the van taking any money and jewelry, and some of the most valuable tools that didn't have serial numbers on them. There was a .357 magnum in the glove box and Tellar took it as well. He looked around and made sure no one saw him this time. He pulled his van out and drove away from the factory in a different direction.

Tellar drove through the town across the State lines and looked for victims. He saw some people in a box car on a slow moving train, and he shot the three that he saw. There were three more that he couldn't see having sex at the back of the box car. Two of the ones that he shot fell backwards into the box car, but the woman fell off face first, into the swamp they were crossing. She may never be found. The train had actually crossed into three more States before the two dead men were found by the others in the box car, as they had fallen asleep after having sex.

There were many old factories and warehouse facilities around, most were used by kids and homeless people to hang around in, with the typical drug hangout being favored in places like these. Once Tellar had pulled off at one of them and was eating his lunch when a hooker walked up to his passenger door and opened it. Without thinking Tellar shot her in the forehead and she recoiled away from the shot. She was dead before she hit the ground. He got out and dragged her body over to an old furnace and opened the door. He lifted her body up and pushed her in, then closed the door. There was a splash as she hit the bottom of the furnace, it was filled a quarter of the way up with water. He walked back to the van, kicked dirt and debris over the blood spots, and had resumed eating when this greasy looking guy walked up to his van. He wanted to know where Doris was, but Tellar said that he didn't know her. Greasy said that he should, because he sent her over here to date Tellar when he drove up and parked. Tellar said that he didn't know what he was talking about. Greasy yanked the vans door open and pushed the button on his switchblade. It opened with a loud click. He reached for Tellar but Tellar fired five rounds as quick as he could dropping the greasy pimp right there. The pimp yelled a loud "FUCK!" as he laid there. Tellar took aim and put another round between his eyes. Tellar disposed of him in the same furnace, after searching him of course. He took the switchblade and six hundred and thirty dollars. He took the drugs that he found, opened the bags and dropped them into the furnace.

Driving away from the abandoned factory, down a small country road, he spotted three tweakers walking up from the road to a run down trailer. They sat on the steps in front of the trailer and waved at Tellar as he was driving. On a whim Tellar pulled up to the trailer, put his pistol in his waistband and got out. There were two guys and a woman, all three looked liked they had been through hell. They talked and the woman asked if he wanted a blow job. Tellar said that he would like the watch the three of them have sex, and would pay for the pleasure. One had produced a crack pipe and they were passing it around. The woman offered it to Tellar who said that he had to get back to work so he couldn't right now, but would come back for a rain check.

They went into the trailer, it was just as filthy and smelly as Tellar imagined it to be. They walked to the bedroom and the three tweakers got undressed and laid in the bed. She started performing oral on one, while the other started to take her doggy style. Both tweaker males came quickly and then collapsed on the bed. The woman turned towards him and was shot. Tellar watched as the men freaked and started begging for their lives. Tellar shot them both in the guts and watched as they writhed in agony. They cried and begged Tellar to not kill them. Tellar laughed, and then the smell in the trailer got to him and he almost vomited. Tellar shot both in the head and fled the trailer. He jumped in his van and drove with the windows down. Five miles down the road he pulled over and vomited violently under a tree. He should have just shot them on the porch outside the trailer.

Once he got home, Tellar put the money he had into the appropriate jugs and went and took a bath. He felt better by dinner time and decided that he would take his mom to the Wharf, her favorite restaurant. She asked him if it was a special occasion, and he told her that it was. It was his way of showing her that he appreciated her and loved her. She smiled and was filled with joy that her boy had turned out to be perfect. They had a fine meal and finished it off with baked Alaska's. He helped her up into the van and drove her home. He hugged and kissed her then went to his apartment downstairs. When he thought that she might be asleep, he slipped out with his bike, his crossbow and two suppressed pistols.

He rode his bike quickly through the streets, in his dark camouflage BDU's. He had a balaclava that could be swiftly pulled over his head in any configuration of concealment. He let the electric motor run and could reach a top speed of 28 miles per hour. He cut the motor and lights when he saw a Cadillac turn off onto his road. There were no street lights here and the driver had turned on the over head light in the Caddy. Tellar could tell by the way he was dressed that he was a pimp, and the three women were prostitutes. They were handing him money and he was yelling at them. The pimp got out of the car and told the women to get out and line up against the car. He started searching them and taking money out of their orifices. Now he was talking quietly to the whores and they looked afraid.

Tellar positioned the 9 mm pistol in his pocket for a quick draw and made some noise. The pimp and whores looked in his direction as he pedaled nearer. As he got closer he stopped and looked them over. The pimp asked him if he saw anything that he liked . Tellar said that he did indeed, and that he would like to have all three. The pimp laughed and said "how much chu got, boy?" Tellar blinked and said that he only had thirty dollars. The pimp laughed even louder and said for that he usually wouldn't even get a hand job, but that he was going to do Tellar a favor and let him play with two of them while the third blew him. Tellar agreed and handed the pimp the thirty dollars. He opened the door of the Caddy and told Tellar to stand behind it while the girls did their thing. The women had pulled their tops off and were getting in position, when Tellar shot the pimp, the whores were in shock and just looked at the pimp lying crumpled on the side of the road. Tellar quickly shot them before they could react. He searched the pimp and found a gold plated Springfield Armory .45 caliber M1911. The pimp also had more than twelve thousand dollars on him. There was another gold plated Colt .38 snub-nose in the glove box. Tellar took everything, and all of the gold jewelry the pimp had on.

Tellar couldn't believe that this piece of filth had so much fine jewelry, including an expensive gold watch. Tellar mounted his bike and started the electric motor and sped away as fast as he could. He rode through streets and through fields and yards giving himself as much distance as he could from the pimp-mobile. Up ahead he could see a large figure moving to intercept him. Tellar slowed so that he could maneuver the bike easier, and then the large man was in front of him. Tellar drew the other suppressed pistol. It was a .45 caliber and started firing at the large hulking man, who jerked every time a bullet hit him, but the man did not fall. He grabbed Tellar as he tried to pass him, and Tellar found himself on the ground staring up at the huge dark figure. Tellar emptied the pistol's magazine into the mans head, who eventually collapsed backwards. Tellar was shaking and jumped back onto his bike and high tailed it away from there. He was shaking and disoriented and didn't now where he was or which way to go. He rode towards the sound of traffic and eventually came to West Avenue. He was a bit calmer now and could figure out where he was at, he stopped and changed the magazine to a fully loaded one.

Tellar wondered how any man could get shot fifteen times by a .45 automatic and remain standing. He was sweating with exertion and fear, and Tellar realized that for the first time in his life, he had actually been terrified. Tellar took a few deep breaths as he let the electric motor do all the work, and was soon over his panic attack. He turned off the motor and was pedaling again, when he saw a man and woman up ahead, walk into an alley. As he neared the alley he slowed, then stopped. The woman was leaning against the wall, the man on his knees before her. Tellar looked around but saw no one else. He pulled the 9mm and shot her in the head, because of her stance and the fact that the man was bracing her, she did not fall. Her head fell forward, blood pouring from her head. Tellar fired into the back of the mans head and his arms went limp, their bodies supporting each others. Tellar turned and was face to face with a Police Officer who couldn't believe what he just saw happen. Tellar fired several times, hitting the Officer in his vest and spinning him around. Tellar got closer and put two rounds into the back of the Officers skull. Tellar rolled the Officer over and grabbed his badge and Duty belt and rode off down the alley. He stopped long enough to put the duty belt in one of the carriers.

Tellar knew where he was now and which way to go. He was no longer panicked, but strangely calm. He rode home, unlocked his doors and went inside. He locked the doors and parked his bike. He started taking his clothes off when he noticed that his BDU top was bloody. It had to be from the huge freaky dude. He was emptying his pockets when he found the watch. He looked it over carefully. It was the one that he took from the pimp, a Rolex or knockoff , he thought. Now that he looked at it carefully, it was a very special looking watch. It was gold with a gold band and the face of it said Breitling. On the back was a serial number and engraved into it were the words "NAVITIMER

RATTRAPANTE EDITION LIMITEE A 250 EXEMPLAIRES TESTé 3 BARS". He set it aside and put all the money that he had into the water jugs. He washed up and brushed his teeth and then went to bed.

He spent the next few months between school, work and side jobs. He had started going into random banks and getting a couple hundred dollars in change in small bills. Then would sort them when he got home. He would take a few hundred dollars every few days to the bank and deposit the money between his accounts. He was still selling his sexual favors to the older women who worked with his mom and they would also refer him to other ladies as a "Handyman Extraordinaire". He had quickly paid Mr. Fraser off for the van and had upgraded to the vans interior and stereo system. Tellar flew his mom first class across the country to visit her sister, and gave her some spending money. She bragged on him constantly while she was there.

Tellar showed the watch to Mr. Fraser, who told him to go see his brother in law, who owned a Fine Jewelry store. Mr. Schwab was older than Mr. Frasers sister, but she had married him anyway. She was his trophy wife and she was swimming in luxury. Mr. Schwab looked the watch up and told Tellar that it was a Navitimer 1 BO3, 18 karat gold band and case with 46 jewels. The value was $55,650.00 and that he would have to run the serial number to see if it was stolen, before he could either buy it or sell it on consignment. Tellar told him to go ahead and do it and that if it wasn't stolen, then he would let Mr. Schwab sell it for him, for ten percent commission.

Two days later, Mr. Schwab said that not only was it not stolen, but he had actually found a buyer for it with an offer of fifty thousand dollars, certified check. Tellar told him to accept the offer and that he would drop by later that day. Tellar checked the Jewelry store out before parking, just in case it was a set up. It did not seem to be, so Tellar entered the store. Mr. Schwab greeted him cordially enough and called him over to a corner of the store. They spoke to each other softly and then shook hands. Mr. Schwab handed him a certified check for the full fifty thousand dollars, and Tellar gave him the watch. Tellar asked him about other jewelry that he had, some was probably not fine enough for him to buy while other pieces were very nice indeed. Mr. Schwab said that as long as it wasn't anything like the watch, he could and would pay cash, no questions asked. While he was there he bought his mother a beautiful diamond ring four total karats in weight. The center diamond was a full one karat. He would give it to his mother upon her return home.

Tellar took the Certified check to his bank and deposited it. They informed him that with amounts that high that there would be a seven day hold on the funds before they were deposited, and did he need the money before that time. Tellar knew that there would be a hold and wasn't worried about it. He said that unless an absolute catastrophe occurred, he would not need the funds. Tellar's bank account now totaled over one hundred thousand dollars and still he had stacks of cash back at his lair. He bought more and more change and small bills from other banks and soon had the jugs filled to over flowing. He used the two wheeler and brought them in one by one and had the money sorted and counted, and deposited into his bank accounts.

Before he knew it, another Summer was over and Autumn was in the air once more. The town was once more hosting the Punkin' Chunkin' contest, but it was illegal to leave your machine unattended without being locked down. It had been awhile now since Tellar had killed. He remembered the look on the kid Jerrold Nadler's face as he sailed through the air, before hitting that window. Tellar had the urge to kill another kid or two. He remembered seeing some boys playing in the storm drainage ditches not long ago. He packed up several magazines of subsonic ammunition and one of the suppressed 9 mm pistols. He went shopping for some toy guns for the kids, then went hunting.

It took him a couple of days, but early on Saturday morning he saw the same boys playing. He rode his bike to where he could get down into the ditch and then rode up to the boys and gave them the toy guns. He talked them into breaking up into teams of four each and then chose their "forts" between the uneven grounds and broken concrete of where the ditches ended. There were walls standing here and there and others that had fallen. At first their were attacks and counter-attacks between the teams. They would throw dirt clods like hand grenades. Tellar told his team to lay low and defend the fort. He was going to reconnoiter the enemies fort and try to take it. The boys hid their heads down occasionally peeking over the wall. Tellar worked his way around quietly to the other teams fort. They were collecting dirt clods to mount an offensive against him and his team. Tellar drew the 9 mm, and shot the boys in their faces. Then he ran back to his fort and was talking to his "team". Tellar looked at the three boys, then shot each of them in turn. The last boy was crying and scared. He had urinated and defecated his pants. Tellar pointed the gun at the boy, who begged for his life. Tellar smiled at him and told him to leave, and when the boy turned around to run, Tellar shot him in the base of the skull.

Tellar picked up the brass casings and then the toy guns. He put them in a culvert and then rode away on his bike. He rode for several miles before exiting the ditches near some strip malls. He rode behind them stopping from time to time to look at boxes and crates stored behind the shopping centers. Behind one was a Police Officer talking to a young girl who he had caught in the act of solicitation. She was giving him oral sex hidden behind some dumpsters. Tellar shot him and then cut through the buildings and away as fast as he could without looking suspicious. He was far enough away before the girl realized that she was giving oral sex to a dead guy.

Tellar made it home and lay upon his bed. He could remember each and every kill. He counted them and was surprised to find that his body count was fifty one. Tellar smiled despite himself, tomorrow he would go hunting again. He rose early and packed a lunch in his pack. He took the 9mm suppressed pistol and several magazines full of ammo, two knives and two grenades. Tellar decided to ride his bike in search of yard sales this early Sunday morning, as he really enjoyed just riding down the roads. He rode the same way the morning that he saw the Armored car. What surprised him most was that the Armored car was there again, on a Sunday morning, before it was light. The only difference now was that the Guard walking around had an M4 carbine. Tellar crept into the bushes and watched. The Guard that was trying to change the canisters was jumping at every sound, and was having difficulty in trying to get the canisters in. Tellar drew the suppressed pistol and took aim. There was a sound from the far side of the armoured car and both Guards jumped. The one with the M4 walked around to see what it was, carbine at the ready. Tellar shot him in the head and watched him fall. The other Guard jumped up and was trying to get inside the front of the truck, Tellar put five rounds into his back. He fell forward. Tellar ran and retrieved the three canisters and took them back to his bike in the bushes. The back of the Armored Car was open and there was a bag in there. Tellar was tempted to go back for it, but thought better of it. Suddenly the canisters started to emit gas and dye, Tellar moved away from them, grabbed the M4 and rode away.

Tellar knew it had been a trap and he was lucky to have escaped it. He rode as fast as he could to clear the area. He heard a Police cruiser headed his way and he rode behind a large hedge. It sped past heading for the ATM and crime scene, he wrapped the M4 in his hoody to conceal it. Tellar decided to go back home and get his van. He took a longer way home and put his bike inside his house, stashed the M4 in a closet and locked the doors. He got in his van and started it up. The sun was above the horizon now. He was feeling anxious and didn't know why. Maybe it was the fact that he almost got caught again. He put Beethoven's Moonlight Sonata in his CD player and drove out to the next county to see what he could find. He found a lot of hunting equipment this time at all of the yard sales. Even found a few rifles and one old lady had six revolvers and two automatic pistols that used to belong to her husband, who had been a State Trooper for thirty five years. They were still in their factory boxes. He had helped move a large piece of furniture and they were in the top of it. She found them and offered to sell them to Tellar, who told her he couldn't pay what they were worth. She asked him what he could pay her and he said that he only had four hundred dollars on him and she told him that she needed the four hundred dollars more than she needed the guns. Tellar gave her the money and she gave him the guns, which he quickly stored in the hidden locked strong box in the van. He had dozens of crossbow bolts, arrows and various points for them both.

On the way back he stopped off at the local super store, just inside the front doors they had arrows and bolts for just one dollar each, with packages of six points for just fifty cents. Tellar took the basket and rolled it through the store to the Sporting Goods Department, where he found more knives and points on sale. He put everything in the basket and rolled it to the counter. The girl behind the counter, Rayleigh, was flirting with Tellar and not really counting the arrows and bolts, nor anything else in the basket. She only rung up fifty dollars worth of merchandise. Tellar paid, and they exchanged numbers, then helped Rayleigh bag all of the merchandise. He rolled it to his van which was already filled with hunting gear. He was no longer anxious but was excited with his great fortune today.

As he was driving back to his house, he saw a new business with a grand opening sign out front. He stopped and looked around. It was a knife store with swords, knives, mediæval weapons, shields armour, and things of that sort. He was surprised at the display on the wall which had a shield in the center and knives and swords radiating outward from it. He purchased a similar shield and two halberds, six swords and ten each of six different knife styles. He was particularly interested in the Holbein Dagger design. It had been created by Hans Holbein for Henry the Eighth as a hunting dagger. Later the Nazi's had appropriated the design for several of their daggers. The Proprietor, Michael Miller, showed Tellar several reproduction Nazi daggers. Teller bought a dozen of each. He loved the SS and SA style as they were the same as the Holbein, but with fancy chain from which they hung. But the SA Feldherrnhalle dagger was even more beautiful, being a variation on the Holbein Dagger. A slightly longer handle, with a longer thinner blade. Michael told Tellar about some original Nazi daggers that he had for sale, none had the chain on them, but Tellar purchased all five of them. He was going to design a special display back in his apartment for them. He also purchased a Norman kite shield with a Nazi Navel Banner design painted on the front of it. Tellar was now very excited and was anxious to get home and get to work.

He stopped off at Frasers Hardware store to buy some hooks and wires to hang the daggers and swords upon the walls. He had been shown how the display had been done at the knife store and it was done with just cup hooks and wire hangers. He had to cut one of the Halberd staves in half so that they would lie flat on the wall beneath the shield. Next he hung the shield and then started to arrange the dagger and swords. It took him until well after nightfall to get them arranged and mounted but the effect was very striking. Tellar looked on line and found other displays and how they were arranged. Most also had flintlock rifles and pistols as well, and Tellar gave serious consideration to purchasing a few to enhance his display. He mounted two of his crossbows and six of the bows that he had acquired from yard sales as well. It was he thought, a fine display even without the flintlocks.

Tellar was in a fairly good mood and decided to give Rayleigh a text and see if she wanted to go out tonight. He asked if she wanted to get something to eat and hang out, her response was "I would love for you to eat me out!" with an emoji of a smiley face looking up. Tellar was smiling as he got into the shower, and he turned to let the powerful water jet hit him at the base of his skull. The feeling was amazing and hypnotic, as the heat penetrated the skin, the water massaged the nerves, he relaxed. The faces of all those that he had killed paraded through his mind, and his pleasure increased. The faces were parading into his mind's eye from the left, and smiley faces were cascading in from the right, one for each kill. He felt the desire to get tattoos of smiley faces, one for each kill. Kill marks are what the Military used to call them. Tankers, Artillery Gunners and Pilots used to mark their barrels and fuselages for their kills, Tellar remembered reading about it once. He finished his shower and dried off.

Tellar checked his text messages and Rayleigh had texted him four more times, plus she had sent him a picture of her vagina. Unlike most American and Canadian women, who shaved their pubic hair like licensed prostitutes, to control lice and scabies, Rayleigh had a very full and thick pubis, which really got Tellar excited.

He found it disgusting that a woman was so nasty and unclean that she had to shave her pubic area to keep it clean. It was the reason why he was more turned on by more Mature women, who may trim the area, but not shave it bald. The thought of a bald pubis and the nasty creatures that inhabit a diseased vagina, literally made him shudder. It was sure to turn him off. He looked at her picture, then took a picture of his erect penis and sent it to her, she responded with a great big heart!

She was waiting for him when he drove up and she barely let him stop, before she opened the door and jumped in. "Drive to the park down by the ball fields!" She commanded and he obeyed. She reached over and freed his penis from his pants and started sucking it. Damn she was great, he thought. Not once did her teeth scrape his shaft, and her mouth was hot and felt like liquid pleasure. He had gotten parked under a tree and had pushed his seat back, to make it easier for her, and she took his hard shaft deeper into her throat, and he couldn't take it any longer. He orgasmed hard, into her mouth, and she refused to release it from the hot, prison of her mouth. She drank him in, which was a lot, as it had been a while since he had had sex. She kept him in her mouth until every last drop had been drained from his cock. She smiled and tried to kiss him, and he let her kiss him passionately. Most guys wouldn't dare let you kiss them after you just sucked their cock, but Tellar was different, and it turned her on even more. She saw the bed in the back of the van and smiled at him. She walked back and lay upon it and spread her legs. Tellar could see the thick cream oozing from her quivering, aching pussy, and was between her legs in no time licking and sucking, trying to do for her what she had just done for him.

She lay back and felt his hot mouth and tongue moving in and around the folds of her pussy and her thick bush. It was magical and he definitely knew how to eat pussy, and it wasn't long before she was having her first, second and third orgasms. He did not seem interested in stopping and acted as if he were a starving man and her pussy was an all you could eat buffet! She was finally able to pull him up and they kissed, this time with pussy cream all over his face. She kissed and licked him, cleaning her sweet cream off his face and mouth. His penis was hard again and it slid into her easily. They both moaned and kissed the other more passionately. They were no longer in a hurry and he took his time making love to her.

As they were driving back into town to eat, she saw Ms. Herring, her Teacher of the Women's studies class at school. She pointed her out and said "I would love to shoot that fucking bitch! She's such a fucking cunt, nobody can stand her!" Tellar smiled and asked if she would really kill her, "fuck yeah!" was Rayleigh's response. They stopped at the Whataburger and got something to eat, and talked about anything and everything that popped into their heads. They talked until Rayleigh had to get home. She kissed him passionately for a few minutes until her father turned the porch light on. It was his signal to come inside. She said that she would call and text him later and that she had the best time ever. He told her the same and kissed her one last time. He watched her get inside before he drove home.

He was now working more for himself than for Mr. Fraser, but made it a point to go in every morning early. Most of the Professional Tradesmen would be there standing around the counter drinking coffee and putting each other down. They always perked up when the saw Tellar, and kidded each other that they all needed to hire a dozen like him, then maybe the work would get done and done correctly. Then they would all purchase their supplies and go to their first jobs. Tellar would sweep the store and talk with Mr. Fraser about the new tools and gadgets, or about jobs that needed to be done. Mr. Fraser was only taking a referral fee for the jobs that Tellar did for him, and it was only a small fee and was insisted upon by Tellar. The other guys were not taking a fee, because he was doing them a favor and was doing a great job and made them look good. Tellar told Mr. Fraser that he had a job to do at three thirty that day, and Mr. Fraser smiled and told him that would be fine. Tellar worked hard around the Hardware store and kept it neat and clean, and Mr. Fraser wished his other employees would be as diligent and hard working as Tellar.

Tellar drove to Rayleigh's school and followed Ms. Herring home. He watched the house with a FLIR scope and then through the windows. She was sitting in a large comfortable looking chair. In front of her on the TV set, she was watching lesbian porn. It was a disturbing film where the women would murder men and the fuck on top of their bloody corpses. He watched a car drive up and a young woman got out and walked up to the door. The door opened and she walked in. They went into the den where the chair was, Ms. Herring was dressed in black latex and the woman had stripped nude. Ms. Herring slapped the woman hard across the face, then pushed her shoulders down. The woman went down in front of her, and Tellar could guess what she was doing. Tellar looked around for a place to snipe her from. There was a road just a hundred yards away. It was a Service road and little used, and there were trees along it to provide some cover. This would do nicely he thought. He would meet Rayleigh, they would have dinner and sex then her would get the rifle set up for her and she could kill the sick bitch.

The next couple of days were very busy with jobs for Tellar. He and Rayleigh talked when they could and texted each other in between the calls. They made arrangements for dinner the next night, and since it was a school night she would have to be in by ten. Tellar didn't mind, he was just happy to be with her. Tellar surprised everyone when he drove into the driveway and walked to the door and rang the bell. Rayleigh's father answered the door and he introduced himself. He was invited in and he introduced himself to the rest of her family. They asked him a lot of questions, all which he answered politely. Her parents were impressed with Tellar and appreciated that he took the time to meet with them. He told Rayleigh's father that he would have her home by ten, and to everyone's surprise her father said ten thirty would be fine and to enjoy themselves. Rayleigh's father tried to give Tellar some money, but he thanked him and refused and said that he earned a lot of money in his work and could take her to nice places and treat her well. They went to the Whataburger again because Rayleigh loved their burgers and fries. Afterwards Tellar drove her up to the Service road and showed her Ms. Herrings house.

They were looking through binoculars, through the big den window and could see that she had the sick anti male porn on her TV again, but couldn't see her. Tellar got his FLIR scope and looked around the house. She was passed out in the big chair in front of the TV. He noticed that her car wasn't in the drive and told Rayleigh that she wasn't home. He opened a panel in his van and removed the Bravo 51 Sniper rifle and set it up in the opened the side window. Tellar told her that she wasn't home and that they should shoot her window and TV out. She laughed and wanted to do it, she wanted to scare the shit out of that bitch. Tellar lined up the rifle and had to guess where her head was. Once he had the rifle positioned, and told her all she had to do was pull the trigger. Rayleigh looked through the scope on the rifle and was puzzled that it was aimed at the chair. Tellar told her that way, they could break the window, tear up the chair that she sat in to watch TV and blow out the TV as well.

Rayleigh looked through the scope and Tellar told her to gently squeeze the trigger. The shot was not as loud as Rayleigh thought it should have been, and Tellar told her that it was a suppressed weapon and that anyone close by would still have heard it, but that not as far away as Ms. H's house. She looked through the scope again. There was a hole in the plate glass window and it was shattered like all safety glass shatters. There were no huge shards, but the glass was an intricate web of tiny pieces that remained in the frame. Accentuating the hole in the middle of the glass. The TV had shattered and was no longer playing. Tellar looked with the FLIR scope and wasn't able to tell if Ms. H had been hit or not. Tellar took the rifle and put it back in it's hiding place.

They drove away laughing and went down to the ball field and made love. Tellar got her home right at ten thirty and kissed her good night. Tellar wondered what the next few days would be like when Rayleigh had found out whether or not she had killed Ms. H. If so, how would she feel about it.

The next day Ms. H did not show up for work, nor the next day or the next. Rumors had started to spread about the videos found in her house and how she had committed suicide when she had gotten caught with them. Though the Police were trying to keep everything hush hush, the titles of the videos had somehow gotten out. Rumors were flying about where she was and if she had really committed suicide or had run away. No one seemed to know anything, and the Police weren't talking. It was also rumored that her Lesbian lover had found her, some accounts say with a married influential man and had tried to kill them, or had just come in and found someone well known standing over her dead body. The stories got pretty wild, still Rayleigh never even considered that she might be the one to actually have killed her.

Rayleigh texted Tellar and invited him to a party at a friends house this Friday night. Tellar told her that he would pick her up at seven thirty. He was a little early, but that just meant more time with her. He drove over to the superstore where she worked and parked way out in the parking lot by other vehicles. They got in the back and made love, then drove to the party. Rayleigh introduced him to all her friends and the girls all remarked about how cute he was. Some of the kids were passing around weed and pills. Rayleigh took a couple of pills and took a hit off a joint and handed it to Tellar who looked at her with a horrified expression. "Come on baby, it'll be fun!" she told him. He told her that he didn't do drugs and she wouldn't either as long as she was with him. She looked at him then blew the smoke from the joint into his face. "BYE." is all she said then turned and ran hand in hand with another boy into another room.

Tellar was furious and left. He drove to Rayleigh's house and spoke with her father, who followed Tellar back over to the house in his own car. When they got there Rayleigh was in the middle of four other boys, sitting on one who had his penis in her vagina, the one behind her was fucking her in the ass, and she was taking turn sucking two other boys off. Her father threw the boys off her one by one and then pulling her off the last violently. He forced her to get dressed and then had Tellar call the Police, which he did. She cussed him out the whole time her father was leading her to his car. He thanked Tellar and shook his hand and told him to leave quickly before the Police arrived. They went their separate ways with Rayleigh yelling one last insult at him before her father drove away. He knew all the guys that she was having sex with, and the one who provided the drugs, and he would make them beg to die.

The one who provided the drugs was a known pedophile and was only their for the underage sex. Tellar knew where he lived and knew that he had left the party as soon as Rayleigh's father had shown up. Tellar put on a tight shirt and some torn jeans and rode his skateboard up and down in front of the pedophiles house. It wasn't long before the pedophile was looking out and watching Tellar. Tellar had made himself look as young as possible and dressed like the other freaks around here. He even had a Hello Kitty backpack, with a change of clothes and a suppressed nine millimeter pistol. The pedophile opened his door and asked Tellar what he was up to, and Tellar told him that he was looking to get into something, which meant that he looking for drugs and sex. The pedophile asked him what he liked, meaning boys or girls, and Tellar's response was "everything" which meant that he liked both boys and girls.

   The pedophile stepped back and opened the door wide. Tellar kicked his skateboard up and walked inside. The pedophile squeezed Tellar's ass when he walked past. Tellar didn't even flinch. The door closed behind him and when Tellar turned around the pedophile was naked with a definite erection. He walked over to Tellar who reached out and took his erect penis in his hand and started playing with it. The pedophile rubbed Tellar's bulge and smiled. He pulled Tellar's penis out and lead him to a bedroom close by. Tellar pushed him onto the bed then slowly started to get undressed, while the pedophile stroked his own cock. When Tellar was nude he unzipped the backpack and the quickly pulled out the pistol and shot the pedophile twelve times as fast as he could pull the trigger. The pedophile lay dead and Tellar policed his brass, making sure that he found all twelve casings. Tellar walked into the kitchen and got a butcher's knife to cut off the pedophiles dick, which he shoved down his throat, turned his body over, then shoved the knife up the pedophiles ass. He looked around and found the pedophiles stash of drugs and cash and he put it in his back pack as well as some jewelry that he found. He made a mess and made it look like a robbery, got dressed then left.

   He went to find the four boys that Rayleigh had been fucking, turned out that they all four played on the football team. He poisoned some of the pills and gave them to the boys and told them to try them and that if they liked them, then he could hook them up and that they could supply the product their friends. He gave them each one pill and told them to try them, and they would see how superior his product was and that he would sell strictly to them and that they could make a fortune off the other kids. Tellar went with them behind the stadium at school and took the pills underneath the bleachers. The drug worked very quickly and they were soon unconscious. Tellar undressed them and placed them in a position of sexually compromising position of looking like they were in a four way suck off. He left them there and they were found by other students who took a bunch of pictures and shared them through text with other students, before reporting it to the Police, which caused a lot of controversy and trouble.

The school's Principal asked them where they got the drugs, but they wouldn't tell him, couldn't tell him because they didn't really know Tellar, and Tellar had told them that his name was Nomad. He also told them that he was a new student, and they thought to themselves that they would look for him at school and settle this themselves. However, they were dropped from the football team and suspended from school for the drug use and sex on school property. The police arrived and took them to juvenile detention for the drug use. Their parents would have to pick them up.

The police found Tellar's DNA at the pedophiles house. They came to see him at Fraser's Hardware and questioned him about his connection to the pedophile. Mr. Fraser let them use his office for privacy. Technically, since he was underage, they could not question him without his parents being present. Since his mother was out of state for a visit Mr. Fraser sat with him. He told them how he had been asked by the man to do some repair work on a couple of interior doors and what he charged. Tellar said that the man had agreed to his price. The man showed Tellar the doors and Tellar looked them over and found nothing wrong. He told them that when he turned around the man was nude and started fondling Tellar. Tellar started crying while relating his story to the Police, and said that he had kneed the man in the groin and ran away. He said that he didn't tell anyone because he was too embarrassed. Tellar told them to please not tell his mom because it would only worry her. They told Tellar that the man was dead and that they were only following leads and that his DNA had been found at the scene. Tellar gave them a shocked look. He said that he didn't know someone could die from a knee to the groin, and that he did not mean to kill him. The Officers looked at each other and then at Mr. Fraser, then back at Tellar. They told him that he had been shot and then mutilated. Tellar looked at Mr. Fraser and then back at the Officers, and asked them what they meant by mutilated. The Officers said that they had no more questions and told Tellar to not get upset, that he obviously wasn't involved and that they were sorry that he had to experience something so awful.

Back out in the store they thanked Mr. Fraser and said personally, the bastard had gotten what he deserved, as he was a known pedophile. Mr. Fraser agreed with them and shook their hands and thanked them. Mr. Fraser told Tellar that he would never mention it again, but if he ever needed anything or had trouble with anyone that he could always come to him and he would help Tellar any way that he could. Tellar thanked him and said that he was proud that Mr. Fraser was his friend. Mr. Fraser smiled at him and told him to take the rest of the day off. Tellar returned Mr. Fraser's smiled, thanked him and drove to mall.

Tellar went into the Hot Topics store and was looking around, He found a cool long coat that fit him and some pants with lot's of pockets. They also had a belt with several pouches on it. Tellar noticed a very beautiful, petite boy watching him and kinda following him around. The store was oddly shaped and Tellar went around a corner, ducked down and watched for the boy. The boy came around the corner acting as if he was just shopping, and looked around for Tellar. He walked to the back corner where Tellar stepped out of the clothes rack and put his arms around the young man, who gasped and turned in Tellar's arms. He was shorter than Tellar and had to look up into his eyes. Tellar kissed him on the lips and the beautiful boy returned his kiss. The kiss became passionate, but they had to stop because they heard someone coming. They stood there looking at a t-shirt and talked softly about the graphics. Tellar told the beautiful boy "Come on, let's go eat." They left the mall together and Tellar drove to the back of the parking lot and parked, so that they could talk.

Tellar looked the boy over, he was very small for a boy and quite beautiful. He was soft spoken and effeminate. Tellar introduced himself and asked him his name, Robbie Holt, the boy told him was his name. His voice was high and soft like a females, and he could pass for a girl with no trouble at all. Tellar asked him if he had a boyfriend, and was pleased to find out that he didn't. Tellar took him by the hand and lead him to the back of the van, laid down and pulled Robbie down on top of him and looked deeply into his eyes. They kissed again and Tellar could tell that Robbie was really into him. They made out like the teenagers they were, and they eventually found themselves nude. They started in a sixty-nine position until Tellar was so turned on that he had to make love to Robbie. Robbie lay there, legs spread waiting as Tellar rubbed Vaseline on the tip of his hard cock and Robbie's virgin anus. Tellar was gentle, and before he knew it, he was inside Robbie who seemed to be enjoying it. Robbie was so beautiful and sexy, and he turned Tellar on so much, that he could no longer hold back and he exploded inside of Robbie and collapsed on top of him. Robbie held him and enjoyed the feel of Tellar on top of him. He kissed and licked Tellar's ears and neck.

After a few moments, Tellar started moving again, he was still erect and still very much turned on. They kissed passionately, and Robbie was the best kisser that he had ever met. Tellar made love to Robbie who came while Tellar was giving him long slow strokes with his very hard penis. Robbie's small, beautiful, uncut penis exploded, shooting his semen all over his own chest and face. Tellar licked it off and started kissing him again. It did not take Tellar much longer before he was having his second orgasm, which he pumped deep into Robbie's anus. He collapsed beside Robbie and pulled him over to him and they kissed while Tellar held him. Tellar looked Robbie in they eyes and asked him how he would like to become his girlfriend, Robbie kissed him passionately in response. He straddled Tellar, who was again erect and ready, and eased himself down Tellar's hard shaft. Robbie rode him and it wasn't long before Robbie was coming again. Tellar yanked him forward and took his penis into his mouth and drank every drop from Robbie, who was shaking with the force of his orgasm. He responded like a woman, and Tellar was totally fascinated by him. He wanted to be with him and did not want to part from him. Robbie could pass for a twelve year old boy or girl, but the fact was, he was eighteen even though he did not, could not pass for his real age. He would graduate this year, while Tellar was still in his Junior year.

Tellar asked for Robbie to spend the night, but Robbie said that his Mother wouldn't allow him at such short notice and that she still worried about him. Robbie had an older brother Dwayne, and two younger sisters Angela and April. But his mom worried about him the most, because he was so small and effeminate, and was pretty sure that he was gay. She worried about older perverts and HIV, and was just really afraid for her little boy. Tellar took him back to his place where they made out for a little while longer. Robbie sucked him off and Tellar returned the favor. They cleaned up and Tellar drove him home. He walked Robbie to the door and waited to meet his Mother. He introduced himself to her and told her all about himself. He told her that they had met at the mall and had become fast friends and just wanted her to know who he was hanging out with. He gave them both his business card, and told Robbie to call him so that they could hang out and do things. Robbie's mother was impressed by Tellar, like everyone who met him. He was very charming and people liked him immediately. Robbie told him that he had to go visit his father and would be there the whole weekend, but maybe they could hang out for a while Monday afternoon. Tellar said good bye and really wanted to kiss Robbie who felt the same, but Tellar waved and turned away and walked back to his van.

Saturday morning, Tellar received a call from Robbie's mother, Angie. She said that she had a bookshelf that needed repair and asked Tellar how much. He told her that it depended on what needed to be done, but that it shouldn't cost very much at all. He told her that he was free now, and asked if he could come take a look at it. She said that now was a great time. Robbie and his mother could have been twins, except that she looked older than him, otherwise they looked almost exactly alike, and both were tiny. Tellar arrived at the house shortly and she showed him the bookshelf. Tellar tried to move it and could tell that it had become loose and just need to be tightened back up. It had been put together with nails instead of screws, and Tellar told her that it was a very simple fix. He got his tool box, some short wood screws and some corner brackets from his van and soon had it fixed. When she asked how much, he told her "No charge." She was trying to argue with him but he just shook his head.

She asked if he wanted some tea, and he said that he would love some tea, and a chance to get to know her better and for her to get to know him better. They talked and she showed him some pictures and he asked to see pictures of her when she was young, she laughed and said that he really didn't want to see some ancient photos of her. Tellar reassured her and soon they were pouring over pictures of her and the kids. Robbie and her were identical. When she was between the ages of twelve to eighteen, she looked exactly like him, and there was no difference in her appearance at those ages. He complimented her on her looks, and she acted as if she were an old hag, which couldn't be farther from the truth. She was enjoying being with Tellar and talking to him, and she was more than a little attracted to him, and she was aching to make love to him.

She remembered that the closet door in the boy's room was almost falling off, and she showed him. The screw holes were wallowed out and the screws no longer fit in them. Tellar told her to get some toothpicks while he got some slightly larger and longer screws. He broke the toothpicks off in the screw holes then put new screws in one hole at a time. When he finished the door was closing and staying closed, and was no longer falling off. She looked at what he had done and he was explaining it to her, and she was very close. He took her in his arms and kissed her. Her arms were around his neck and she was returning his kisses. He picked her up and took her to the bed across the room and laid her upon it and lay next to her, without ever breaking the kiss.

His hands were under her blouse and he was fondling her small breast. Her nipples were very large and very, very hard. She moaned while they kissed. It had been five years since her and her husband had divorced, and she hadn't been with any other man since. She was rubbing his erection through his pants, until he unbuckled his belt and opened his trousers, freeing his throbbing erect penis. He lifted her skirt and rubbed her clitoris through her panties, she almost came. He pushed her panties aside and slid his tongue over and around her wet, creamy pussy, and it was too much for her to stand, she had her first orgasm and he licked her clean. He pulled her panties off and slid his very hard and aching penis into her hot, wet pussy. He slid in so easily, and she moaned with the pleasure of it. He rolled over, taking her with him. She straddled him and rode his cock, while he removed her blouse, and massaged her breast. She was enjoying the feel of his hard cock inside her, and was riding it slowly trying not to cum again so soon, when he leaned forward and started sucking one of her small breast and huge nipples. She was overwhelmed and she had an extremely powerful orgasm, so much so that it brought tears to her eyes, and she cried with the force of her orgasm.

He asked her what was wrong and she could only shake her head, until her orgasm subsided somewhat. She kissed him passionately and told him that was the first real, full body orgasm in a long time. He fondled her buttocks and moved her around continuing to make love to her, until he had to roll over on top of her and pound into her. She was moaning loudly and telling him to fuck her pussy hard and told him to pound her pussy good, and was soon having another orgasm, Tellar gave two more mighty thrust and exploded inside of her, and collapsed. She held him like Robbie had their first time, it was like making love to Robbie, except for her incredibly creamy pussy and her huge nipples and small breast. They lay there talking, kissing and exploring each others bodies, for a while. They made love two more times, and once more in the shower, just before he left.

She asked if he would like to do it more often and he said that he would love to, but that she had to promise never to tell, or let on in front of Robbie. She promised and said that she could never discuss sex with her kids. They kissed once more and he left. Tellar felt ten feet tall, and decided to drive around, and soon found himself headed out of town. He drove down the highway and turned onto a smaller two lane road. Through some trees he could see three boys swinging on a rope swing out into a large creek, where they splashed around. He pulled over and parked his van behind an old abandoned house. He got his Bravo 51 out and took careful aim at the rope where it was tied around the branch. The boys were seeing how far out they could swing before letting go. Tellar fired the suppressed rifle and the rope snapped as it got to the end of it's outward arc, sending the boy flailing into the opposite bank of the creek. He hit hard then tumbled into the water and sank. The other boys looked at each other and drove into the stream looking for their friend. They were frantically trying to find him. He watched them through binoculars. The boy never surfaced, the other two ran as fast as they could towards a house that Tellar could barely make out on the other side of the field beneath some trees. Tellar stowed the rifle and binoculars and drove away.

Tellar drove around and then finally went home. He looked around and then remembered the M4 that he had stashed in the closet some time back. He checked and it was still there, still wrapped in his hoody. He took the rifle out and walked over to the fridge and slid it out and went into the tunnel behind it. He had to duck his head as it was a bit low. He unlocked the door on the other end of the tunnel, then unlocked the gun vault. The guns leaned against the walls and Tellar had planned on building racks for them. The plywood and lumber that he had purchased was still there. Tellar fetched his power tools and then cleared the room of the weapons. He covered the walls with the three quarters inch plywood built, shelves four feet high, then made a low rail, on top. He drilled holes every six inches along two walls, then put wood glue on the pegs he had cut and lightly tapped them into the holes. On the third wall and on both sides of the door, he built shallow railed shelves, that he could lean the pistols on barrel towards the wall, butt of the handle faced outward.

Tellar sorted the rifles and pistols by caliber and type and then grouped them together. He had used three layers of the fire proof Sheetrock behind the plywood to help make the room more sound proof and fire resistant. Now he moved the dehumidifier to it's permanent resting place and was finished. It looked great and like a real arsenal should. He sorted the magazines for the pistols and rifles and stored them under the gun it had been made for. He kept very few loaded magazines as they tended to lose spring tension after a while, which is why you should unload then from time to time and let them rest. He had seen speed loading equipment and then found a link on how to make them on a video hosting site. Under the videos in the comments section were the specifications and measurements. Tellar took pictures of the specs and would purchase the materials tomorrow. Before he quit, he rigged the entire lair to blow up with the explosives that he had taken. He rigged the switch and then ran more explosives along the tunnels and into his house. He couldn't let this place ever be found or taken. Lastly, he rigged a gas valve so that it could be opened remotely. It was getting late and Tellar was getting tired. He locked everything up and then went back to his apartment.

 He got in the shower and let the hot water massage the base of his skull, until he was relaxed. He washed himself then rinsed off and dried himself with a thick, luxurious towel. He got a glass of tea and sat down in comfortable wing back chair that he had found at a yard sale. It was thickly padded and filled with real goose down. He was sitting there relaxing when his phone rang, it was Angie. She told him that she was still thinking about him, and how much she enjoyed today, how wonderful it had been to be with someone. Tellar told her he felt the same way. Tellar asked her to come over and spend the night, but she said that she couldn't, but with just a little persuasion, he talked her into it, and it wasn't long before she was knocking on the door. Angie was there with a long coat on and a small suitcase. He invited her in and she put the suitcase down. He offered to take her coat, and was surprised to find her naked underneath. He hung up the coat and came over to her, took her in his arms and kissed her passionately. In between kisses, she told him that her pussy was sore, he asked if she would rather not have sex, to which she replied that he "had better feed her hungry little pussy that hot sausage and make sure that she wouldn't be able to walk tomorrow". They made love all night, into the wee hours of the morning and fell asleep before dawn.

She woke and kissed him, he pulled her to him and slid easily into her. They both came quickly, she kissed him and then dressed and left. Tellar lay there only a moment longer, turned on the coffee pot then got into the shower. He lingered a while under the hot water as it massaged the base of his skull. It sent tingles up and down his spine. Reluctantly he dried off and poured himself a cup of coffee. He dressed and then went out to clean his van. He remembered that his Mom would be returning from her Sisters house next week, and when he finished straightening up his van, went to check his mom's house. He dusted and vacuumed the main areas, then went to get himself something to eat. He thought of Robbie and Angie, both were such a turn on to him.

He got into his van and drove South out of town towards the warehouse district in the nearby city. He parked and put two suppressed semi-automatic pistols into his waistband and pulled his hoody over them. He put on a cap with long hair sewn around the bottom of it and walked away towards the warehouses. He had heard that there were a lot of homeless and transients around and he wanted to hunt them down. He didn't have to hunt for long. The first warehouse contained several shoddily built "rooms" each with a sheet for a door. He could hear people sleeping behind the closed curtains, several snored. He carefully looked into the ones that had no snoring coming from behind the curtains, sure enough, there were sleeping people in each. Tellar couldn't tell their sexes due to the heavy coats and blankets, and it didn't matter, he took aim and shot them in the head, one by one.

The last one was snoring so loud, he wondered how anyone else could sleep. Tellar peeked in and saw the dirty face of a scraggly bearded man lying on his back. Tellar smiled and aimed for his left nostril, which was huge, and squeezed the trigger. The man's body jerked once and the snoring stopped immediately. He put another round up his right nostril, and the top of the mans head blew off, spraying blood all over his pillow and the cardboard wall. The bullet and some of the brain matter going through the bullet hole in the cardboard. Tellar smiled, he had just killed eight people. Excrement thought he, human refuse that needed to be destroyed, trash and he was the Trash man. He was humanity's Sanitation Worker, he thought, I Am A Man, and you, you are just trash to be collected. He was walking along, lost in his own thoughts and almost walked right into a girl. She smiled at him, he fired the .45 from inside his pocket, and the bullet hit her under the chin. The large round blew the back of her head off, and she jerked backwards and fell to the ground dead.

"Andrea?" Another girl that he couldn't see was emerging from one of the makeshift rooms. She had seen the girl jerk and fall back, and ran to her side. Tellar was ready for her as she knelt down beside the girl he had just slain. She looked up at Tellar and he shot her between the eyes. He policed his brass as usual, and reloaded his pistols. He heard some commotion at the back of the warehouses, and went to check it out. He was being careful not to be seen or heard. He came upon rows of shelve made to hold great amounts of weight. He climbed up to the top shelf and continued onto the end. There were two men sitting outside the door, obviously armed, and guarding the door from unwanted visitors. He watched them for a moment from behind some crates stacked at the end of the shelves.

Tellar looked for something that he could throw, to distract the guards, but all that was up her was some scraps of wood, and none were very large. He picked the largest and threw it as far as he could, and it clattered lightly when it hit. The guards looked in the direction of the noise, and both said "rats" at the same time. The closest one to the noise got up and walked past the shelves and when he was out of sight of the other guy, Tellar shot him in the back of the head. Tellar moved as quietly as he could and looked at the other guard. He was reading a magazine and Tellar shot him in the right eye, and he fell from the chair that he was sitting in. He started to get up and was moaning, and Tellar took careful aim and put four bullets into his back where his heart should be and one in the head. He was dead, Tellar could tell, for certain this time. Tellar climbed down by the first guard that he shot, he searched him and took a gold necklace, two gold rings, an expensive Audemars Piquet watch and a Glock 19, and two magazines.

The other guard had two gold necklaces on, four gold and diamond rings and Jaeger-LeCoulter watch, this guy however carried a Sig-Sauer Legion, with an extended threaded barrel. On his other hip he carried two extra seventeen round magazines and the silencer in a special holster. Tellar took it all, then listened at the door. It sounded as if five or six men were playing poker inside the room. There were windows, but they had been painted the same light green color as the walls. He found a place where the paint had been scratched away, and he peeked in. He could see five men sitting at a table, drinking and playing poker. He could see the rest of the room and no one else was in there, and that at least two of the men were armed.

Tellar went to the door, which swung outwards and checked the knob. It wasn't locked, so he turned it and jerked the door open, and yelled "Freeze!". The men looked at him, and the biggest started to get up, Tellar shot him in the head. He fell back, but did not immediately die. He lay there trying to move, and making some sick moaning and gurgling noises. The other men didn't dare move. All of them were looking at Tellar, their hands upon the table.

"Look kid, just take the money, you made your point, no one is going to challenge you further. Go on take it." Tellar shot them all as quickly as he could. He took their jewelry and money, and then fled the scene. He knew, somehow, that he had just robbed a Mob game and had killed the members of the local Family. He left as soon as he could. He changed his route home and doubled back and made sure no one had followed him. As he was driving the back roads, he saw a motorcycle cop ahead, coming towards him, he put the Mob guards Glock pistol out the window and shot the Officer several times. He saw a boy on a bicycle that he thought had just witnessed what he had done and he shot the boy several times as well, then accidentally dropped the Glock. The boy lived, but could not explain what happened to him, or who had done it. The Police and FBI, were linking them as a Mob hit, and knew that the gun belonged to one of the dead Mobsters at the warehouse. Tellar had just caused the entire area to become a war zone between Families and had alerted all of the State and Federal Law Enforcement agencies.

Tellar awoke early, showered and dressed and drove to the airport to pick up his mother. She had spent two months with her Sisters and Family, and was finally arriving home. Tellar was excited to see her. He waited at the airport, and the news blared from all of the television sets about the Gangland war that was going on and about all of the Agencies involved with trying to investigate the murders and retaliation killings going on. Tellar knew that anything that happened would probably be immediately investigated and that he would most likely be caught. It was as if something inside of him just "switched off", and he became a "normal" boy awaiting his mothers arrival. She came through the terminal and he waved excitedly at her then ran and picked her up and hugged her, and swung her around. They kissed a few times and each told the other how much they had missed each other. She asked what Tellar had been up to and he said that he had been very busy with work and school, and didn't have much time for anything else. He told her about Robbie and told her that he was his new best friend, and about Robbie's divorced mom, and how he had been taken care of by them. Tellar's mom was proud of her son and how sweet and kind he was. Tellar asked about her trip, and his mother talked to him the whole way home about what a wonderful time that she had had, and what a real treat it was that Tellar had sent her to visit her family.

At home She was anxious to fix him dinner, and he let her. All had to be from the freezer or cans, as she had been gone for so long that there was no fresh food in the house. Still, it was delicious and he was pleased to have his mother safe and sound back home again. They sat next to each other on the couch and Tellar had poured some wine for them. He hugged his mother to himself and kissed her from time to time on the forehead and cheeks. They had never before had a problem kissing each other on the lips and soon Tellar was kissing her over and over upon the lips. Both had become inebriated from the wine and soon, Tellar was massaging his mother's breast and kissing her passionately, and she was responding. She had not been with another man since Tellar's father divorced her for a young woman when he was six. Tellar mad love to her and she was too engrossed in how good it felt to realize what they were doing. After several orgasms, his mom fell asleep. Tellar got up and went into the kitchen and poured himself a glass of milk, then went back into his apartment and fell asleep.

Tellar awoke early the next morning and took a shower. He got dressed and drank some coffee. He was reading the paper and wound up reading the real estate ads. There was a horse farm that was up for sale, and Tellar decided to go have a look. He arrived and the house was not occupied. He looked around, peeking into windows, the house was empty and no furniture remained inside. There were stables and Tellar looked around there. The stables were made to be climate controlled, to help with extreme weather, but could also be fully opened to allow for a breeze to cool the stables naturally. Both the Stables and house had separate emergency generators, as well as solar panels. While he was walking around the Owner drove up. Teller introduced himself and told them that he was interested in the place. The owner showed him inside the house, which was beautifully designed. The kitchen was large and made to look as if it were from the 1600's with large counters and a large fireplace at one end. It was large enough to walk into and had iron hangers of various sizes and shapes. You could actually cook in it if you had too. The huge stove and four ovens were at the opposite end of the spacious kitchen. There was a large Dining/Family room off the kitchen and that connected to the Den. There was a dedicated Library next to the Den, and a restroom between the Den and formal Parlor at the front of the house. On the other side of the grand entry hall was the conservatory.

Up the stairs in the entry hall was the living quarters. Four huge bedrooms, three with large walk in closets. There was a large full bathroom for the three bedrooms, with a huge antique copper tub and a full glass enclosed shower. The master bedroom had a full bath as well, but had a closet large enough to be called a room. The closet room was attached to both the bedroom and bath. There were shelves and hanging bars to fit half a clothes store here, plus towels, wash clothes and bath essentials aplenty. The closet room was lined in cedar, with a cedar floor. All shelves were made of cedar as well, as it deterred creepy crawlies.

The owner showed him a secret panel inside the fireplace, which lead to an atom bomb radiation proof shelter, in the subbasement, that was built in the nineteen fifties. It was very spacious at forty five feen wide and one hundred and twenty feet long. It had it's own generator, and was connected to a spring deep underground. There were several rooms here and a separate green house of fifty feet by fifty feet, with ultraviolet growing lights. There was a survival library here and charts on the walls with useful information, including how th use the grow lights to generate the vitamin D in your body. There was a hydroponics lab to turn waste fluids into growing fertilizer for the greenhouse. You could live here indefinitely in case of a nuclear attack. The library was stocked with all kinds of books and materials from the Civil Defense Department of the U.S. Government, all from the forty's, fifties, and sixties. Tellar was very interested in this place. It had everything that he could want and more.

Tellar thanked the Owner and took his information and said that he was going to check with the bank. The owner believed that Tellar was too young, but didn't know the circumstances, nor that Tellar could easily get approved for the loan. Tellar was incredibly excited and drove directly to the bank to apply for the financing. The bank knew Tellar, knew of his investments, but he was still to young to purchase the Horse Farm. Tellar would have to get his Mother to co-sign the loan, which she was happy to do. The bak arranged the purchase and the transfer of funds from investments to escrow. It was only a matter of time now, and as far as everyone was concerned, Tellar had just purchased the Horse Farm.

Tellar was more excited than he had ever been before. He loaded two suppressed pistols, one .45 caliber and one .9mm, as well as several bolts and his crossbow. He drove out two counties over before sun up, telling his mom that he was going hunting. He put on his hunting vest and walked carefully and quietly through the woods. He could smell someone having diarrhea. He looked around and heard the hunter up in his tree stand. Tellar looked up and saw the mans very white arse sticking out between two rails. The man's diarrhea was ballistic and liquid as it shot from his backside. Tellar raised his crossbow and took careful aim through the scope, and let his bolt loose. It sailed swiftly up the mans anus, pitching him forward and over the opposite rail of his stand. The man feel thirty feet, landing on his head with a sickening sound as his neck broke and his skull crushed into pulp.

Tellar looked around, No other stands in sight. He carefully approached the man and searched him. Took what money he had, two hundred and fifteen dollars. Tellar replaced the mans wallet, covered him with branches and leaves, and climbed the tree stand. Here he found the compound bow with sights, silencers on the strings, counterweights, and anything else the man could get on it. It had to worth over three thousand dollars.

There were twenty four arrows in a box, with easy access for a quick draw and nock. Tellar waited until after sunrise and was looking around. He spotted another hunter not too far off, in another tree stand, and took careful aim. The bow almost acted by itself, almost aimed itself and delivered his arrow with amazing precision. He pinned the other hunter to his tree.

Tellar looked through the binoculars. The man was still alive with a shocked expression on his face. He tried in vain to remove the arrow, but it was too deep in the tree. Tellar knew the man would soon push himself forward to free himself from the arrow. Tellar nocked another arrow and let it fly, hitting the man in the other side of the chest. Both lungs were now deflated and the man had a horrified, excruciating look upon his face. Tellar nocked one more arrow, took even more careful aim and put this arrow into the mans mouth. He had aimed for his forehead, but this was just as good. Tellar had severed the mans spinal column, killing him instantly. Tellar lowered all the gear down from the tree by a rope and climbed down. He added it to his own gear and hiked over to the other tree.

From the ground Tellar couldn't see the man, pinned to the tree like a crazed science experiment. Tellar quickly climbed the tree. He searched the man and took everything of value. This hunter had a crossbow, and a dozen bolts. Tellar took his cooler, that was also a backpack, and put everything in it. He lowered everything down out of the stand then climbed down and picked up all the gear. It was almost more than he could carry. He was sweating and breathing heavily when he reached his van. He opened the back doors and loaded the equipment into the van, and had closed the doors when he noticed a car under a near by tree. Two young women were in the car and both were looking at him. They waved and he waved back. He gave them a nervous smile, knowing that they had gotten a real good look at him. He pretended to hike up his pants, while actually repositioning his pistol for a quick easy draw.

The girls opened the doors as he approached the car. They smiled and made small talk, he smiled back and leaned against a tree. They talked easily enough and he could tell that they were flirting with him but he really needed to leave before the hunters were found. He squatted down to get a better look at them when a guy in the back seat leaned forward.

"Hey Tellar! You freak!" he said. It was Jerry Borden from school. Tellar drew his weapon and fired into the vehicle killing both girls and just wounding the guy. He emptied the .9mm into them, but didn't kill Jerry who started to scream. Tellar drew the .45 and shot through the glass in the rear side window, until Jerry was silent. Blood was everywhere, and so was Jerry's head. One of the girl's in the front seat moaned, and Tellar shot them both in the head, blowing their brains out, all over each other. He tried to police the brass but he was almost panicking. He only found a few and he thought that he heard another car coming. He jumped into his van and sped away out the other side of the parking area and down the road.

After a few miles and checking the rear view mirror a few dozen times, Tellar started to relax. There was no traffic and it was still very early. Up ahead in the distance he saw a person walking down the road toward the him. He drew his pistol, rested it between the window and mirror as he drove towards them and fired. The first couple of bullets missed, and they were unaware of the maniac in the van driving towards them was shooting at them. It was an older man who really wasn't paying attention to the van, until the first bullet hit him in the shoulder and spun him around. Blood was gushing from the wound and the man was crying. Tellar pulled up to him and stopped. The man turned to look at him, tears streaming down his face, and the man barely able to speak because he was crying so hard. Tellar shot him between the eyes, his head jerked back as his brains exited from the back of his head. The force of his head jerk tumbled him into a ditch on the side of the road. Brains and blood dripping off the leaves of the trees behind where he stood.

Tellar drove on. Down the road he spotted a police cruiser under a large tree with low branches. The cop had pulled over to take radar and had fallen asleep. Tellar drove a little ways down and pulled off the road. He walked quietly back to the cruiser, the Officer snoring softly. Tellar drew his weapon and pointed it at the Officers head, who suddenly opened his eyes and looked up in surprise. His eyes wide open now and a frantic second trying to draw his weapon before Tellar shot him. The Officers body was spasming as he quickly died. Tellar ran for the van and drove off, getting off this road as fast as he could.

Tellar figured that he had had enough excitement for one day and he drove over to see Robbie, but it was the weekend that he visited his dad. Tellar almost drove off, but decided to knock on the door. Robbie answered it and took Tellar by the hand and pulled him inside. He kissed Tellar passionately. Robbie was dressed like a Catholic schoolgirl, with the short, plaid skirt, the saddle Oxfords, and thigh high white stockings. There was a two inch gap between the bottom of the skirt and the top of the stockings. He wore a white blouse and pig tails. Tellar was very excited and returned Robbie's kiss. Robbie lead him to his room and Tellar threw him into the bed and climbed in on top of him. They made out until Tellar just had to screw Robbie. He did it in the missionary position, which was Robbie's favorite. Tellar came hard and Robbie was just about to, so Tellar took his hard cock into his mouth and swallowed his cum. Tellar collapsed on top of Robbie. They kissed and talked some more until Tellar got excited again.

They made slow love to each other for quite a while. Taking their time and kissing a lot, making sure the other was happy and getting what they wanted and needed. As they lay in bed, Tellar told Robbie about the horse farm. He said that he wanted Robbie and his mom to come live with Tellar's mom and him. Robbie said that they wouldn't be able to have sex if they were in the house, but Tellar told him about the secret room. Tellar got dressed as Robbie changed into regular clothes. His mother didn't know for sure and Robbie didn't want her to know yet. They kissed goodbye and Tellar went home to talk to his mother.

When he got there she was upset about what they had done. Tellar tried to tell her that it was no big deal, because they loved each other and it was only natural. Tellar's mom ranted about it being very unnatural and that it was an abomination and that he was sick if he thought it was natural. She was yelling at him and then she was silent. Tellar had shot her while she was yelling at him. He couldn't understand what was happening. His mom was dead, there was blood everywhere. Tellar panicked and then ran into the bathroom and showered. He changed his clothes and left.

Tellar drove for hours, trying to comprehend what happened and how it happened. He found himself in front of Robbie's house, just sitting when Angie drove up. She walked over to his van and knocked on the window. Tellar jumped violently, which scared Angie as well. She invited him in. All he could do is just shake his head. He followed her into the house, and she asked him what was wrong. Tellar just shook his head. She mad him some hot tea with honey and amaretto. He sipped it. After two cups he seemed to calm down. Angie questioned him and he finally opened up to her. He told her that his mom was dead, how she was just lying there, not moving, not breathing. Angie asked him if he had called an ambulance, but he shook his head no. She was asking why not and reaching for the phone telling him that they had to call the police and paramedics and that she would be there with him, but she fell to the floor dying. Tellar had shot her as well, but she had already dialed 911 and he could hear the Operator, he shot Angie again in the head, killing her instantly.

He left the house and drove to the hardware store. Mr. Fraser could see that he was upset. Sheriff Bonner was there, and had been talking with Mr. Fraser. They started asking him what was wrong, was he okay? Tellar shot them both, first Mr. Fraser and then the Sheriff. The Sheriff was hit in his vest, which stopped the bullet, but knocked him off his feet. Tellar shot Mr. Fraser again then turned his attention to Sheriff Bonner.

After the fifth .45 round slammed into him, but didn't kill him Tellar realized that Bonner was wearing a bullet proof vest. The Sheriff had the wind knocked out of him and was unable to draw his weapon for the bullets slamming into his armour. Tellar pointed at Sheriff Bonner's head and killed him. People were running from the store, with Tellar firing after them. Several fell, one girl fell after a bullet severed her spinal cord. Tellar reloaded and fired from his vehicle, as well as running over several people. It was all falling apart now and Tellar was no longer in control. He fired into an oncoming Sheriff's cruiser as it passed him, killing the deputy and sending the cruiser into the crowded sidewalk, killing five and wounding eight more.

Tellar was almost home. He drove over the curb and over the sidewalk and ran over a pregnant mother pushing a stroller. Tellar opened the glove box and pulled out a grenade. He pulled the pin and tossed it into the van and ran. As he reached the door, the grenade exploded, sending shrapnel through the sides, roof and floor of the van. It blew glass down the block. Several people trying to help the lady and baby were killed by the blast. The van erupted into flames, as he slammed his door. He went to his electrical panel and opened the cover. He opened the gas valves, which sent natural gas flooding into the Lair. He loaded weapons and checked windows and the doors. He pulled out the refrigerator so that he could get into the tunnel, and that's where he had the switch that would blow everything up.

Unbeknownst to Tellar, the gas was also filling up the house next door. The family died of asphyxiation as the gas filled their house. The Police, Sheriff, and FBI were pulling up at Tellar's mothers house. SWAT teams pulled up and took positions around the house. Tellar ran up and down stairs throwing a hand grenade from an upper story window on different sides of the house. He blew up two cruisers and the FBI's SWAT van. They fired tear gas into the windows, but Tellar would fire at them from other windows. Everybody was wondering if there was more than just Tellar in the house.

Tellar had the Thompson sub machine guns and the MP40's located in front of windows and would run from one window to the next firing out the window wildly. He caught a glimpse of the SWAT teams making a push towards his door, and he unloaded several automatic weapons at them. He killed and wounded eleven Officers and Agents, but they backed off. Tellar could now smell the gas and retreated into the tunnel and pulled the refrigerator closed. The FBI could tell that Tellar was no longer in the house and was probably trying to make a run for it. He watched them on closed circuit. When they came streaming into his mothers house and through his door, he detonated the explosives. With a three story house, a cellar, and the explosives, the combined explosion leveled the buildings on his block. The buildings across the street was hit with debris, flying bodies, and body parts, parts of cars, chunks of concrete and other things that were suddenly being removed by the extreme force of the explosion. Everyone on the streets or in the windows of adjacent buildings were either dead, dying or critically wounded. The news helicopter was knocked from the sky as if it were an insect, killing all on board.

The devastation was massive. From over head it looked as if the street had been hit by a bombing raid. In the middle was a huge crater, all the buildings around it were severely damaged, with several collapsing. No glass for blocks around the blast zone was intact. Car windows were shattered for two blocks, and you could see the debris field from overhead. It was unbelievable. You could see where debris had been thrown for a dozen blocks, in open areas the debris scattered itself out in straight lines. Where the blast and debris met interference, it either stopped the debris, or added to it. There was a huge column of fire that burned until the fire department and utilities company could get it under control and then turn it off.

Evil had a face. It was Tellar Monroe's, and he had unleashed Hell, Death and Suffering upon this particular part of the Earth. We see the same type of devil that dwelt within Tellar in the politicians that we elect and the sycophants that surround and elect them. We see it in the people who run the Media outlets, and those that they chose to put in front of the camera's. But we will not accept it, because then it is a threat, and we as Americans are happy little sheep that joyfully follow the wolves to our own slaughter. We are the evil, it lives inside us all.

7
LYCANTHROPOI

Some people say that there is no god. When they speak of the one created by the Bedouin tribe of Judea, while in exile in Babylon, then they are correct. The Judean's took the Sumerian and Babylonians religions mixed them together, changed the names and started Judaism. Christianity is based on a cobbled together religion from more ancient religions. Then circa 600 bce, a cave dwelling homicidal maniac began a crusade to forcefully spread his version of Judaism, which he named after himself mohammedanism, and war has raged ever since. The gullible Christian is deluded into thinking that the terrorist state of Israel is the land of god's "chosen" people, to brainwashed to see the truth that even the jews admit is a cobbled together religion. And of course the moslims are just bloodthirsty savages like their "prophet", and all are just as happy tearing the others throats out and killing the others children in the name of a god that never existed at all.

Then there are those that say that there are no gods at all. They are all wrong, I know, for I am the son of Zeus, who may be accurately described as a "GOD". While I can't give you proof to their existence, look at the magnificence that was Greece. If it had not been left to the degeneracy of humanity, we would have tamed the solar system a thousand years ago. Thousands of years ago, beings so far advanced and from a different dimension, learned how to control energy, and how to achieve total energy conversion, and to use it to move among, between and around the dimensions of space, time, distance, and what humans perceive as reality. They are for all intents and purposes Gods. They warred amongst themselves and the great philosophers told the tales as did the ancient priest. Creatures great and horrible that men now call myths, actually exist.

The Olympians won that war many millennia ago. Their Titan

fathers and brothers were banished from this dimension, but their stories remain. The Olympian Gods took refuge for a while upon this idyllic little speck of dust in a backwater area of the Universe. They created man from the rough-hewn men that were here. They gave them intelligence and taught them to love the Gods, and then they gave us free will, a spark of divinity so that we would know them for what they are. However mankind did not have the knowledge that the Gods had, nor the powers, and so the spark of divinity became a curse that was explained as Pandora's box.

The worst part of the spark is that man wants to believe in the divine, and it's easier to believe in a monotheistic religion, than the truth. I know the truth, as I said, I am the son of Zeus. I have spoken to him, and the other Olympian Gods. I have traveled, with their grace, from this dimension to others, and I have been to Mount Olympus, and I have sat among the stars. My mother Kallisto and I, bear the curse and wrath of Hera, the wife of Zeus. I have met the great Goddess Artemis, and have spoken with her at length. I have statues and a dagger forged by the god Hephaestus himself and presented by him to me when I visited his forge. And for five thousand years, I have been pursued by Hera and her agents and monsters, just because I had the honor of being born the son of Zeus and Kallisto. I am Arkus Nonakris, the first Lycanthropoi, father of all the other Lycanthropoi, and **We Walk Among You**!

I am Arkus Nonakris, and I am for all intents and purposes immortal. I am also Lycanthropoi. I have suffered the pains of death more than a thousand times, always to be turned away by Charon, never allowed to cross the space-time barrier that they call the Styx, and be returned to my fathers home. This is my curse, and the curse of Lycanthropoi, I have passed on to humanity by accident. It was a thousand years before I realized what was happening, and only after Hera explained it to me. She did it so that I alone would bear the shame and guilt of the curse of the Lycanthropoi. Over the remaining millennia, I have been able to form secret cabals of Lycanthropoi, for their own protection, much to the annoyance of Hera. I alone know the truth, I also know that soon, I may lose my immortality, Zeus willing.

Arkus Nonakris walked into the club. These days it was filled with hipsters, none over thirty, and almost all were Werebles. Well, that was the term two hundred years ago among the Lycanthropoi. Arkus was old, far older than any of these Lycanthropoi Atomica. It used to be that the curse brought with it the ability to live to very old age, usually two to three generations. Some live six to ten, if they didn't commit suicide before then from depression, remorse, regret, madness, and loneliness.

All of that started changing when humanity started intentionally poisoning their water, air and food. Plus the whole Atomic and Nuclear testing really shortened the life spans of everything. Arkus could smell the poisons in the environment and he could not drink the water in towns and cities because of the fluoride. So much has changed in four thousand nine hundred and ninety nine years.

He paused inside on the landing, just inside the door and looked around. The music was the crap that all hipsters listened to these days. It had no soul, it was just as dead as the brains of those that listened to it. Not much had changed in the bar though, but then Alexei wouldn't allow it to change too much. The Bartender was new, Arkus didn't recognize him. He was a hipster Lycanthropoi, what could be worse? He walked down the nine steps into the bar, and across the floor. All of the Werebles could smell him, but couldn't process what they were smelling.

Their sense of smell was so keen, just like a bloodhounds, that's why they could find each other, and like wolves, they were social creatures.

The non-Werebles were all female. Arkus could smell each and every one of them. He could tell when they were in a fertile cycle or bleeding. He wasn't interested in any of them though, he smelled another smell, another female, and he saw her sitting in the alcove where the waitresses sits overlooking the bar, where she could see everyone and respond if they needed something. She was in her early fifties, very attractive and smelled wonderful. He walked over to her table and sat down. She put her book down and looked him over.

"I'm sorry Sir, but no one is allowed at this table except Staff." She said smiling at him.

"I know, I built this club and I am the primary Owner of it. Alexei is my Partner, and he's not here today." Arkus smiled back at her.

"Can I get you anything, Sir?" She asked with an enticing little grin on her face.

"Yes please, some of the Blue Mountain coffee." Arkus was very intrigued by her. She was human, and the most attractive he has ever met. He watched her get up and walk over to the coffee maker. He admired her shape and the fact that she had a little more meat on her than all of the girls in the bar.

She came back and put the coffee on the table along with the cane sugar and a spoon.

"Like what you see?" She asked him smiling and reclaiming her seat. He returned her smile while he made his coffee.

"Very much so. I much prefer women to little girls." Arkus smiled again and smelled the coffee before taking a sip. It was perfect. He narrowed his eyes and savored the flavor of the coffee.

"Mmmmm, now that's great coffee." Arkus said in obvious satisfaction.

"It's so difficult to get great coffee these days unless you make it yourself. All of these coffee stores use substandard beans, over-roast them and then, get kids to make the shite and call it coffee." He says looking her in the eyes.

"Please excuse my manners Miss..." He says waiting for her to answer.

"Sandra Oliva, but everyone calls me Sandy."

"Well, Sandy, I am Arkus Nonakris, Owner of this bar, this refuge from the world, though I see that the insanity has invaded my little realm of escape. So what brings you to my little corner of the world?" Arkus has maintained his eye contact with her which has made her anxious, he could feel it and smell it.

She reached for a menthol cigarette and lit it, and blew her smoke away from Arkus, which he appreciated.

"A girls got to survive doesn't she?" She said returning his stare. Arkus shook his head in agreement.

"So is the apartment rented to you or is there a special arrangement between you and Alexei?" Her eyes widened a bit and she took another nervous draw on the cigarette.

"How did you know I lived upstairs?" she asked off guard. He took another sip of coffee and enjoyed the taste.

"I didn't. I just guessed, you answered with your response. So are you and Alexei... involved?" Arkus asked again and taking another sip of the coffee which was now cooler.

"No Alexei and I are not involved. Unlike you, his taste runs to 'little girls', the younger the better." Sandy answered. Arkus drained his cup and Sandy took it and made him another cup and returned. He nodded his head in thanks.

"I thought that Alexei had better taste than that. Well, it's obvious then that he doesn't appreciate the finer things in life." Arkus smiled widely and took a sip of the coffee. She returned his smile occasionally taking a draw from the cigarette. When she finished it she put it out then dumped the single butt in the ashtray into the trash.

"And you prefer the finer things do you?" She flirted with Arkus now, and he could smell that she was excited.

"I always enjoy the finer things, and occasionally a very fine woman, such as yourself, but they are far to rare these day." Arkus smiled and drank some more coffee. She smiled at him and got up and made him another cup of coffee and set it on the table.

"Hey Bitch! Hey old bitch! We've been trying to get your attention, but your old boyfriend has you too distracted! We need more beer before you guys have old people sex and make us vomit!" It was one of the girls at the table he passed on the way in. She smelled of rank blood, which meant that she was bleeding. Sandra turned and started to go, but Arkus took her arm gently. She looked at him and he shook his head gently.

 Arkus rose and walked to the table. Everyone's smiles faded. He stood over them looking at each and every one. There were three Werebles all males, and the three girls were starting to get really nervous, unconscious reactions to the pheromones in the air. The three young boys rose, Arkus made a barely audible growl in his throat, so low that none but the Werebles would hear it. But that growl conveyed a world of information to the other Werebles in the bar, for all had heard it and all were watching what was happening.

All of the younger Werebles flinched, including the Bartender, which just established Arkus as a very dangerous Alpha. Arkus' scowl was sinister enough by itself, the growl was a omen of death and suffering before it overtook the unfortunate idiots that dared stand against him.

"Leave!" Arkus softly commanded. The Werebles grabbed the arms of their girlfriends and pulled them up. They were too scared to protest. One laid a twenty on the table for the drinks and before he could close his wallet Arkus said "TIP" another twenty was thrown on the table and all of the table sitters scurried out of the bar. Arkus picked up the two twenties and took one to the bar tender and gave it to him telling him it was his tip, and brought the other to Sandra, presenting it to her. She took it looking at Arkus. He could smell her fear, but it was fading.

"What did you say to them to make them jump like that?" Sandra looked at him with a strange expression on her face.

"Well, I didn't *say* anything, sometimes the best communication is just a meaningful stare." Arkus gave her his best intimidating stare, which only made her smile.

"What? Aren't you intimidated by my stare?" Arkus broke into a grin.

"Should I be?" Sandra asked smiling and lighting another cigarette.

"Absolutely! I am a very dangerous man, can't you tell, I have lived this long, so I must be very dangerous!" Arkus smiled at her again. Sandra got up and went to the bar and got a bottle of Amaretto and two glasses. She sat down and opened the bottle and poured two glasses.

"Do you drink anything stronger than coffee?" She asked, her voice now had a sultry note to it. Arkus was very aroused. More than he has been in a very long time. He picked up his glass and held it in front of Sandra. She picked up hers and they touched them together, and drank. Neither drained their glass. Arkus savored the amaretto just as much as the coffee.

They continued to talk and drink until the bottle was empty. While they sat there, another Waitress came in and clocked in and slid into a chair between Sandra and Arkus. Sandra introduced her replacement Tiffany, a young bleached blond bimbo with fake breast and a bad attitude. Sandra stood and Arkus could tell that she was intoxicated. She clocked out and was just a bit unsteady on her feet.

"Let me help you up stairs." Arkus smiled and put his arm around her waist to steady her. He could tell that she was turned on, just as much as he was. It had been a very long time since any non-Wereble had attracted his attention. He lead her to the back steps behind the Servers station and opened the door to the stairs.

"How do you know your way around?" She asked him with a bit of surprise in her voice.

"I told you, I built this place." Arkus said picking her up and carrying her up the short flight of stairs. He took her to her apartment and put her down, took her key and opened her door. He walked her to the couch and she plopped down.

"How did you know which was my apartment?" She asked in confusion, she was drunk and he would probably have to answer all her questions again when she was sober.

"Because the other one is my apartment." Arkus answered her. She stood up and met him half way between the couch and front door. He could tell she wanted him, the whole apartment was flooded with pheromones and they were driving him crazy. He ached to take her, and he grabbed her and pulled her to him and he kissed her with a passion and hunger that she had not known before. He tasted her kiss. He could barely taste the menthol of the cigarette, and strongly taste the amaretto, and could taste the pheromones in her saliva. She kissed him back with the same enthusiasm, the same passion. Arkus picked her up and carried her to the bedroom and undressed her. He let his hands and mouth wander over her soft flesh tasting her, smelling her. He wanted to release the beast inside him that would ravish her, then ravage her and turn her into a Lycanthropoi. It was so strong this urge, that he trembled. He laid her upon the bed and took his time, trying desperately to control himself.

    He made her orgasm several times with just his mouth, before she finally pulled him up and she rode him to two more orgasms before collapsing next to him. She was now much more sober. She looked at him in the fading light. Ran her fingers through his white beard, and smiled at him.

"You're pretty good for an old man." she said teasing him. "How many times did you come? I lost count of mine." She said smiling with utter satisfaction.

"I haven't yet." Arkus returned her satisfied smile. He was gratified that he could still please a woman.

She leaned forward so she could look him in the eye,

"You haven't come yet?" Arkus shook his head. "Well, we will have to remedy that!" She said and kissed her way down. They kept eye contact the entire time. She felt him starting to tense up, could hear the change in his breathing, felt him explode in her mouth. She made sure that he was drained before kissing her way back up. She straddled him, and he easily penetrated her as he was still erect, and she was still very wet. She kissed him and he returned the kiss with such ardor, that she was once again ready to continue. He did not jerk his head away like most guys would have after a woman went down on them, but then she realized that he wasn't like any man she had ever met.

He awoke before dawn and went into the bathroom to relieve himself. When he came back, he stood there and admired her form in the moon light flooding in the window. It was just past the full moon, which is a dangerous time for Werebles, most Werebles at least. His curse was just that, a real curse, from the Gods.

His mother had been Kallisto, Zeus' lover and she and her child had been cursed by Hera. Kallisto had been a companion to the Goddess Artemis, until her pregnancy was revealed by bathing with Artemis and her Nymphs. Artemis was upset, but Hera was furious and Zeus stepped in and turned Kallisto and Arkus into bears, but that didn't fool Hera, who ordered Artemis to shoot them. Zeus turned them into stars and that way they escaped Hera's wrath, or so Zeus thought. Hera left Kallisto in the sky, but plucked her son Arkus out of the night sky and forced Kallisto to watch as she cursed Arkus with the curse of Lycanthropoi and near immortality, knowing what a curse it would be for a demigod. The only powers that Arkus had was his immortality, Hera made sure of that. Forced him to watch his friends and loved ones turn old and die. She knew that the loneliness and loss would drive him mad and knew that suicide wouldn't be a viable option for at least five thousand years. His immortality was finally drawing to an end, and he could feel freedom nearing at last.

Mortal men were incapable of truly understanding the curse of immortality. You will never meet another immortal, the Gods see to it that you don't. The loss of friends, family and loved ones adds up. It's compounded with every relationship until, like Atlas, you are bearing the weight of the universe, your universe, upon your shoulders. Arkus sighed deeply and slid back into bed next to her. The next morning Sandra woke and went to the restroom. When she saw Arkus in the bed, the memories of their passion came flooding back into her mind. A broad smile crossed her beautiful face. She could see Arkus' erection under the sheet, as he was on his back. She got back into bed and mounted him. He woke to the feeling of the heat of her vagina as it slid down his erection. He moaned and reached out and took her hips. She rode him slowly and their pleasure built equally until they both had an orgasm at the same time. She laid on him and they kissed deeply for a while, then she slid off him, turned over and lit a cigarette.

"Let's go to Athens restaurant for Breakfast. They have amazing eggs Benedict." Arkus said matter of factly.

"I need to shower before we go, and I need coffee." She said to his back. He was already in the kitchen making a pot of Blue Mountain coffee. She had an older coffee maker, the one in the bar had been upgraded to a single cup maker. He brought her coffee, mildly sweetened and with a splash of amaretto. She could smell the amaretto in the coffee before tasting it, it was perfect!

"Mmmmm, it's perfect! How'd you know?" She asked delighted by the coffee and his making exactly the way she likes it.

"Just a lucky guess. That and the fact that you keep amaretto next to the coffee pot." He said smiling. She sat cross legged in the bed and they drank the coffee and talked for a moment, then Arkus got up and headed for the shower. He turned on the water and adjusted it and got in. When she had finished her first cigarette and cup of coffee she joined him in the shower. They washed each others bodies and took turns washing each others backs. He pulled her to him and she could feel his stiffening penis between her soft round buttocks. She leaned forward and he slid inside her. He took his time enjoying the feel of her flesh and the silky water flowing over their bodies. She orgasmed first and knew that he wasn't far from another one, she turned and got on her knees and finished him off. They turned off the water and dried each other off.

He opened her front door and walked over and unlocked his door, she followed him. More out of curiosity than any other reason. His apartment was much larger. It was filled with antiques. Some seemed very ancient indeed. He dressed as she looked around. In the corner of the next room was an altar. It had three statues on it, Zeus, Artemis, and Kallisto, though she didn't know their names, she guessed at Zeus and Artemis, they were kind of obvious, but she didn't know the third. They looked to be ancient, all three were very finely made in bronze, and had been cast by Hephaestus himself, a gift for the fate he would suffer. There were some seemingly common stones upon the altar as well as a small meteorite. There was also a large ancient glass vessel filed with ancient gold coins. Arkus walked up behind her and took her in his arms.

"They are Zeus, Kallisto and Artemis. Kallisto was one of Artemis' hunting companions until Zeus seduced her.

Hera caught them and Zeus changed her and her son into bears to protect them from Hera's wrath, then turned them to stars." Arkus told her.

"You seem to know a lot about the past. Are you an Archaeologist or Professor?' She asked turning in his arms.

"I was. I was the Professor all the kids never wanted to get. They all dreaded my classes. All except Alexei. He was an exceptional student. He got his PhD, and we became friends. Academia went on to become nothing but a political indoctrination center and we both left, tired of fighting the lies and politics of the mentally insane. Alexei wanted to start a bar and I owned this building. It was the perfect place. Alexei lived in your apartment for many years then bought himself a house in the suburbs. We ran this bar together for a while, then I became restless and decided to ride with my Brothers in the Werewolves."

"The Werewolves? Really? You don't seem like a one percenter. You do seem like a Professor." She said smiling at him again and kissing him once more.

"Come woman! You starve me! I need food! Go get ready." He said kissing her once more and then pulling away and slapping her ass cheek! She smiled and enjoyed the sting of his swat. She walked over and got dressed and put on the bare minimum of make up. She didn't need much at all, she was a natural beauty. Her auburn hair was below her shoulders with some curl to it. She had brown eyes the color of amaretto. They met in the hall and he handed her a motorcycle helmet. She smiled, it had been a while since she had ridden a motorcycle. She had owned a Hardly Worthit once, but had to leave it behind when she and her boyfriend broke up. They went down the side steps and out into the street. Beneath the awning was his trike. It was beautiful Honda, red and black flake with silver flake accents, and very little chrome. He helped her up onto the back seat and then mounted the drivers seat. It was then that she noticed the Werewolves cut he was wearing. He donned his helmet. The front had a sculpted snarling werewolves head and behind it was real wolf pelt. He started the trike and they rode out onto the street and down the road.

    He pulled up to Athens Restaurant and there were at least thirty motorcycles outside. All bore the markings of the Werewolves MC's distinctive colors and markings, and every one had the one percenter diamond. The Werewolves were one of the oldest Motorcycle Clubs in the world. They were at Hollister, California when the term "One Percent" was coined by the local American Motorcycle Association. They were a small club and one that was well respected by the other One Percenter clubs, you had to be Lycanthropoi to be a member. They did not claim territories, so they were accepted by the other clubs. Plus they were always there with valuable commodities that the other clubs wanted or needed. While the Federal and local Law Enforcement agencies tried, they could never arrest any member of the Werewolves for any crime. They never had drugs, illegal weapons or ever broke any laws that they could ever detect. But they knew that they were an integral part of the Outlaw Motorcycle society.

Arkus pulled up to the restaurant, then backed up to the curb. He dismounted and helped Sandra off. They left their helmets on their seats and went into the restaurant. The Bikers made a ruckus when they walked in and all got up to greet Arkus. Arkus was brought tea and eggs Benedict and Sandra was served the same. The women greeted her and introduced themselves. All of the women were Werebles as were all of the Bikers. And all were at least one hundred and fifty years old, the oldest biker was Bëorn, at two hundred and seventy years old. He had served with General Washington in the Revolutionary War. He had met and known the Founding Fathers. Only Arkus was older. Everyone knew that Sandra wasn't Wereble, but they treated her with the respect that the girlfriend or wife of the Founder deserved. None of this was known to Sandra. Only Werebles knew, and they never told anything to non-Werebles. They ate and talked for only a short time. Bëorn Sigurdsson was now the President of the MC. Arkus would ride next to him then the Vice President, Gryff and Road captain Snatcher, and then everyone else behind them.

Arkus helped Sandra up onto the back of the trike and then mounted up himself. They snapped their helmets on and started their bikes. Arkus allowed Bëorn to pull slightly ahead and then pulled out next to him. They rode to the highway and then South, they were going to make a delivery to another MC. The reason no one had ever been caught, is because they used dead drops. They were rented storage facilities and the President would deliver the key, location and number of the storage facility at the meeting and collect the cash. Only two to three people ever knew where anything was at, and thanks to the great abundance of storage facilities in existence, they always had a new place to store the goods. Later the other MC would go in a rental truck and retrieve the merchandise. The Manager was usually one of the wives of a Member, who knew which ones were empty, and let them use them freely. It was a simple and elegant solution to avoid traps by the Law Enforcement Agencies.

They rode South for over an hour and Sandy enjoyed the ride very much. She was happy to be on a bike again, even if it wasn't her own. They turned into an older paved road that went into a wooded area and came to a large metal wall and gate. It was painted with scenes of Vikings and the Viking Gods, and above the gate was a wrought iron legend "TIL VALHALLA!" The motto of the Sons of Asgard MC. The gate was opened and everyone rode in. A cheer went up from the SOA members that were cooking out on huge grills, and drinking. The motorcycles were parked and everyone was handed a large horn tankard filled with a sweet mead. Sandra went with the other women and they all got food and sat down and started eating. Bëorn, Arkus, and Dyth, the VP, met with their counterparts in the Sons Of Asgard MC. The VP of the SOA, handed Dyth a thick heavy bag, and Bëorn handed Valgard, the SOA President a chain with a key on it. They whispered to one another and then embraced. Women of the SOA brought the Officers huge horn tankards of sweet mead and they toasted each other and drank. Valgard roared the named "ODIN" at the top of his voice, everyone except Sandra returned the shout of "TIL VALHALLA!"

The demeanor of the Officers immediately changed and they joined the table where food was brought to them. The rest of the day was spent eating and partying and when Arkus tired, he and Sandy were lead to a surprisingly clean and comfortable room. The young woman pointed out that they had a private bathroom. Arkus and Sandra both knew that they were being treated like royalty. Sandra came out of the bathroom and Arkus had disrobed by then and pulled back the covers on the bed. Sandra came to him and kissed him passionately.

"Are you too tired Old Man?" she teased. He could tell that she was turned on and wanted it badly.

"Tired yes, Too tired, hell no! I'm not dead yet!" He pulled her to him and kissed her as deeply as he could. He grabbed her ass and pulled her up and she wrapped her legs around him. He turned and walked her over to the bed. He threw her onto it and then stood over her and ripped off her blouse. She wasn't wearing a bra and he leaned down and sucked one of her breast. She grabbed a handful of his hair and moaned loudly. He reached down and unfastened her jeans. He ran his hand under her panties and through her ample bush to her very wet vagina. She moaned even louder and whispered for him to take her. He put his creamy finger in her mouth and she sucked it and licked the rest of his fingers. He repositioned himself and removed her jeans, then tore off her thin cotton panties. He buried his face between her legs and was soon giving her an orgasm. She pulled him up between her legs and thrust her pelvis up to meet his, and impaled herself on his rock hard erection. They spent the next hour slaking their desires. Sandra fell asleep and Arkus dressed, and went and got a tee shirt from the back of his trike for Sandra. He asked Valgard if the Biker store down the road was still in business, Valgard confirmed that it was, but had closed for the evening. Arkus thanked him and went back to Sandra.

Arkus opened the door and there was another woman sleeping naked in the bed with Sandra. Not an uncommon occurrence in the biker community. Officers often had threesomes and foursomes. Arkus undressed and slid into the bed next to Sandra, who immediately threw her arm over his chest and snuggled closer to him. He fell asleep with her in his arms, the first time that it's happened in two thousand years. He let his mind wander back to Rome. He was a General under Julius Caesar, then. He had been called back to Rome from the outer reaches of the Empire and was enjoying his time in Tuscany at the Estate of a low ranking Senator. Honoria Antonia, was his daughter and was quite a Tuscan beauty. The Senator was happy to see his daughter and I so familiar with each other. He was hoping to have me on his side if anything happened. Rome was being torn apart by internal strife, and a General and his Legion of cohorts could come in quite handy. It was, he now remembered with her, just like this, when a messenger brought word of the murder of Julius Caesar. Unfortunately, Honoria's father was allied with Caesars murderers. Her father was forced to fall upon his own gladius, and Arkus gained possession of the house and lands. Honoria's mother fed the entire family poison before Arkus could return and let them know that they were safe. Arkus knew it was Hera that made her poison her own children.

Arkus awoke and turned over, tears burned his cheeks. Sandra was spooning the other woman now, her arm thrown over her waist. Arkus brushed away the tears and slid closer to Sandra and spooned her. His erection finding the warm, wet spot between her ass and thighs and he penetrated her easily. He lay there inside her waiting to see how long it would take her to respond. It took a few minutes and soon enough she was moving her hips and moaning softly. The woman woke and rolled over. She moved the hair out of Sandra's face and started kissing her. Sandra returned her kisses and was moving her hips faster. The woman kissed her way down and started licking and sucking Sandra's clitoris while he took her from behind. Sandra had a powerful orgasm. Sandra pulled her up and they kissed again. Sandra lay back and the woman turned around and positioned herself in the sixty nine position over Sandra and they began eating each other. Sandra took hold of Arkus' penis and guided him into the woman's vagina. It wasn't long before they were all having an orgasm. Arkus pumped his seed into the woman held in place by Sandra, who kept him from pulling out. When at last she let him collapse, she moved between the woman's legs and licked her vagina clean of Arkus' seed.

The woman snuggled up on one side of Sandra while Arkus lay at her other side. The woman introduced herself as Joanie and took turns kissing both Sandra and Arkus. She gave most of her attention to Sandra. Arkus got up and relieved his bladder then got dressed and went outside. Another woman handed him a large cup of coffee, but it wasn't Blue Mountain. Arkus took it nonetheless, and put some sugar in it and some cream and joined Valgard, Bëorn and Dyth at the table. They were talking about guns, but they stopped when Arkus joined them. Valgard told them about the two Doctors that had recently joined the SOA, and the addition of the Operating room they had just built. It was now fully equipped and the Doctors could do full surgeries there. It would be very useful, and he wished that they had been so lucky when he was younger. Things sometimes went terribly wrong and

Hospitals were no longer an option, especially since they had to report gun shot and knife wounds to Law Enforcement. Arkus told them about the Military Field Surgical kit that he kept in his first aid kit on his trike. He also told them how it had saved his life on more than one occasion.

Sandra remained in the room with Joanie and they had played around some more. Joanie said that she was looking for a steady job, and better rent. Sandra said that she would put in a good word with Arkus at the bar, and that she could share her apartment. It had three bedrooms and one and a half bathrooms, plenty of room for her, and half the rent still wasn't as much as she was paying now. They kissed once more and got dressed and joined the rest of the people outside. Some of the men were cooking breakfast on a large flat iron grill, it smelled wonderful. Sandra got two cups of coffee and joined Arkus and the men. She handed him the coffee cup and kissed him then sat down next to him. Some of the other Ladies were coming out about that time, though none seemed to be as awake as Sandra. Several of the younger women, came out of one of the buildings, in various states of undress. Sandra lit a cigarette as Ingrid joined them at the Table. Valgard had met Ingrid in Denmark a few years ago when he had gone on an run there for recruiting purposes. They had fallen in love and he brought her back to America for a year and then married her. They returned to Denmark for the Wedding, along with forty seven of his Chapter Brothers.

Once the Sons of Asgard got established in nine different countries, they all changed their bottom rocker to "MIDGARD". Now they were in Finland, Norway, Sweden, Denmark, Iceland, Greenland, Ireland, Scotland, Estonia, Latvia, Poland, Lithuania, Czech Republic, Germany, Austria, Luxembourg, Switzerland, Slovakia, Romania, Hungary, Bulgaria, Albania, Italy and America. One of the first International Chapters had been in Rhodesia, started back in the middle nineteen sixties. Valgard had been at the founding of every chapter, and had a collection of rockers to prove it. He had been given a cut from Rhodesia and had served for a year in the Rhodesian Army. Upon his return to America, he was immediately drafted for Viet Nam. Instead, he was recruited by the CIA for special missions in Laos and Cambodia. He saw action in Viet Nam, as did all the operatives, but Valgard was special. He had killed NVA Generals and Politicians and had their identification papers and pictures to prove it. He also had the newspaper articles that said how they had died from some sickness or heart attack, stroke or some other excuse. Never once does an article claim that the person had been assassinated. He had even fragged a smart assed Lieutenant straight out of college ROTC, who was arguing with an experienced Sergeant who had fought in three wars already and was a hero ten times over. The Lieutenant wanted his men to walk down the center of a road that was known to be mined from time to time, and the Sergeant knew better. The shave tail Lieuy, was ordering the Sergeant to follow his orders when Valgard walked up. Colonel Valgard wore no rank upon his uniform, which was smart because snipers loved to shoot Officers. When he approached the Lieutenant turned his wrath on Valgard because he thought that he was a lowly recruit. Valgard pulled his pistol and shot the Lieutenant in the head, then showed his ID to the Sergeant before he had a chance to shoot Valgard. Valgard instructed the men that the Lieutenant had been shot by a sniper, and that they would now be taking orders from the Sergeant who would keep them alive if they would listen to him and follow orders. It was during his time in the CIA that he had met Arkus. They had been friends ever since that day.

All of the spy tricks that they had learned, had served them well in the Biker life. Arkus had lead a shadow life for nearly five thousand years, he had to, it was a matter of life and death for him. But since he was immortal, death was never permanent. Imagine having your throat cut and feeling all of the fear and pain until you bleed to death and your lungs fill with your own blood. Now imagine twelve hours later, coughing up the blood and having to hide the wound. Now try hiding and getting away and changing your identity so that no one can recognize you. There was the time in seventeen ninety one, that he had taken up with a married woman, although he didn't know that she was married. Her husband was a Sailor and was away, and she neglected to tell him. When her husband returned eight months later and found his wife with another man, he and his friends seized Arkus and hung him from a Yard arm in the Harbor. The woman later hanged herself, much to the dismay of the Sailor. Arkus had revived and had to cut himself down, dropping into the water and swimming away. He later tracked down each of the four Sailors and hanged them.

Arkus lived as a law abiding Citizen when he could, and lead the double life having to depend on the Underworld to supply him with new paperwork, which was getting more and more difficult nowadays! He had amassed a great fortune in the years that he had lived. As an Archaeologist and Professor he could use all of the knowledge he had learned over five thousand years to "find" lost treasures and civilizations. He had cashed in on his knowledge by selling the information to treasure hunters as well. It had been Arkus that had sold Lord Carnarvon and Howard Carter the location of King Tutankhamen's tomb. Lord Carnarvon paid him well, and even fulfilled the bargain struck between them. Arkus had become incredibly wealthy. Carter and Carnarvon offered to share the credit with Arkus, but he had refused. Arkus knew to keep his head down and not seek the spotlight. It wouldn't do for an eighty year old rival to see that he was still alive and very healthy and unaged.

As CIA operators Valgard and Arkus knew who to buy what from and who to sell it to. It was Arkus that showed Heinrich Schliemann where to find Troy.

Arkus and Sandra were ready to leave. Sandra had to get back to work, at the bar. Arkus howled and the other Werewolves responded. Everyone said their goodbyes and Arkus invited the SOA back to the bar. Joanie rode with one of the Ladies that had her own bike back to the bar. She had a small bag with her, it was all that she owned. She waved at Sandra, who leaned in close to Arkus' ear and whispered;

"Just because she is going to be living with me, do NOT get the idea that the three of us are going to be swinging all the time." she squeezed him around his waist and laid her head on his back. Though she couldn't see it Arkus was smiling broadly at the thought that she had already claimed him. He turned his head and said;

"Yes Ma'am!" He started his trike and they rode out, down past the steel gate and down through the forest and out to the mundane world. They didn't drive straight back to the bar and those that were following were just along for the ride. They stopped for fuel and then for ice cream later at the Custard Shack at Crossville, then back to civilianland. Everyone parked outside of the Great Bear bar.

It looked like your typical eighteen hundreds building. Two stories above ground with a cellar entrance at street level that lead down narrow steps. It was a popular design. A family lived upstairs and ran a business out of the first floor. Stock was delivered through the cellar. The store front was very ornate and elaborate, with bay windows upstairs and down, and a large balcony that shaded the front door and windows. Arkus had designed and built the building himself. Later during WWII he added two lower levels which were enlarged and fortified with lead sheets in between layers of concrete, when the American craze to build bomb shelters happened. It didn't hurt to tell the contractors that back in the Cold War. Now he had two fortified, reinforced bunkers that doubled as treasure vaults. He stored here his most valuable objects and treasures, some so rare and priceless that they could be sold for any price he dared to ask for them. Here he kept every Military Honor he had received in his incredibly long life. The Greek gold laurel wreaths, some presented by Herodotus, Eratosthenes, and his Spartan, Roman, Greek, Phoenician, Egyptian, Viking, German, British, Scottish, and Russian weapons and decorations. He had been awarded one of the very first Purple Hearts by General Washington himself, He had one of the first Medal of Honors from the War Between the Sates. He received it again in WWII, One in Korea, and one in Viet Nam, as well as a slew of other medals. All under different identities. Here was his armor from every nation that he served in.

Vast amounts of gold and silver and bronze coins, but the most valuable and deadliest of all, were silver ingots and coins from the

Temple of Artemis. It was the purest silver in the world, which made it the most deadly to all of the Lycanthropoi in the world. All except for Arkus Nonakris. Since his mother had been a divine Nymph and hunting companion to Artemis, he was immune to it's deadly effects. Hera had not thought to give him that particular curse. He had cast bullets in several calibers from the silver and carried magazines loaded strictly for Lycanthropoi. Werebles could see it even in total darkness, for it shown like moonlight. For Werebles, it was like watching a nineteen fifties TV program, where the light reflections left streaks as it moved. It scared them all. They would be spellbound by the sight of it and terrified at the same time. But deadlier still was the five inch blade made from this purest of silvers, which Arkus carried for those Werebles that got too close, and were too stupid to back away.

The first Lycanthropoi were soldiers and warriors that survived an attack from Arkus, even in regular combat. Hera's curse for them. After a few years of their lycanthropy, they would seek Arkus out, having been convinced by Hera's priestesses that it would cure the curse. Of course every month at the full moon they would change and they would attack humans. If the human survived, they became a Wereble. Not always a wolf, sometimes it depended upon what kind of animal that Hera decided for them. Later it was whatever beast resided within their spirits. Some were hunted down and killed, others banded together for survival. At one time, the entire Vatican was inhabited by Werebles. They started the Spanish Inquisition, as a way to keep safe and feed their insane desires, as many often went insane. Even Lycanthropoi are no match for the black plague, and thousands died. Now, we try and stay to ourselves. We have places to go where you are reasonably sure that you can find safe haven, like the bar. One of the all too common side effects of being a Lycanthropoi, with your extra strength and extended life, is insanity. Usually manifest in different degrees of paranoia, but some become outright homicidal. Some of the serial killer cannibals were Werebles, and were given injections that contained pure silver upon their execution in Prison.

Sandra had taken Joanie upstairs to show her the apartment and the

Werewolves filed into the Bar with Arkus holding the door. Inside were other Werebles, including three very large ones. Tiffany had been trying to avoid their advances all day, and they had pushed customers around and hassled them. The bartender had had enough of them and told Arkus that Alexei had been trying to find him to help get these creeps out of there. Arkus walked over to their table and asked them to leave, they looked at Arkus and laughed. Arkus kicked the chair out from beneath the dominant male, and he fell. The other two came out of their chairs at the ready, but Arkus jabbed the closest one in the throat and he dropped to the floor gasping for breath. The second sprung towards Arkus who sidestepped him and used his momentum to slam him into the Werewolves, who piled up on him and pinned him to the bar. The Dominant Wereble grabbed Arkus from behind and put him in a choke hold. Arkus slammed his heel down on the knee of the dominant one and dropped him. Arkus spun and delivered an open hand punch to his throat, which ended his resistance. Suddenly all eyes were upon the silver dagger that Arkus wielded. It appeared as if by magic, in his hand. It shown like lightning and sent chills through every Wereble. He picked up the dominant Wereble and slung him against the bar. He placed his arm across his chest and held the dagger millimeters away from his skin. It made his skin tingle and he was breathing fast and shallow. Arkus was calm, he knew the silver would burn their skin like acid, it would leave a permanent scar. The only thing that would. Arkus spoke softly, but everyone heard him.

"Look at it, dead meat. So pure and beautiful, just like liquid moonlight made material. Blessed by Artemis herself, Goddess of the moon. Just a touch is enough to cause excruciating pain. I know that you can feel it, so close to your skin. All I have to do is touch you and you will be scarred for life. Cut you, and you die as it courses through your veins. What, I wonder, happens if I stab you? Care to guess how excruciating your death would be?

Want me to stab one of your butt sniffers and let you watch them die? No?" Arkus taunted him still more until Arkus licked the full length of the blade. Every Lycanthropoi gasped, knowing that Arkus was about to die horribly. But he doesn't. He held the knife up and looked around smiling and all were looking at him. He placed the blade on the left cheek of the dominant Wereble who half screamed, half howled in agony. Arkus slammed him to the floor and told the three ruffians to leave the state, and that if he ever saw them again, he would kill them. They picked up their wounded friend and ran through the door, you could hear the car doors slam and the squeal of their tires as they sped away.

Arkus sheathed the dagger. Everyone still looking in horror at Arkus.

"Why aren't you dead?" Bëorn said hoarsely. Arkus looked around at everyone, they were all very afraid. It was if a person had a bottle of cyanide and arsenic and curare and had turned it up and drank it all, with no more effect than that of a glass of water. Arkus smiled at them all shook his head just a little and said;

"Well, I am after all, ME!" Arkus waved his hands as if to wave away smoke and exhaled in exasperation.

"I am immune to the effects of silver. I don't know why, I just am!" The jukebox came on and the theme from Highlander by Queen started playing, Arkus sang along.
"Come on everyone, drink up!" Arkus grabbed a bottle of amaretto and three glasses, and went to the Servers table and sat down to await Sandra and Joanie. Things seemed normal, but Arkus could tell how much he had frightened everyone. His back was to everyone but he could hear their whispers. All but the Werewolves had left, and still they whispered. The jukebox continued to play which helped to hide the whispers. Joanie and Sandra came through the door and sat down. He poured them drinks, he toasted them and they all drank. The Werewolves left by two's and three's, until all were gone. The bartender told them that he was leaving and that he would lock the door behind him. They waved and told him goodnight. Sandra and Joanie were pretty drunk by now. He helped them upstairs and into their apartment, kissed them both, but lingered in Sandra's arms looking into her

beautiful face. She offered to share her bed with him, but he declined, even though he longed to be with her. He felt old, very old, and as if the weight of all the centuries had descended upon him. He hugged her tightly, as if to draw her inside of himself, to become one being, and drive out the thousands of years of loneliness. They remained two separate people though, and he kissed her passionately, and she returned his kiss with equal passion. Joanie had succeeded in dropping her dress, and shoes and falling onto the bed and falling asleep. Sandra looked over at her and then back at Arkus, and smiled.

"Want me to come to your apartment?" She asked, both of her arms around his neck. He kissed her again and told her no, to get some sleep, and that he would see her in the morning. They kissed one last time and Arkus went to his apartment. He heard Sandra close the door behind him, he was aching to be with her, but was bothered still by how everyone had reacted to his little show. He went to the small altar and talked to his Mother, Father and to Artemis. He told them what had happened and how he felt about Sandra, and for the first time in millennia, he begged them to protect someone he loved. He went to his bed and collapsed upon it and was soon fast asleep. At some point in the middle of the night, Sandra woke, crossed the hall and joined him in his bed, and fell back to sleep.

 Just before sunrise, he woke. He was pleasantly surprised to find Sandra in his bed. His delight turned quickly to cold fear. He hadn't set the alarm, he hadn't locked the door, and he hadn't awakened the moment it opened. It had never happened before, and it bothered him, almost as much as the stunt that had backfired on him last night at the bar. He couldn't let this happen again, it was totally the opposite of how he had been all of his life. While he may be immune to the poisonous effects of pure silver, a silver bullet to the heart will still kill him. A silver bullet to the brain would definitely kill him. He remembered a cool morning one September back in 1862. It was the seventeenth and he was at a small town called Sharpsburg, camped near Antietam creek, along with the rest of General Robert E. Lee's Army of Northern Virginia. He had risen to go relieve himself, and had walked into a small patch of woods on Lee's left flank. Before he could get his pants unbuttoned, he smelled them, then he heard them, coming through the cornfield. He ran back to camp and gave the news to General Lee himself. The Sentries started reporting movement in the cornfield and the camp was roused. Battle was engaged almost immediately. It was General Hookers First Corps attacking. They had also fought them recently at the Peninsula Campaign. Lee's Army was also fighting a holding action at the Sunken Lane, at Lee's center. The fighting was intense, Arkus could remember vividly the sound of the guns, the smell of the black powder, and the sounds of artillery shells exploding all around him. Occasionally a bullet came so close to his ears he could actually hear the whine of the bullet as it sped past his ears.

Then came the blinding moment when the fifty-eight caliber minnie ball slammed into his head, breaking open a hole through the bone and lodging in the space between his brain lobes. He woke later, surrounded by Union and Confederate men, all dead. He was on a stretcher being carried into a Union Medical tent. The Doctor was shocked, but acted quickly. A bullet was placed between his teeth and he was tied down. The Doctor probed into the wound, which caused Arkus to pass out. The Doctor was able to extract the minnie ball and sewed up the wound. The Doctor was pleasantly surprised by the recovery and quick healing. He called it a miracle. He kept Arkus around for six weeks while he convalesced. The Doctor was also surprised at Arkus' knowledge of classical literature and languages and they spoke often in Latin and ancient Greek. Arkus liked the Doctor and wanted to tell him that the reason why he knew so much about the classics was that he had been there and had actually learned from the great Philosophers in person. He had heard the Colonel of an Infantry Regiment order the Doctor to write Arkus' release orders, so that he could be transported to a Prisoner of War camp. Arkus made his escape that night, with help from the Doctor.

When Arkus found out that his entire Unit had been wiped out, he wept for the loss of his friends and Comrades in Arms. He transferred to an Artillery unit from Memphis, Tennessee that had been started by wealthy Attorneys, and served out the war in that unit. After the war,

Arkus changed his named and served on the merchant vessel Triton's Fury, and sailed around the world again. He had sailed away after so many other wars. On 23 July 1745 he sailed with Prince Charles Edward, son of James, named the 'young Pretender' by the English, and landed on Eriskay Island off the west coast of Scotland. Almost a month later, on 19 August, Charles 'Bonnie Prince Charlie' was able to gather his men at Glenfinnan, with the support of some of the Catholic Mac Donalds. He raised his standard before all gathered and his Father was proclaimed King James the Third and Eighth. The Jacobite army later captured Edinburgh and defeated the British at the Battle of Prestonpans on their march south. By December the Jacobite army had reached Derby, a mere one hundred and fifty miles from London, only to be stalled and then withdrawn back north. The last battle to be fought on English soil was the skirmish at Clifton Moor, on 18 December, 1745. The retreating Jacobites met the Duke of Cumberland's army at Clifton in Penrith. Amazingly only twelve Jacobites and fourteen English soldiers were killed. The English received a decent burial in the nearby churchyard, while the Scots received a mass burial under an oak tree, that became known as 'the Rebel Tree'. By February, the Jacobites capture Inverness, and stay there for two months, while the Duke of Cumberland's army closed in. On 16 April, against the advice of all of his Chiefs, Charles lined up his army, tired and starving, on the flat moor of Drumossie, and in less than an hour more than a thousand Scots lay dead, The wounded soon died from their wounds. They were separated by clan and buried in mass graves. Bonnie Prince Charlie escaped with a bounty of 30,000 pounds on his head. Arkus made his way back to the sea and sailed to the New World, America which would all too soon be at war with Britain.

    He would serve valiantly with General Washington and receive one of the new 'Purple Hearts' issued by the General. He would fight in the Revolutionary War from the first Battle at Lexington and Concord, all through the war to the last battle at Yorktown. Arkus had fought in so many battles, in so many lands under so many famous men, or as a famous leader, that he could no longer remember all of the names. War was ever present, and never changed, only got more terrible with each advance in weaponry, and now his body was finally aged enough to preclude him from further wars, but none excelled at it like Arkus. Always though, he came face to face with those sent by Hera, who was determined that he would die, and she would place his head on a golden platter, and his still beating heart, his soul, in a magic golden box made by Hephaestus, in her Temple on Mt. Olympus.

Sandra rolled over and shook Arkus from his reverie. He looked at her beautiful face. He reached out and gently moved a lock of hair and gazed upon her. The clouds outside parted and moonlight illuminated her nude form.

"Was this the face that launched a thousand ships and burnt the topless towers of Ilium? Sweet Helen, make me immortal with a kiss." Arkus whispered as he looked again at her face. He leaned in and kissed her lips gently, trying to resist the urge to part her lips with his tongue, it was Sandra's tongue that parted his lips as her arms closed round his neck. She pulled him to her and they kissed more passionately. He made love to her and she tried to keep from making too much noise. At last, when both lay slaked in each others arms, they kissed and talked softly.

"What was that you said before you kissed me?" Sandra asked. She ran her hand over his chest and snuggled closer to him.

"It's from a Christopher Marlowe play, Doctor Faustus, in reference to Helen of Troys beauty. 'Was this the face that launched a thousand ships and burnt the topless towers of Ilium? Sweet Helen, make me immortal with a kiss.' I said it because you are the most beautiful woman that I have ever met! I can tell you for certain that 'Fair Helen' was never as fair as you." Arkus said, for he had seen Helen of Troy, had fought in that war, though at that time he was known as Achilles.

"Oh you can say that for certain, huh? For *certain*? Well how can you be certain?" She teased him.

"Because the heart has eyes that the brain knows nothing of! Besides I just know some things at my age." Arkus looked her in the eye and then kissed her deeply. When they finally broke the kiss she looked at him and said

"Okay 'old man', what ever you say." She was throwing her leg over him, he grabbed her and thrust into her once again. She gasped with the surprise and delight and started making love to him again.
"Old man, huh?" He thrust hard and continued until she was arching her back, her small breast bouncing, and they both cried out with the force of their climax. She collapsed on him and he loved the feel of her body on top of his. They kissed and held each other until they both needed to empty their bladders.

They both got up and walked to the bathroom, Arkus let Sandy use the toilet first, while he fetched thick, luxurious towels from the linen closet on the other side of the bathroom. He smiled at her and went to the shower and turned the water on. She finished and got in the shower, while he voided his bladder, then joined her. They kissed then washed each others backs. Joanie came into the bathroom and joined them for the shower. When they had rinsed Arkus walked, dripping wet to the linen closet and got another thick towel and dried off. He used the towel to dry up the trail of water and then placed it on the floor outside the shower. Sandra dried Joanie off and Arkus dried Sandy. Joanie kissed both of them good morning and walked back to Sandra's apartment. Sandra kissed Arkus and followed Joanie.

Arkus dressed and went to Sandra's apartment but the women were gone. He heard them down in the kitchen of the bar. Sandra had made them all breakfast, Arkus smiled at them and grabbed juice and three glasses and disappeared, only to return with a freshly brewed pot of Blue Mountain coffee and three cups. He jerked his head toward the upstairs, and Sandra and Joanie followed him. At the end of the corridor was a door that Sandra had never noticed before. It was incredibly obvious now as it stood open. What lay beyond was a pleasant courtyard of verdant moss covered brick walls twenty feet high, with a large tree growing from the center. A marble bench surrounded the tree. Sandra looked around. No other doors or windows marred the twenty foot high walls, just three alcoves with human sized statues in them. No outside noise seemed to penetrate the green shade and cool air of this oasis of tranquility.

Arkus had set the table in the courtyard with a tablecloth and dishes.

Sandra was in awe at the courtyard.

"I have worked here for six years, and lived here for five of those years, I never knew this place existed." she said in soft, almost worshipful tones.

"This is probably my favorite place on the earth." Arkus said looking around and breathing deep.

"It's like... coming home again." He said in a softer tone. Arkus took a sip of the coffee and smiled. They ate their pleasant meal in relative silence, enjoying the tranquility and the calm, peaceful mood that it inspired.

They finished their meal and still they sat, in silent contemplation. Arkus could feel the weight of five thousand years, heavy upon his spirit, and yet at the same time, he felt as if he finally had something to live for, Sandra. He couldn't keep her out of his thoughts, and he wanted to be with her all the time. He had really, truly loved only three women in all those centuries, with the exception of his Mother and Artemis, but that was a totally different kind of love. He knew beyond a shadow of a doubt, he was head over heels in love with Sandra. When a five thousand year old man fell in love he fell hard, fast like a meteor falling through the atmosphere. He had done that too, five thousand years ago. It was no use fighting it he knew, but while she may be attracted to him, he didn't know if she could fall in love with him. As much as he wanted to rush this, he didn't want to rush it and lose her. That would be too damned difficult, and maybe he would have to let Hera win, and kill himself.

Arkus, told them that they are welcome to use the courtyard, as long as they never brought anyone else there, and that they never defile it with garbage or damaging any part of it. They promised him that they would treat it with the utmost respect. Both said that it was like being in a church or sanctuary, and that it seemed so 'holy'. They carried everything back into the kitchen and Sandra and Joanie started the opening duties for the day. Arkus kissed Sandra deeply and said that he would see her later, that he had business to take care of, now that he was back in town permanently. She told him to have a good day and to be careful. She hugged him tightly and kissed him once more before they reluctantly broke their embrace. He walked out the front door and locked it. He had to meet up with Bëorn and Dyth to divide up the money and to convert it to gold, silver and other tangible assets and to deposit some into his account. This would still leave a significant amount of the cash to be deposited later, in several transactions to avoid the questions large amounts of cash tended to bring with it, now that the federal guidelines made banks report transactions over a certain limit.

Arkus got on the trike and started the engine, looked around carefully and pulled out into the street before speeding away. He headed towards the clubhouse of the Werewolves, known to everyone as the Lair. It was outside of town and protected by high concrete walls. It had once been a government facility where they controlled secret weapon manufacturing. At it's heyday it had twenty one buildings, a huge parking lot and several walls, fences, and gatehouses. Now the only building that remained was the huge factory. It had been partitioned off to make apartments, a clubhouse, and a fully functioning garage. Most of the acres of concrete and asphalt parking lots had been cut and stacked outside of the main building, or used to fill unused gates, and to make crash-proof barriers. The gates were now retrofitted with automatic security gates, controlled by remotes, you didn't have to be right up on the gate when you activated the remote, so that it would be opened before you reached it. However when Arkus reached the outer gatehouse, the gate was chained and padlocked. The power had been turned off so that the gate couldn't be activated with the chains in place. He shut off his trike and got his phone out, he was damned sure going to get to the bottom of this.

He called Bëorn and asked what the hell was going on. Bëorn asked him to meet him at the Sons of Asgard's clubhouse and that something happened that needed to be discussed. Arkus agreed and started the trike and headed towards the SOA clubhouse, he knew this couldn't be good. He rode the distance and tried not to let his mind fill with all that could be happening, overwhelm his thoughts. He arrived and all the SOA members acted as if nothing had happened, maybe they didn't know and maybe they did. Maybe this was an ambush. Valgard greeted

Arkus just the same as ever. They shook hands and embraced and Valgard handed him a cup of coffee. Arkus thanked him and took a sip. Valgard pointed to the Chapel, and looked at him with a questioning look.

"Later, I promise." Arkus told him, and handed the empty cup back to Valgard.

"We go back a long time, Man, you need us to take care of business you let us know." Valgard nodded at the Chapel, and looked Arkus in the eye. They both knew something heavy was coming down, but neither knew what.

"I hope it doesn't come to that, but stay sharp." Arkus shook Valgard's hand again and walked towards the Chapel.

Bëorn and Dyth were facing the door and rose out of respect when Arkus walked in. They embraced and shook hands like always, but Arkus could feel the fear, could smell it, it was so tangible. They sat down facing each other.

"Arkus, man you scared the shit outta everybody the other night with that stunt! So much so that everyone wants to go Nomad for a while. Take a trip down south and visit the Soggy Bottom Chapter, just for a bit. I tried to talk them out of it, but they are just too freaked man!" Bëorn was still visibly shaken especially for a man of two hundred and seventy years old. Arkus slumped in his chair, he was tired and they could tell.

"JESUSGODMOTHERFUCKINGDAMNCHRIST!" Arkus sighed deeply. When he looked up again, they saw the determination in his eyes and knew he was about to lay down the law. Arkus took a deep breath and began.

"Right. You tell them they got themselves a one month vacation, anyone not ready, willing and able to come back after that had damned well find a Chapter in another country, or turn in his cut altogether! I won't have any more dissension in the ranks, they toe the fucking line or reap the fucking Reaper! You got that? I'm not going to fuck with a bunch of terrified crybabies who run at the first real bump in the road they come to. They are supposed to be **WEREWOLVES**, if they can't hack it, tell them to turn in their cuts and lose the ink! This ain't no girly show, this is the fucking trenches, welcome to the A-Bomb detonation! ***BOOM, MOTHERFUCKERS!***" Arkus clapped his hands loudly with the 'BOOM' and Bëorn and Dyth both flinched. They gave Arkus a key and told him where his cut of the cash was. They got up and Arkus turned his back to them and walked out. Bëorn and Dyth looked at each other and knew that Arkus was serious. There were now about thirty SOA members in the clubhouse, all watching the Chapel doors open. Arkus had reached the middle of the room then turned suddenly to face the other Werebles.

"Valgard, the other Werewolves are on 'vacation' for a month. During that time, make it known that they are not welcome at any SOA clubhouse, not until they get their dicks back!" Arkus and Valgard embrace and turn to look at Bëorn and Dyth, who suddenly feel the warmth of friendship leave the room. They rushed out and roared away on their bikes.

"Sorry everyone, they turned to pussies after this last job. Hopefully they will man the fuck up again real fucking soon!" Valgard and Arkus say goodbye and Arkus rides out on his trike. He headed back to the bar. Alexei's Maibach is parked in front of the bar when he got there. He pulled up and backed the trike to the curb. Alexei is in the Office checking receipts and the books. He smiles and gets up when he sees Arkus come in. They greet each other with great affection. They make small talk while they walk up to the bar. Tiffany is tending bar and sets two glasses down in front of them and pours them each a shot of Pritchard's Whiskey. They intertwine their arms and drink Russian style. They discuss business and how well the bar is doing. Tiffany pours them another round every so often. Alexei tells Arkus that it is good to see him again then excuses himself to finish the books.

"Alexei, one other thing," he waves Sandra, Joanie and Tiffany over, "No Werewolf of this Charter walks into this bar with his cut on for one month, you got that?" They look at him in wonder. Alexei is a member and was one of the founding members with Arkus, but all say they will enforce his decision. Tiffany and Joanie wait on the few customers there while he walks up to the Servers station with Sandra. He pulls her behind a curtain and kisses her passionately. She returns his passion and he pulls her through the door and up the stairs. She is breathing hard and is excited by his aggression. He takes her to her apartment and opens the door and drags here in and kicks the door closed.

He roughly pulls her shirt up to expose her breast and sucks first one then the other roughly. He spins her around and pushes her over a table. He grinds his crotch into her ass and she is moaning with the desire that he is rousing in her. He reaches around and unfastens her pants and yanks them down followed quickly by his. He thrust himself into her, easily. She is so turned on that she is dripping wet. He buries himself as deep as he can in her, and her breath catches in her throat. He holds it deep, then withdraws and plunges in again with animal ferocity. He pulls her hair and rams two more times and she comes hard. He pushes hard for a few more moments and then spins her around and pushes her to her knees. She takes him deep into her mouth and sucks for all she is worth. Her hand finds it's way down to her bush and she starts rubbing her aching clitoris. Soon she is climaxing again.

He grabs her hair and pulls her up and kisses her savagely. He dips down grabs her by the knees and almost flips her onto the table. He pushes her legs up and thrust his face between her legs and licks as much of her cream as he can, She is moaning loudly and both are terribly excited as he thrust into her again and pounds her until she climaxes yet again, he only allows her a few moments to enjoy it before he pulls out, She slides down in front of him and takes his throbbing erection in her mouth and he explodes. She drinks every drop and he becomes weak with the force of his orgasm. His knees buckle and he sinks to the floor to lie on his back. She continues her attention to his still erect cock, then kisses her way up his body, until they kiss again. She is lying on top of him and he kisses her once more.
"Wow! What a pleasant surprise! I like it rough!" she says and kisses him again.
"Well you ain't seen nothin', yet, Baby! Stay tuned to the same Bat Time and same Bat channel, you might be even more surprised later on!" He said to her. They got undressed and went to her bed and spent the rest

of the afternoon and evening making love and taking turns pleasuring the other with their mouths.

    At some point they end up on the couch and fall asleep. They are awakened by Joanie, who tells them that Bëorn and Dyth are in the private dining room, without their cuts. Arkus yawns and stretches, then kisses Sandra and gets up and dresses. He puts his cut on. He unbuttons the pocket and pulls out the old Werewolf pin and pins it above his Chapter patch, but below his one percenter diamond. He kisses Sandra, and Joanie grabs his cut and kisses him too. He slaps both of their behinds and walks out, while Sandra starts telling Joanie about their afternoon.

    Arkus opens the doors and Bëorn and Dyth stand up, they are both wearing a hangdog expression on their faces when they see the Werewolf pin.
"Arkus, we..." Bëorn starts to say something but Arkus cuts him off. "Do you know how old I am? Take a guess, how old do you think I am?" Arkus ask. Bëorn and Dyth look at each other then Dyth answers; "Maybe two hundred and fifty, same as us, or there-about..." Arkus is shaking his head.
"You don't know, you can't know. I am four thousand nine hundred and ninety-nine years old! I am your Grand-sire! I am the very FIRST Lycanthropoi! All of you are here because of ME! Because somewhere down the line you survived an attack from a Lycanthropoi, or the curse passed through your bloodline. But thanks to Hera, I am the first. We all know that most don't survive very long after the transition, they get themselves killed or go mad or both. Only the strongest survive, only the smartest. That's why I searched them out and started the Werewolves. We three met again in WWI, as Pilots. Both of you were there after World War Two when we formed the first Charter. The Army was practically giving away the Motorcycles. I still have three crated up, and an original Trike. I also have a German Zundapp with the sidecar and MG 40. Jesus Christ on a jewish cracker! I know how hard it is! Think how much harder it is for me! And now to make things more difficult, I have fallen in love with a non-Wereble, and I honestly don't know how much longer that I have to live." Arkus was suddenly

deflated he sank into a chair and put his head into his hands. Bëorn and Dyth stood there in stunned silence, looking from Arkus, to each other and back again. It was difficult to process the information that Arkus had just shared with them.

"What, what do you mean, you are the first? What are you saying, how could that be?" Bëorn was trying to puzzle out the reality of it. Dyth and Bëorn sat down at his table and looked at him intently. Arkus raised his head and looked into the eyes of the men that had been his friends for more than two hundred years.

"Five thousand years ago, the Greek Gods walked this Earth the same as you and I. They were considered Gods because they could manipulate matter and space. They arrived upon this planet in primordial times, and they created everything. My mother was Kallisto, a Nymph, semi-divine, who was a hunting companion to Artemis. One day Zeus took the form of Artemis to seduce my mother who was the most beautiful Nymph of them all. Several months later when they were bathing beneath the full moon Artemis discovered my mother was pregnant, when asked who the father of the child was, my mother answered that it was Artemis herself that had come to her and seduced her. Artemis became enraged and banished her from her sight and turned her into a bear, later discovering that it was her father Zeus that had transformed and seduced my mother. Hera had found out and was searching for my mother, who by this time had given birth to me. Hera sent both men and beast to find and kill us. It was only when Hera caught up to us that Zeus intervened and placed my mother and I into the heavens as constellations. Hera learned how to draw me back down to Earth, but could not bring my mother back. So for five thousand years, Hera has tormented me. For a while, I went mad. I traveled the Earth and those who incurred my wrath either died or became Lycanthropoi. You would be amazed at how many mortals can really piss you off when you are half-mad and have a jealous, and crazy Goddess pursuing you. Many of the people that she sent after me became Lycanthropoi. Until all over this world, there are legends of White men where there weren't before, and legends of Werebles. But I, I am the first, the Primus, the Archon, the original Alpha. I am immune to silver because of Artemis, it was her way of telling me that she was sorry for what happened to my mother and I. It was she who gave me that dagger, made by Hephaestus himself and infused with moonbeams. And now you know, you two are the only other living people that know. The Gods are real, as am I. I see that by your looks you think me utterly mad, maybe I am, if I am how do you explain this?" Arkus pulls out the dagger and cuts his hand with it and puts the tip into the wound. That action would have killed any other Lycanthropoi instantly. Bëorn and Dyth eyes wide with horror, then surprised when he doesn't die. Arkus runs the flat of the blade over the wound and it disappears. He lays it on the table in front of them. "There you have a weapon made by the god Hephaestus, right out of the Greek legends. I have held the sword of Perseus, I have seen the Gorgon Medusa's head, another tragic victim of the Gods. You and everyone you know have been indoctrinated from birth with this false god and prophet of a desert Bedouin tribe who stole everything in their holy scriptures from the Babylonians, Sumerians and Zoroastrians, changed the names and places and added some nonsense and had that religion forced on others by the sword and the spear, *upon pain of death*! The big three religions, that destroyed every civilization it encountered. There is nothing true about the big three. Unlike the Greek gods, whom I have actually met, that I am descended from. You have seen it yourselves in battle. How many wars? How many times have I been shot, bayoneted, hit with shrapnel, and still survived?

Remember World War One? We were Pilots in the new fangled flying machines, How many crashes did I survive? Five! Why? The same reason as you, I am immortal. Though you can be killed a lot easier than I can, and my immortality is coming to an end, I can feel it. I am tired, more tired than you can ever even hope to imagine. Now all I want to do is grow old with Sandra and be burned upon my pyre when the time comes. When it happens make sure that it's under an Autumn moon when Ursa Major and Ursa Minor are above the horizon. Watch those stars and see if they don't shine brighter while my body burns. I will return to the stars." Arkus had a strange look of peace on his face. Dyth and Bëorn looked at each other once more, not knowing what to say. They didn't know how much to believe, after all, they were Lycanthropoi, and most people knew that they were just fiction, never suspecting the truth. It was Dyth who spoke first.

"Eighty years ago, when we had the Blood Moon Initiations into the Werewolves, you only partially changed, I assumed it was because you were the one speaking and needed to stay in mundane form to speak. You didn't change because you are a bear. Then why are we wolves?" Arkus smiled and looked him in the eye.

"Each Wereble changes into the predator that is most like his spirit, most are wolf like. Some are bears, Lions, tigers, pumas, there have even been two huge cobras. Even an Eagle. I am a bear, it is my nature now, chosen by the gods themselves. Now what are we going to do about the Werewolves?" Arkus asked weary once again. He could feel the weight of five thousand years fall upon him and crush him under the weight. Bëorn smiles broadly and slams his fist upon the table, and half yells it out.

"**Blood Moon Ritual!** Bring them back into the fold and remind them just who the *fuck* they really are! Road trip to Iron Mountain, the Birthplace of our Club!" Dyth could feel his chest swell with pride and the desire for a good old fashioned Blood Moon Ritual! They all three stood and howled at the tops of their voices. They had a renewed purpose and they put the word out for all available Members of all Charters to meet in one month at Iron Mountain, Mandatory meeting. Only the death of a loved one would be accepted as an excuse, though no member would dare miss a mandatory meeting. Only members of the International Charters were excused from coming, though many of them would be coming.

 The ban on wearing their cuts for the Mother Chapter was still in effect, and it was embarrassing for the members who would now have to ride at the back of formations. Only Arkus wore the cut. There was nearly two thousand members world wide, and Arkus called the Manufacturer of the Werewolf pins and ordered three thousand of them, to be delivered to Iron Mountain Ranch, known as the Wolfsschanze, or Wolfs Lair, as soon as possible. He paid extra for rush status and was promised them in three weeks time. They would drive up two weeks before and check on the Ranch, even though they knew that the local Charter there maintained it. New construction on bunkhouses would be needed. They would hit the large Army Surplus store close by the Ranch for cots, and bunks, and everything else they needed.

The next couple of weeks were a blur of activity, and Arkus had called the owner of the Army Surplus store and made a huge order for necessities, Including a full field kitchen, blankets, beds, cots, sleeping bags, and anything else that the Owner thought might be useful. Arkus grabbed Sandra and told her to pack that she was about to be taken to the Ranch with him. He was leaving a week earlier than everyone else to supervise the construction at the Ranch. He had a plush building, called the Wylfsschanze, built for the non-Wereble women and had it insulated and sound-proofed. Arkus seemed to be renewed in his spirit and he was definitely feeling the blood rush. He was almost animalistic with Sandra, who liked the rough sex. The days were filled with building and logistics and preparing. He had ordered the fire pits and bar-b-cue rotisserie frames and had them built. He ordered whole cows from a near by farm, to be delivered to the Ranch prepared for cooking on the rotisseries.

There was a large cooler installed in a new building that would chill the alcohol and beer ordered. A seventy five gallon plastic container of mead showed up and was loaded into the cooler. It was designed so that tap lines could be attached to it and it could be drawn at the bar from a tap. The boxes of Werewolf pins arrived and Arkus checked them out. The original pins had been captured in Germany near the end of the War, when his unit encountered the Regimental HQ of the Wehrwolf SS unit. It was a copper and black pin with a skull and crossbones and a red "W" under it. The repros were very nice but did not quite match the original pins. All of the Original Members had them, or did at one time. Pins have a tendency to get lost off a vest, especially with as vigorous use as an MC cuts get.

The "pinning" ceremony would be one way of re-instilling that feeling of Brotherhood, it would be heralded as important as the receiving of your "Rockers". The International Members that couldn't come will be treated to a similar ceremony in their own country, and the pin would be sent with their Chapter President. Sandra would be given one, and any President could request one for his wife or sweetheart that he wished to honour. He also had ordered Sandra a sexy leather cut with the Werewolves back emblem, and no rockers. Unlike most one percenter groups, the Werewolves did not have a patch for women saying "property of". They did wear a patch that Identified their man, and a patch that said "Wylf" and their name. Sandra's cut had the back emblem, and on the front was the patch that said "Arkus" and on the right breast was her "Wylf Sandra" patch. He would also propose to her after the pinning ceremony.

The women were to be sequestered in their clubhouse until after the ceremony. There were after all, a few non-Werebles. All the men would shape-shift into their Wereble form, and would pledge their oath once more. The Mother Chapter would be pardoned at that point. After all had changed back, the women would join the party. Sandra had been put in charge of the Wylfsschanze, and she had made it a real comfortable place, even making Argus purchase an over-sized air conditioner unit for it. It was a two story comfortable get away from the loud rowdy scene that Church, tended to be when patching in someone or this pinning was going to be. There was also a "Chapel" to discuss strictly top secret business. It was wired to make it impervious to listening devices and had "white noise" makers through out the building. It had cell phone jammers located on all four walls, which meant absolutely no cell phone reception, even though you were required to drop them in the cell phone slots outside of the building. The jammers also kept any "wires" from working, just in case there was an infiltrator from one of the Federal Law Enforcement Agencies amongst the members. Business would be discussed at some point, and they were damned sure going to keep it private.

The main entrance was just off the road, which was well marked as a private drive, no entry. Above the Compound gate, was a gate stolen from a "work camp" in Germany after the end of WWII. It's motto did not fit here; Arbeit Macht Frei. Above that had been added in wrought iron "Wolfsschanze". Across the metal gates was the German word

"VERBOTEN", also repurposed from the work camp. Several large Nazi Adlers had been seized by his unit as well as wrought iron SS runes. The Ranch had been fitted out with many original signs, banners and metal items, which were lying around free for the taking after the war.

The bar was thirty feet long and made in a right angle. There were hundreds of different Nazi pins and medals inlaid into the surface of the bar with a three inch thick piece of glass covering them. There were items and uniforms of major Nazi officials, probably worth somewhere in the millions of dollars to collectors. Here were artifacts from Wewelsburg Castle, Original Party Standards, and what was purported to be the original spear of destiny, and was sealed into an acrylic block six feet tall and two feet thick. During the final days of the war in Europe, at 2:10 PM on April 30th, 1945, Lt. Walter William Horn, serial number 01326328, of the United States 7th Army, took possession of the Spear in the name of the United States government, or so he thought, but in actuality he had seized a clever forgery.

The full moon had arrived and Arkus could feel the Βράσιμο αίματος, (Vrásimo aímatos) or Blüt Kochen as the Germans called it. It literally meant "blood boiling", because that's what it felt like, He had to change, had to hunt, had to kill. It hadn't affected him this hard in centuries, but then again, he was in love and his body chemistry had changed with it. He had desires and passion again. The beast had awakened inside of him, and he wanted blood. He had left Sandra a note and had ridden out without her knowing it. He rode to the nearest city and hunted. He found the hangout of a latino gang with a bad reputation for murder and other atrocities, and he hunted them all. He had killed ten of them, individually and now the house that they were partying in was left without guards on the outside, only those inside were left alive.

He approached the back door but it had a two by four as a barrier bar across it. One of the windows close by was open, the music was deafening. He looked inside. Two latino women were pleasuring some gang-banger. Arkus partially changed, ran and leapt through the window and was tearing out their throats before anyone knew what was happening. The loud music covered the noise. He had collected all of the weapons on these freaks as he killed them and had quite a collection so far. He added the two pistols from this asshole to the bag outside the window. He opened the door just a crack, no one was in the hall. He went into the room across the hall, four men and one woman were engaged in rough sex, and it didn't take him long to tell that she was being gang raped. He could smell her fear and desperation. He tore out the throats of the four mexican bastards. He covered the girls mouth and put his finger to his lips to let her know to remain quiet. He got her some clothes and took her to the room across the hall and helped her out of the window.

She slumped down against the wall in shock. Now his blood was really boiling and he changed fully, He tore through the house with such speed and ferocity that he literally tore the mexicans apart. He gathered the weapons that they never got the chance to use and took them out the back door. He changed back to his non-Wereble form for the dazed girl outside. He had two duffle bags of weapons that he stashed in a culvert out back, as well as money, drugs and jewelry, most of the jewelry was high content gold, all was of the Jesus Malverde, with one having a matching ring, bracelet and necklace with Malverde Sinaloa on them. He went back in one last time with two ounces of thermite and some gasoline. He doused the bodies and furniture, and a small shrine dedicated to Jesus Malverde, laid a trail of gasoline to a pile of rubbish and then lit the thermite on the rubbish. He closed the back door carefully picked up the girl and ran. He took her to his trike and put her on the back seat.

He retrieved the guns and put them in the back of the trike, and took her away. He stopped a block away from a fire station and carried her in his arms up to the station and said that he had found four men raping her and that she needed medical attention. The Paramedics quickly got her in an ambulance and took her to the Hospital. He told them where he found her and said that the house was now on fire. Just then the Station got the call to be dispatched to a burning residence , the same one he just stated was on fire. Arkus sprinted away as the Firefighters scrambled to get into their turnouts and jumped on the fire truck.

    They conveyed everything they knew to the Police that showed up, and told them that the man had claimed to take her from this very house, where no less than twenty three bodies lay torn apart and burned. Another ten in the culvert behind the house. The cops said that they should pin a medal on this guys chest, but took a description of the man, to put out an all points bulletin. They retrieved video from the Fire House, but oddly enough he had successfully avoided getting his face on camera.

    He changed his clothes and cleaned up before returning to Sandra. He was excited on so many levels that he was practically shaking. When he returned to the Wolfsschanze, he found Sandra in their room reading, He came in and grabbed her, picked her up and kissed her with force. He carried her to the bed and threw her down on it, practically ripped his clothes off and forcefully disrobed her. He took her from behind, hard and savagely, pounding into her. He squeezed her breast and pulled her nipples, she moaned in extreme pleasure. The more she moaned the harder he pounded into her, until she screamed with the force of her orgasm. He flipped her over and tasted her ample cream, until he mounted her again. She was shocked and amazed at his ferocity, and very pleasantly surprised. He was pounding her faster and she was trying to hold her orgasm but couldn't and was coming again. A low guttural scream welled up from her as she orgasmed, which triggered his orgasm. He thrust one last time and exploded with a growl that became a roar. Neither had ever experienced such a primal and powerful orgasm before, and they both collapsed into a heap upon the bed. Every ounce of energy went into that orgasm that both fell asleep immediately.

    The next morning, Sandra had taken the jeep that was kept at the Wolfsschanze, and had driven down to the farm down the road that sold fresh produce. She purchased carrots, corn, green beans, sweet peas, and Lima beans as well as four freshly butchered chickens. She came through the Dining Hall and into the kitchen where she and two other of the Wylfs started cutting the vegetables and cooking the chickens in two huge stainless steel stock pots. Soon there would be some delicious chicken noodle soup, which she knew was a favorite of Arkus. Several Members had arrived, which only two had a Wylf, and they had gathered with Sandra when she came from shopping. Once the soup was made, the Wylfs set the tables and made tea to drink. The coffee pot was turned on and the coffee made, with the knowledge that there would be more arriving at any time.

 The Wolfsschanze was immaculately clean, barrels around gathering areas were constantly burning, and were for throwing your butts into after finishing your cigarettes and cigars. There were recycle barrels for glass, cans and paper. This wasn't your typical gathering spot. Everywhere were signs telling you to keep the Lair clean, and any violation was met with a hefty fine. The Wolfsschanze had only ever been raided once. All of the Werewolves stood at attention in Military precision with fully loaded rifles at shoulder arms. The FBI, ATF and DEA were invited into the compound and every place they wanted to search was opened to them. Of course there was nothing to find, there never was, and there never would be, not here and the Feds knew it.

 Arkus and the other few men had finished with every preparation that they could think of. Since there was no smoking within the Dining Hall, the women had stepped outside the back door and had just finished with smoking when they heard the men come in. They extinguished their cigarettes and put them in an old coffee can that would be dumped into one of the burn barrels later. Arkus smiled at Sandra and she returned it in genuine affection. He walked around the tables and up to her. He took her in his arms and kissed her deeply while grabbing her buttocks, she hummed when he did it. He broke the kiss and looked around, everyone seemed to be waiting on him, though they were pretending to talk softly to the Wylfs.

"What is it, it smells fantastic!" He said realizing that he was very hungry and reached for a bowl. Sandra grabbed his hand and told him to sit down and she would bring him some. She was setting a precedent for the Wylfs, who would be expected by the men to follow her lead. The men sat and the women served them and brought their own to the table. Everyone had food and a drink, and no one ate until Sandra sat down at the table. She could feel the savagery of their love making in the soreness that she felt. She reveled in the feeling. Arkus looked into the bowl and was pleasantly surprised to see the chicken noodle soup. He looked at her and smiled. He took a bite after cooling it off and praised the ladies for such a wonderful meal. All talking stopped, and a chorus of slurping ensued.

Around eleven in the morning you could hear the motorcycles from far off. The members were arriving by groups of twenty to sixty, with quite a few bearing fried chicken from various fast food joints. Some brought fried fish and even pizzas. The Wylfs worked hard making sure that the food was accessible, and that there was plenty of coffee, tea and of course ice cold beer. Sandra asked some of the Wylfs to take the Jeep into town to get paper plates and plastic ware and cups. Plus chips, dips and whatever else they wanted to get. She handed them a thousand dollars that Arkus had given her when she asked for the money to go shopping. The Wylfs returned an hour and a half later with a full Jeep and five hundred dollars change. The Prospects were working hard to keep everything stocked and cleaned. The women didn't have to work any more, all they had to do was call for a Prospect who would do the dishes, kept food and drinks stocked, cleaned up, cleaned the toilets and whatever else any Member or Wylf could think of.

Wylfs were respected and treated like royalty by Prospects and other Members. They were Wives and committed lovers. Bambi's were just party girls that hung around and were fair game for anything, as long as they knew their place. If they stepped out of line, they faced quick and often harsh punishment. They would often be made to perform lesbian sex shows for the amusement of the entire club. Prospects could have sex with them, only after asking permission of every patched Member present. Usually it was very early in the morning when most Members were asleep, when they got to have sex with them, and only after several men had had them first. Prospects were harassed relentlessly. You could call them up at 0230 in the morning and tell them to bring you a single ice cold beer and they would have to get up and get dressed, although most stayed dressed, go get the beer and deliver it to you, ice cold!

Menial task were the bread and butter of the Prospect, and

humiliating them was the best game around for a patched Member. They were the ones that cleaned up the puke when a patched Member had drunk way too much and could no longer hold it down. They cleaned up blood, shit, piss or any other mess the patched Members found. They washed their cars and trucks, shined the chrome, ran errands for Wylfs too busy with kids and work. They picked up and payed for dry cleaning and no matter the task, duty or humiliating job they could never complain about it.

The Pinning Ceremony

   The day had finally approached. Prospects were running back and forth to the Airport picking up International Charter Members. Buses had been rented to accommodate the Members and their luggage. Most Airlines would not allow you to fly with your Colors on, so they were packed with care in a carry on, and as soon as you were outside, the Colors were on your back. The Feds had found out after the third plane landed with Bikers on it. They arrived after several buses full of Members had already been picked up. They were trying to film each and every member as they came out of the Airport and donned their colors. That fact was relayed to Arkus, Bëorn and Dyth when the Prospect returned to the Lair. Nothing could be done, as no laws were being broken, but the Feds did what they could legally do.
   When all the Members had arrived, some twelve hundred Bikers with three hundred women, the Lair was pretty crowded. A section of the wall was removed and tents were set up in the field behind the lair. Eating was done in shifts and one hundred port a johns had to be ordered to handle the necessities of biology. The port a johns were lined up to help block the campsites from prying eyes on neighboring farms. The day was one huge party, with Members playing their own instruments and providing music for everyone there. Women danced and performed for the Members, prospective women wanting to become Wylfs showed their bodies and talents trying to find a Member to take them as their old lady. Drugs were forbidden and none made it to the Lair. Dinner was handled in shifts with the Presidents and Vice

Presidents and their Wylfs eating first, other Officers and on down the line to Bambi's and Prospects. The party went on all day and up until just after dark. The great thing about being outside the city, when night came, it was really dark. Arkus stepped up on the stage, and the Wylfs and Bambi's followed Sandra into the Wylfsschanze, and when the last female had entered, the door was locked from outside, making sure that no one would "accidentally" open it.

In 1780 serving as a Scout in Tennessee, Arkus had met the Great Chickamaugan Chief Tsiyu Gansini. The Colonials and British knew him as Dragging Canoe, War Chief of the Cherokee. Arkus and Dragging Canoe became friends and blood brothers along with Dragging Canoes real Brothers, Little Owl, Badger, and Turtle at home. Arkus had been gifted with many great items, and Arkus in turn had given them some of the finest weapons made. After Dragging Canoe saw Arkus in Bear form, he gave him a very fine silver buckle with the totem of a bears foot upon it. Arkus wore it on the the most special of occasions. Today was one of those occasions, and he donned it today in anticipation of the ceremony. He ran his fingers over the buckle for good luck and inspiration.

"Brothers, Welcome to the Wolfs Lair! Tonight we renew our old bonds of kinship. We will renew our vows to the Club, we will re-pledge our heart and lives to what we have built for ourselves. In blood will we pledge it and those that cannot pledge, cannot accept the Brotherhood, then you will have to go from us, after you pledge your oath that you will never speak to any non-Werebles. To do so would bring you dishonor and death. First we will have a patching ceremony for those that have earned their Rockers. Sponsors will bring their Prospects into the circle now." twenty seven Prospects are brought forward and then lead out to the gate.

All the Patched Members form a double sided line and the prospects must run the gauntlet of flying fist and feet. They have to make it to the center of the circle to get their Rockers, only twenty four made it, which means the other three have to remain Prospects for another year or leave. The Members start a low growl as the men run the gauntlet, and it builds into a roaring howl when they reach the center. Everyone is changing into their Werebles form. With the exception of three, all are wolves, two are badgers, and Arkus alone is a bear. But not just any bear, He is huge! He has become a Kodiak Bear, huge and ferocious with massive fangs and long, sharp dagger like claws. All of the Members are surprised to see a bear, even though they thought that if anyone would have been a bear, it would have been Franz Müller, from the German Chapter. He stood at a whopping seven feet three inches tall, and proved to be the largest badger ever.

The Banner of the Werewolves was brought to the center of the circle. It was Black with a red "Wulfsangel" under the head of a werewolf. Each Wereble drew a knife or dagger and cut themselves and approached the banner, took hold of one of the corners and uttered the phrase "I Swear but my heart, the blood in my veins, and the soul which inhabits this body, that I will ever be faithful to the Club, it's Members, and it's Laws. So help my honor and keep me steadfast in due performance of the same, binding myself under no less a penalty than that of death." When all had taken it save Arkus, he stepped forward and pulled the Sacred Silver Dagger of the Gods and held it aloft. All eyes glowed with the light which shown from it. Arkus stabbed the tip into his paw and smeared his blood upon the Banner. It glowed momentarily, and slowly faded. All eyes were on the dagger until Arkus put it away. He made a full circle in the darkness, but he could see their frightened eyes staring at him. He changed back into his human form before speaking,
"This night before the Gods you have renewed your Oath and Obligation to this Club and to one another. And I know that the Gods were watching you. There are four types of people in this world, Sheep, Wolves, Sheep Dogs, and Werewolves. **WHAT ARE YOU?**" He yelled the last word and it became a howl. The answer was far louder than he expected as every voice rose to it's loudest in answer.
"**WEREWOLVES!**" The shout was so loud that windows and doors shook from the fury of the shout. Bëorn and Dyth brought out the pins and one was given to each Member, and each was told to change back and to keep their forms around non-Werebles. After the last Patched Member had received their pin, the Ladies door was unlocked and they

were told to rejoin the party. After about an hour, Arkus stepped up on the stage and everyone immediately went silent. He waved Sandra over and then met her half way. He kissed her and then dropped to one knee. He gave her her Colors and then asked her to marry him. She started crying and could only shake her head yes. The crowd cheered for them and congratulations were shouted and given by everyone. They were picked up and carried to the stage and placed upon chairs. Bëorn and his Wylf, Mattie Lee brought them each a tankard of mead. Arkus and Sandra intertwined their arms and drank until both tankards were empty. They smashed the tankards against a nearby rock and then kissed again. Again everyone cheered for them. Arkus held up his hand, a pin in his fingertips. He pinned it over Sandra's left breast as a token that she was now his Wylf! They kissed again and the Musicians started playing again. Now the feeling was really festive and things degraded into a drunken feast with the only ones not drinking being the Prospects. After about an hour Arkus lead Sandra away to rude comments about what was about to happen, with even ruder remarks questioning whether or not he would be able to perform.

There seemed to be no problem with either of their performances, and when they had finally had enough pleasure, they fell asleep in each others arms. It had been a long couple of weeks and full of stress for Arkus, with most of the issues resolved, he fell into a deep and peaceful sleep. Tomorrow the Sons of Asgard, the Turks, Lords of Hell, Fuhrer's Bastards and the Brothers in Christ, would all show up and the partying would begin in earnest. While not a One Percenter Club, the Brothers in Christ had a tendency to show up at all the Biker clubhouses and many rode with other groups. Most were just rich boy wannabes, who didn't have the testicular fortitude or the balls to be a One Percenter. They were tolerated as long as they didn't get too preachy, or too intrusive with the jesus freak stuff.

Arkus rose early and kissed Sandy on the cheek softly, trying not to wake her. He let her sleep and left the room silently. The buildings were built with two by eights instead of two by fours, and the walls had extra insulation and sound deafening materials as well as electrical interference lines so that you couldn't aim high power microphones at them and listen to what's being said inside. It was zero six hundred and most were still asleep. Joanie had just arrived by car, and was tired, she had driven here after work. She hugged and kissed Arkus and asked where Sandy was. Arkus pointed out their room and told her that Sandy was still asleep. She walked off to join Sandy in the bed after kissing Arkus once more.

Arkus walked into the dining hall and got some coffee. There were Bikers and Bambis in various states of undress, and one rather large but shapely woman totally nude making coffee. She turned when Arkus came into the kitchen, and smiled her recognition at him. He returned her smile and could smell her, could smell that she was Lycanthropoi.
"Well, well, it's the Great Man himself. The Founder of the Club and the Legend. Why are there no women members in this Club? Is it for men only?" She asked smiling and standing her full height of five feet eight inches, this caused her ample breast to become even more obvious.
"No woman has ever applied, is probably the only reason why we don't have any women members. You are obviously a Wereble, obviously capable, so you want to be a Prospect? Okay, we can make that happen, but first, Who the fuck are you?" Arkus said reaching for a cup and the sugar, the coffee was almost ready.
"Sorry, I'm Ari. I have been around for five years, my brother is a President of the Romanian Chapter. I have my own bike, and I have earned the respect of all the other Members and I get my pick of pussy, like any other Patched Member. Few of the guys could take me in a fight in human or Canto form. What do I have to do?" Ari asked looking Arkus in the eyes. She reached for the coffee pot and poured Arkus and herself a cup of coffee.
"Canto form? What's Canto?" Arkus asked to give him time to recall who the President of the Romanian Chapter.
"It's what the younger crowd calls themselves. Werebles is like saying 'groovy', a bit out of date." Ari chuckled.
"Arabella Codrescu! Vlad's little sister! WOW! How you have grown! Romanian women were always gorgeous! Why hasn't Vlad let you join the Romanian Chapter?

"Some bullshit about no women have ever joined, they wouldn't be allowed. 1450's macho bullshit, I'm sure. I am good enough to fuck, but not join." Arabella said with a growl under her voice. Arkus could smell her pheromones and Ari could smell his, Both were in need of changing, both were still under the effects of the blood boiling. Arkus grabbed her wrist and took her to the Chapel and closed the doors. Once inside he changed into the Kodiak bear and she became a Dire Wolf. She was large and primal and smelled wonderful. Arkus mounted her and let the beast emerge knowing that she could take it. They were savage in their forcefulness and each reveled in the ferocity of the other. Their orgasms were simultaneous and extremely powerful enough to make them collapse and change. After a few moments Arabella leaned over and kissed him deeply. She had needed it as much as he did. They were both too primal too release themselves with non-Werebles, and even with most Werebles wouldn't be able to take the full ferocity of their joining.

Arkus had an idea while he lay there with her. He told her about the gang house that he invaded and what happened. It was on the news as a rival gang war. He told her where the money, guns and drugs were and told her to get dressed and go fetch them, and to bring them to Chapel today at noon. They were going to tell everyone that she had done it under orders of Arkus as her "buy in" to the Club. She agreed and kissed him once more and got up on shaky legs, She giggled and thanked him once again for helping with her Se fierbe sânge, Romanian for blood boiling. He dressed and went into the bathroom and cleaned up a bit then went back to the kitchen for more coffee.

It was almost eight and very few people were up. Arkus went and had a hot shower and returned to the room with Sandy and Joanie, both of whom were still asleep and totally beautiful. Sandy was spooning Joanie their hair spread out and intertwined with the others. He got clean clothes and his cut and dressed quietly, then walked back to the kitchen. On his way a few were stirring, it was now almost ten and at eleven the Officers would be awakened and would have to get ready for Chapel at noon. Mattie Lee smiled at Arkus and joined him in his walk to the kitchen. She put her arm around his waist as they walked and his arm rested on her shoulders. They engaged in small talk and joked around with each other while they walked. Arkus slipped his hand down to Mattie Lees ass telling her what a fine round ass that she had for a hundred year old woman, she laughed and told him 'A hundred and one, baby!'. She started waking up Bambis and Prospects telling them it was time to start cooking. He hugged her and grabbed both ass cheeks and told her that he would love to fool around anytime, (knowing that it's forbidden, but flirting wasn't)

She kissed him and said that she was happy with her old man, but was honestly flattered. She went about making sure that all the dishes were gathered and put through the dish washer and that brunch was being cooked. Arkus went to the Chapel and made sure that it was aired out and that there were no traces as to what had occurred there. He opened the doors and sprayed air freshener in the room and lit his pipe and smoked. It was one of the few places where you were allowed. There were fresh cigars in the humidor, Arturo Fuentes Opus X Lost City. He smoked his pipe and Mattie Lee or one of the Bambis would check on him every few minutes and refill his coffee. More people were up now and some of the other MC's were filtering in.

Matti Lee came in to check on Arkus and he grabbed her and kissed her again. She returned his kiss as they embraced. He picked her up and put her on the edge of the table and pressed himself into her. She could feel how hard he was, and she reached down and freed his cock. She stood up and dropped her shorts and he picked her back up onto the table, while she guided his cock into her. The Blood boiling was infectious and could drive another Wereble into the feverish feelings that would overrule their senses at times, Now was one of those times. He pounded into Mattie Lee and it wasn't long before she was orgasming. He held her as he felt her come. She could feel him about to come as well and pushed him away and dropped to her knees before him and deep throated him as he exploded into her hot throat. She drained him and then rose smiling and licking her lips. He pushed her back up onto the table and cleaned up her creamy pussy, then let her down and they kissed passionately, before she put her shorts back on and left, kissing him once more before she left. The Prospects were busy either doing what Mattie Lee told them to do, or making sure the Officers were up and getting ready. A notice board had long ago been erected and the Rules of the Wolfschanze were permanently displayed prominently where all entering could see.

Arkus pushed a button on the wall that sounded a loud horn outside, a signal to all the Officers to come to the Chapel. He could see out the window that Arabella had arrived and was unloading two dufflebags and a pack. She told a Prospect to bring them in, and he obeyed her without question. They were put just inside of the Chaple doors and Ari waited outside. The Officers for the Various Chapters that made it, filed in and took a chair. There were thirteen Presidents and Vice Presidents here, as well as Alexei and Arkus. Arkus took the Head of the Table, as was expected . He greeted everyone and was genuinely happy to see them all.

"Before we start, I have something that will change the Club forever, and think that you all should have a vote. I have been approached by Arabella Codrescu for full membership and a buy in. She's the sister to Vlad Codrescu, the Romainian Charter's President. We have never had a woman apply and never had one that ever seemed interested or one that was capable, but Ari is all of the above. Those dufflebags contain weapons, the backpack money, drugs and jewelry from that mexican gang that was hit. She did it, and that's the proof. It will also be her buy in. It's up to you." Everyone looked around at each other, not wanting to be the first to speak.

"Ari is definitely capable, she's been riding with us for five years and we all consider her a sister, but there has never been a woman in the Club." Vlad commented.

"I like Ari, but, I ain't sure." Bëorn spoke up, the others mumbled agreement.

"So do you trust her? Do you have any doubts about her loyalty? Do you have any specific reason other than she's a female?" Arkus was trying to pin him down.

"I don't doubt her loyalty one bit, she's totally trustworthy, no doubt about it. She's gone toe to toe with our guys on more than one occassion and even ran jobs for us and performed special duties that only a woman could do, but the Club rules..." Bëorn was cut off.

"Say absolutely NOTHING about women being Patched Members. If she's doing the job of a Patched Member then why not let her have the Patch?" Arkus remained calm and pointed out the logic of it all.

"Well, she's well liked and respected in the Chapter, I don't have any objections, it's up to everyone else. She's proven herself to the Club on more than one occasion." Bëorn finished. Everyone looked to Dyth, who had no objection. "Show of hands for..." Everyone raised their hands for her Membership and full buy in. Alexei got her patches and Arkus tossed him one of the Werewolf pins. The rest of the Club business was discussed on Club, National, and International levels. The contents of the pack and dufflebags were laid out on the table and sorted out. Arkus took a fine pistol, it was a Sig Sauer P226 Legion in .45 auto. After business was discussed Arkus pushed the horn button again which was a signal for all Members to gather outside at the courtyard of the complex. They waited a few minutes to allow everyone to get to the courtyard, and walked in somber semblance to the stage and filed onto it, looking out over all of the members. Arkus nodded to Bëorn to tell the news to everyone.

"Today we are making history in this Club for many reasons. One, this is the most Members ever to attend any meeting or gathering. Two, Thirteen Presidents and Vice Presidents, and ALL of the Original Founders are here. Three, for the first time we are awarding the Patches to one of the most worthy Prospects ever, and one that the Mother Chapter is very familiar with. They have served us faithfully and never questioned anything we asked them to do, no matter how dangerous. They have performed one last amazing feat as proof of their Loyalty and Worthiness, and today we will present them with their full patches. We will order your name tag, because from here on out you will be 'SHE-WOLF", Arabella step up here and take you patches." All the Patched Members form the gauntlet and Arabella smiled. She runs, leaps and dodges fist, knees, feet and elbows making it all the way without being hit once. She leapt upon the stage and stood before

Alexei and Bëorn and took her oath. Alexei handed her the patches and pin then, backhands her. She is taken by surprise and is spun patially around. She turns with a smile upon her face. Alexei returns her smile and tells her that is so she won't forget her Oath.

Everyone cheers as she runs to the Wylfschanze to sew on her patches. All of the women there cheer her for her getting in and help her to sew on the patches with the sewing machine. She kisses a few and tells them that her 'She-Wolf' tongue is at their beck and call. She joined the rest of the crowd outside along with most of the Wylfs, to the cheers of the crowd. Ari immediately grabbed a cute Bambi and pulled her into an embrace and kissed her deeply, to the rude remarks of the other Bikers. The dinner bell was sounded and everyone went into the Dining Hall. The food was Mattie Lees' typical excellent fare. No one would go away hungry and there would be plenty for those arriving all through the day. Most would bring fast food from the town or from someplace along the highway.

As the day wore on and the Bikers partied, the Christian Bikers wanted to prove themselves by drinking and wrestling, typical behavior. Some were making comments about the big tit bitch that got her patches. They were warned to keep their comments about a Patched Member to themselves. Then one of their members started shooting at a bobcat and her two kittens. Arkus told him to stop and the Christian Biker spouted off that that he would after he killed them. Arkus pulled his Sig and shot at the idiots hands. The pistol had been loaded with illegal ammunition that exploded, a favorite of the cartels. Arkus had blown both of the guys hands off. He held up his arms looking at the bloody stumps and screaming. He was grabbed by two of the Werewolves and held while his stumps were tied off. He was taken to an area and given what medical attention that they could give, and was tranquilized. Prospects immediately set about cleaning up the blood around the area and poured diluted bleach over the area to destroy DNA.

All of the Christian bikers pulled weapons and pointed them at Arkus and the closest Werewolves. Arkus yelled at Ari to make sure that the women were safe, and she lead them to the Wylfschanze. All were crying, and Ari got them in and returned armed with a submachine gun. The Christians soon found themselves out numbered and outgunned, and they surrendered. The Werewolves bound them and lead them to a nearby building, while Arkus and Bëorn decided what to do. They had ridden in with the Lords of Hell (of course), and the President was summoned and brought rather roughly to the Chapel. They were told the 'official story' and were told that they would make sure everyone told the same story or else the Werewolves would settle up the damages. Harry 'Putrid Scum' Wilson, President of the Lords of Hell guaranteed the full cooperation of his Club and apologized for the damned Christians.

    Ari and some of the most trusted Members of the Mother Chapter were sent into town to steal a car and kidnap a couple of the mexican gang-bangers. They returned two hours later with four bangers in one of their cars. All were wearing the religious medal of Jesus malverde, which would identify them as members, three were still too young to have a lot of ink yet, while the forth was obviously in charge of training the other three. It was their bad luck to be caught without the rest of their gang. All of the Christians were loaded into one of the buses rented for the gathering. They were driven out of town and Ari asked for the privilege of executing everyone. Arkus laughed and told her to let some of the others have some fun as well. They were given machete's, the favored execution weapon of the gang and driven out away from the Ranch. Out on one of the smaller highways, everyone was unloaded.

    The bangers were put into their car and were told to start it up and drive away. As soon as they put the car in gear, the Werewolves opened fire and shot them all dead. The car rolled to a stop in a ditch. The Christians hands were bound behind their backs, and each one beheaded like the bangers would have done. Two of the Christian motorcycles were shot up and all of their cuts were collected. The Christian Biker who had his hands blown off was held for Ari to have her fun with. The cuts would be put into one of the gang houses the next time that Arkus needed to cool his boiling blood.

Ari and the rest returned with a dufflebag full of cuts. She reported on what happened and was told to go to the old barn and in the Southwest corner was a trap door, down the stairs was the Christian Biker and he was all hers. She smiled and thanked him, and went immediately to the barn. She had taken the dufflebag with her to store until the time was right. The remaining motorcycles, were loaded into a tractor trailer and had been taken into the next town where they were stored in a warehouse, that wasn't associated with the Club. The serial numbers would would be changed and bikes repainted, and some of the premium upgrades would be removed and used for Club Members. Everything was reported to Arkus and when everything was taken care of, he went back to the party and Sandy.

It wasn't long before Ari returned with a huge smile on her face. She winked at Arkus and immediately set her sites on Joanie. They started dancing to the music and Arkus looked down at Sandy sitting next to him talking to Mattie Lee. He went to the bar and brought back three glasses and a bottle of amaretto. He poured the drinks and they emptied their glasses. Joanie and Ari left, and Sandy was soon ready as well. They said their goodnights and left for the room. Sandy was slightly drunk, and was very excited. She was all over Arkus as soon as they were in the room. Arkus took her roughly and it wasn't long before she was loudly coming. Arkus wasn't long behind her, then collapsed next to her. He was spooning her when they fell asleep.

Arkus rose early and after relieving his bladder, walked out to the Dining Hall. Several men were running from the Security Office and the alarm sounded, one stopped to tell Arkus that the cops and Feds had found the bikers executed and were on their way here, because everyone in town had heard them bragging about coming here. "FUCK!" Was the first thing that popped out of his mouth. Everyone assembled bleary eyed in the compound's courtyard. Arkus went over the story again with everyone. Then everyone walked into the dining hall and the Wylfs, Prospects and Bambis started making breakfast. By the time Law Enforcement arrived breakfast was being served. The men on the gates made sure to open them before law enforcement got near them, and everyone acted nonchalant when they came screeching to a halt and running into the courtyard in full combat gear with automatic weapons. Arkus and the rest of the men had stored the weapons and stolen goods in a secret vault under the Dining Hall, and unless they were going to bring in bulldozers and excavation equipment, they would never find the vault. The doors of the Dining Hall were opened for the LEO's, and everyone acted surprised and delighted to see them and cooperated fully. Several of the Federal Agents were well known to the MC.

"Well if it isn't Jack Kolchak, Special Agent in Charge, FBI. How long has it been Jack, two years, three?" Arkus greeted him and held out his hand to the Agent, who took it and shook his hand.

"Arkus, when did you get back in town?" Jack asked surprised to see him.

"Why hell Jack, you really didn't know that I was back in town? Your guys are sleeping on the job. Been back about a month." Arkus said smiling.

"Apparently so. You know the routine, I need everyone outside, we have a search warrant to search your compound." Agent Kolchak was pleasant but matter of fact.

"You heard the man everyone, outside. You didn't need a search warrant Jack, all you had to do was ask, anytime. But thank you for not coming in at the crack of dawn and waking everyone up, we don't get a lot of sleep, but when we do, it's nice not to be scared out of our wits with doors busting down and flash-bangs going off. I had enough of that in boot camp. All we ask is that your guys don't break anything, we will be happy to supply you with keys or open any door for you. " Arkus was the last one out. Agent Kolchak agreed.

The Dining Hall was the first building searched, and afterwards Arkus ordered the women to get all the Agents coffee. The Agents walking around had several agency ID's. ATF, FBI, DEA, SHERIFF, and SWAT. The ladies brought out paper cups and pots of coffee others had set up a table with sugar, cream and milk in containers. As the LEO's went from building to building searching and coming up with nothing, Arkus introduced Sandy to Jack and said that they were now engaged. Jack wished them well and seemed genuine in his congratulations and well wishes. After about an hour, all of the LEO's met out of earshot and reported that they hadn't found anything, no drugs, guns, stolen items, no trace of anyone that was missing, no proof of any mischief. Jack told everyone that they were going to be watching them, and to keep out of the light.

"Well wait a minute Agent Kolchak, what happened to bring you all out here? Did the neighbors complain about the music? I mean you obviously had a reason to come out here, didn't you?" Arkus asked him looking concerned.

"The local Chapter of the Brothers in Christ were found executed, their bikes stolen and their cuts missing. They were last seen with the LOH MC, telling everyone that they were coming here for some kind of epic party. The next thing we know is that some kids from a farm down from where they were executed, found their headless corpses. They haven't stopped crying since. Care to tell me what you know about it?" Agent Kolchak was looking at the faces of the nearest Bikers as he said it. Sandy and some of the women winced at hearing they had been decapitated.

"Well, Hell! I can understand that everyone would be upset about kids finding decapitated bodies, but we don't know anything about their deaths. Truth is they couldn't handle just how epic it got. They got drunk, pulled out some weed, got obnoxious and we asked them nicely, to leave, which they did, on their own accord. We didn't get rough with them and they definitely didn't do anything to get killed over. And we don't decapitate people. We're sorry that happened, but it wasn't us. We will gladly cooperate with you on this one Jack. It's not good for this community, our community. Sheriff, you know that we have never done anything here, we don't shit where we sleep. We have raised money for charities, supported the town, paid our taxes. What do we have to do to prove it to everyone?" Arkus asked and everyone else mumbled in agreement.

"Lose the cuts and biker image, it scares the Hell out of everyone." Sheriff Owens said. He had the same name as Kolchak, John and both were called Jack.

" Afraid we can't do that. We have never intimidated any citizen intentionally, never will. We have tried to stay off everyone's radar, but the Patch grabs and keeps everyone's attention. It was a pleasure seeing you guys again, want to stay for breakfast?" Arkus asked them but they had turned away and were getting in their trucks.

Everyone scattered and searched for bugs. The Security Team got out electronic scanners and searched as well. Nothing missing, and three dozen bugs were found, and some of those wouldn't have been found if the women hadn't been talking, as they were voice activated only. The bugs were collected and then destroyed, Arkus told all the Presidents and VP's to assemble for Chapel. They talked about meaningless things as the Chapel was searched four times with electronic means before anyone said anything of import. Sandra and Joanie brought them two carafes of coffee and some cups before they closed the doors and then left. She and Joanie were talking about Ari as they left.

They spoke only about what they were told by the Agent, still uncertain about listening devices. They did not speak about the Agent not mentioning the car of mexicans and that worried them. They would have to do a little careful investigation. What no one knew was that the LEO's had raided several mexican gang houses last night. The mexicans had found the car and had removed the bodies of their friends. One of the religious medals they wore was still in the car, and it tied the car to the mexicans. The machetes were in the trunk with bloody fingerprints of the now missing dead mexicans, and that also tied it to gang activity.

They would later find out that two of the Brothers in Christ were buying weed and amphetamines from the mexicans and were screwing their underage chiquita whores, and that would tie it back to them as well. So far as the LEO's could tell, it was strictly the Brothers In Christ RC and the mexicans in business that went bad. As much as they wanted to tie the MC's to this, there wasn't any proof at all. One of the VP's found an old style tiny microphone in an out of the way corner. It had two copper wires coming out of the back and since it didn't transmit via signal, it went undetected. The other searches were doubled, but they only ever found that type of mic in the Chapel. They found six in total and they were soon rendered useless. They were connected to off and on switches so that the MC could feed what ever information they wanted to the Sheriff.

The wires had been routed through the walls along the old telephone wires and out to the main line that lead out to the highway. From there it ran a few hundred feet to a Wally's filling station where the Sheriffs Department, had deputized the owner, Wally Stoner. Wally's was a fairly large building for a filing station. There were two bays with lifts, a storage area, two bathrooms, a sales area, an Office, and a small room that Wally let's his Mechanics use occasionally. It was now being used as a monitoring station by the Sheriffs Office. Jack Owens was paying him one hundred and fifty dollars a month to rent the room, and made him an official Deputy.

It was obvious that the LEO's had set up the listening post, ran the wires and then had an Agent run the wires to the Chapel and connect them. It was brilliantly executed, old school and only by luck that they were found. Arkus had a white board brought in and he would write what needed to be said and everyone else would agree. They voted to scatter and return to their territories and lie low for a while. It was also decided that they would find one of the mexican houses in the next state and plant the Brothers in Christ cuts in the house and give the LEO's the 'word" by way of the wired mics in the Chapel.

They called everyone together and told them that the gathering was now ended and that they were to part, stay on the up and up, and to break no laws, not even a speeding ticket, the MC would fine them ten times what the court would charge them for a traffic violation. Arkus stored his trike in one of the temperature controlled garages at the Ranch, and pulled out on the White Wolf, a custom trike that was as long as a truck. As a matter of fact it had a 1961 GMC V12 "double six" gasoline engine mounted on the rear and a comfy two-seater bench in the canopy behind the large drivers seat. The pipes were run out either side and then up in the back in classic flared tail pipes. Everyone gathered around to take pictures. It had been kept up by Wally of all people, although Arkus had parked it here only a year ago.

Sandy and Joanie stashed their stuff under the bench seat compartments. Arkus handed Joanie a helmet, while Sandy donned hers. It was time for them to split up again, and Arkus was getting tired of running, so he made sure that everyone would see him coming and going by riding the White Wolf trike. He drove back to the Bear Bar and pulled around to the rear and hit the garage door opener, waited for it to open and pulled in and killed the engine. He put his helmet on the handle bars and waited for Sandy and Joanie. He walked between them, their arms around his waist. The door in the garage lead upstairs and through what appeared to be apartments.

At the end of the hall Arkus opened one of the doors. It was a utility closet, with a secret door behind the very large mop sink. He pushed past the sink. The women had an easier time because they were smaller. He flipped on the light and closed and latched the door the put a metal bar across it in two metal arms, to barricade the door. They walked single file down the narrow hall and came out another secret door in the hallway where Sandy and Arkus' apartment doors were. No sound came from the bar downstairs which meant that Alexei hadn't made it back yet. Arkus opened Sandy's door and they went in. He went over and picked up the amaretto bottle and took a swig from it and handed to Joanie who took it and took a swig, then handed it to Sandra who followed their lead. He disrobed and started undressing the women. They were kissing each other and soon were in bed drinking amaretto and making each other feel good.

A month had passed and they had raided one of the mexican safe houses in the next state over, planted the cuts from the Christian Bikers, stole all of the money, drugs, weapons and jewelry. The mexicans had just had a successful snatch and grab on a jewelry store, and they had some quality merchandise, as well as more of the Jesus Malverde and Sinaloa jewelry. Alexei knew a jeweler that could swap the backs on the Rolex watches that were in the mexican haul, and those would be given as bonuses to some of the Presidents and VP's of the Charters. Information was 'slipped' to the LEO's via their mics at the Chapel of the Ranch. The Chapter there let it slip as gossip. The FBI raided the house and found the dead mexicans and the cuts. Fingerprints were also planted inside the house from the dead mexicans that were at the scene of the Biker executions. The CIA training really paid off. Alexei had been Russian mob and Spetznaz, and had worked from time to time in the KGB and GRU.

Valgard and Arkus had worked for and with the CIA, CIC, CID, MI-5, MI-6 and other organizations that officially did not exist. They were still regarded as ultra top secret, and the names would come up as civilians when ran through Law Enforcement data banks. No links to any Security Agency would show up, although all of the Agencies would get the red flag. Alexei and Arkus worked at the bar for the next few months, and were watched by various Agencies for three months before the were ordered to stand down, since zero criminal activity could be tied to them. In the mean time, the jeweler had melted all the gold, sorted the diamonds, and had sold everything that he could. He passed them several thousand dollars at the bar, apparently paying for drinks with small bills but passing several large bills with them, until all of the money had been passed.

Arkus asked Sandy to go with him on a road trip, just the two of them out and around, a little vacation. She was happy to go. Arkus had been working a lot lately and trying not to act suspicious. What he didn't know was that Sandra had been approached by the Sinaloa and had sold Arkus out. She had taken over one hundred thousand dollars and drugs from them and would, in turn let them know when they could take him. She believed their lies that they just wanted to talk business with him, a lie and a band aid for her conscience. He had taken the White Wolf trike back to the Wolfsschanze to get his regular trike. While he was doing that, Sandra was packing. She called the Sinaloa on the burner phone they had provided her and she let them know where he was headed. Then she turned it off and took it out back and tossed it into the dumpster.

Arkus had almost made it to the Ranch when two black escalades pulled to either side, windows down and automatic Kalashnikovs out the windows. They opened fire upon him and the trike. He slammed on the brakes, causing the suv's to speed past and slam on their brakes as well. He steered for the side of the road and went over the embankment, and jumped from the trike. He slid down into a drainage culvert hidden under the scrub. The trike burst into flames as it hit the ground, as the large fuel tank ruptured. Everything had been engulfed in flames by the time the Sinaloas had reached the side of the road. It looked to them as if Arkus had been taken with the trike and was now burned beyond recognition. He had been hit several times by the bullets, but nothing serious, and he would definitely survive. They stood on the side of the road and unloaded their weapons into the burning twisted wreck below them.

Arkus waited until dark to leave the culvert. The fire department had already made the scene and put out the flames, but the police wouldn't be able to recover the trike and it's rider until the next day, when special equipment and the CSI team could arrive. He went in the opposite direction and crawled through the culvert and through the underground drainage pipes. When he was well away from the area, he crawled out and started walking to the Ranch. He didn't have far to go, fortunately. The few Bikers at the Ranch were shocked to see him hurt, and wanted to call everyone to let them know. He swore them to secrecy, and told them that he would kill anyone who broke his confidence. He knew that he had been set up and knew also that only three people knew where he was going, and that it had to be one of them, but why? After getting patched up and hiding in the secret bunker under the Wolfsschanze, for a few hours and sleeping, he watched as the police drove into the compound looking for him. The other Werewolves acted surprised to see them and even more upset to hear about the trike and Arkus. He listened to them make threats to the FEDS and Sheriffs Deputies about getting back the ones that killed Arkus.

After a cursory search they left, but Arkus knew that they would be watching the Ranch to see who came and went. Meanwhile, at the Bar, another group of FEDS and Sheriffs had arrived to tell Alexei and Sandra about the wreck. Alexei played it cool and Sandra became hysterical. So much so that Joanie had to take her to their apartment and give her a strong sedative. Jack Kolchak was talking to Alexei and was matter of fact as always.
"Alexei, we recovered three thousand or so, seven point six two rounds. Plus there has been a lot of Sinaloa presence in the area lately.

If Arkus has gotten into something, or the Club, now's the time to tell me, I can help. You know that I like Arkus and I don't want to see him dead, and I really hope he's not, but his body wasn't at the crash scene and there were blood trails through the culverts under the highway. If you hear of anything, give me a call, let me help, Please." Alexei was caught off guard by the Agents sincerity.

Jack held out a business card and Alexei took it and nodded. He was as worried about Arkus as Jack seemed to be. The truth was Jack had never really concerned his self with the Werewolves, as they always seemed to shun the spotlight. He always thought of them as just another group of riders caught up in the life and trying to avoid the reputation of the One Percenters. But somehow, they had crossed one of the worst of the cartels they could run up against, and he figured that they were way over their heads in the shit now! Hell, even the fucking U.S. Government couldn't do shit about them.

The Sinaloas had picked this area as a distribution point, and Jack Kolchak was about to shut that down. He called Quantico and filled them in. A task force was assembled in town and they immediately started raiding any and all suspected drug and gang houses. Sinaloa immediately got the message that they would not have a profitable partnership here, and they moved on.

Sandra had been a mess since the FBI Agents visit the day after her informing the cartel of Arkus' whereabouts. No one had seen or heard from him for a couple of weeks. Arkus had recovered nicely at the Ranch with the help of the few Bikers and Wylfs that resided there permanently. Arkus got one of the guys Tom Sims, to drive into town, with him hidden in the back, to a service station across the street from the bar. During prohibition there were tunnels from the bar to several of the surrounding buildings, the petrol station was one. Tom told him about the unmarked cars everywhere and about cameras mounted in several locations that he could see. Obviously the bar was under surveillance.

Tom pulled into the service bay of the hundred and ten year old service station and parked above the mechanics grease pit. Tom and the mechanic made a production over the fact that the wheel has a shimmy in it. Arkus stealthily left the vehicle and made his way to the storage room, and through the trap door into the tunnel underneath. The mechanic made sure that everything was back in place and Tom handed him a roll of bills. Tom walked across the street to the bar to get a drink. A couple walked in behind him. Tom figured that they were undercover agents, so went to the bar and got a beer. Tiffany was working the Bar and Joanie was working the floor, waiting on customers. Alexei was in the Office chatting up a tiny eighteen year old, who looked twelve.

Tiffany told Alexei that they had a Werewolf in the bar without his Colors. Alexei came out and talked with Tom as if nothing was going on. He introduced the eighteen year old to Tom and they shook hands. They continued to talk, and Tom drank another beer. He handed Alexei a ten dollar bill on which was written the words, ARKUS FINE BUNKER A, ALLS WELL. Alexei read the words, but acted as if it were a normal bill. He started to give Tom change but Tom told him to put it in the tip jar. They shook hands and Tom walked back across the street to the station. The mechanic said that he couldn't do anything until the next day when the part arrived. Tom called the Ranch and asked for a ride.

Sandra had told Joanie in a drunken, drug induced fit of remorse that she had told the cartel Arkus' whereabouts, but said that she had been told that they only wanted to talk business with him, and that she had stupidly believed them. Joanie told Alexei what Sandra had said and he told her to keep quiet about it. Alexei, would tell Arkus about it, if he ever showed up again, and if he didn't show up in a month, he would quietly kill Sandra and make it look like a suicide. Now after learning that Arkus was downstairs, he was going to have to tell his friend that the woman that he loved the most in the world, had sold him out. Alexei went through a secret door and up a wrought iron winding stair case, in a claustrophobic shaft, up to the second story to Sandra's apartment. He was standing outside the door when Arkus came through the door at the rear of the corridor.

Arkus could tell by the pained expression on Alexei's face who had sold him out. His heart broke and in his mind he cursed Hera for her part in all this. He knew that she had manipulated Sandra and that she would have been unable to resist Hera's wiles. He also knew that Hera had a way in to hurt him and to get to him like she hadn't been able to do for millennia. Arkus and Alexei opened the door and walked in. Sandra had overdosed on the drugs she had gotten from the cartel. Arkus broke down and cried. He held her body and wept bitterly for his lost love. This too had been orchestrated by Hera, because she knew that Arkus would have forgiven her. Alexei sat beside Arkus with his arm around him, his head touching Arkus'. He wept for his friends loss.

Alexei helped Arkus move her body downstairs to the bunker. The underground area was massively large. Tunnels and fortified bunkers and warehouse sized rooms, and in one area, a mausoleum. They bore her body there. Alexei could tell that Arkus wanted to be alone with her as he prepared her body for the vault, and so made his way back upstairs. Arkus placed two ancient gold coins upon her closed eyes. He cleaned her body, put her in fine clothes, then bound here in pure white silk. He sealed her within the vault and crudely scratched her name in ancient Greek, then climbed back upstairs.

In his apartment he knelt before the altar, and openly wept as he talked to his mother and to Zeus. He told them that he no longer wished to be immortal, that he wanted nothing more than to finally grow old and die. At long last he had cried himself to sleep. He lay upon the floor before the altar, while Kallisto his mother, Artemis and Zeus watched and yearned to stop his pain. It was in Zeus' power to grant his request, and Kallisto begged for their son to be free of the curse and Hera's hatred forever. Zeus relented, at long last. Zeus confronted Hera and told her that it would end, that very moment, and he absolutely forbade her to ever bother him again. Hera had no choice in the matter, as Zeus was the absolute ruler of the Gods, and she had to obey.

Joanie went up stairs and found Sandra missing. She told Alexei and she and Alexei searched the building. Arkus had gone downstairs when he heard them coming through the door. After a complete search of the building, Alexei allowed Joanie to call the Sheriffs Department and file a missing person report. Arkus made his way back to the service station and back into the truck. Tom was dropped off to pick it up and drove it back to the Ranch. From the Ranch he was smuggled out of the State to another Chapter where he got another trike and rode it back to the bar as if nothing had gone wrong. He had a forged receipt for the sale of the White Wolf, to a Biker who had just been reported missing when the White Wolf had been found.

All the angles were covered and Arkus acted as if nothing had occurred when he walked into the bar, followed closely by the Sheriff and Jack Kolchak. He was told of Sandy's absence and the fact that no one had seen her leave. He was told about the White Wolf being shot up and no body being found with it. He gave them the receipt for the trike, showed them the bag of cash that was supposedly exchanged for the trike, and he told them that he was deathly worried for Sandra, that he was more concerned as to where she was and why the hell they weren't out looking for her. He was genuinely upset, they could see that. They could see that he wasn't faking the tears and emotions, and Jack said that he thinks that she had some how ran afoul of the Sinaloa.

Arkus looked incredulously at Jack. He wanted to know what the fuck did the cartel have to do with anything. Jack told him of his theory that the Christian Bikers and the Sinaloa had been in business together and that they had connected them with the Werewolves because of the gathering in which the Chapter had left and met up with them and that things had gone side wise, one thing lead to another and somehow they had connected Sandra to the group and had probably kidnapped her. He told Arkus that if that was the case, she was probably already dead. Arkus grabbed Jack by the lapels and was shouting in his face as the Deputies tried to separate them. Jack told them to leave Arkus alone after they managed to get him away from Jack. Arkus was upset and that could be bad news. All Arkus had to do was to put the word out and any mexican or south American with in ten states would be a target. Joanie was trying to comfort Arkus, he held her with his face buried into her shoulder crying deeply.

Jack told Alexei to take care of Arkus, and to let him know if there was going to be a war between the Club and the Sinaloa. He also told

Alexei that he had called in every Federal Agency that might have anything to do with stopping the cartel, and that he would make sure that they paid for Sandy's death, if they were responsible for it. He had wanted to arrest Eric Holder and Barack Obama for arming the cartels in the fast and furious scandal that went unprosecuted to this day. The evidence was there, they were obviously guilty and had tied the hands of the Federal Agencies that might do something about it. Even the new President ignored it. Politicians could get away with anything, they covered each others asses because they were all criminals, and the cartels owned them! Jack left with bile rising in his throat from anger and disgust. He may not be able to chop the head off of the beast, but he could certainly hurt the beast!

 Joanie took Arkus upstairs to his apartment and got him something to drink. She offered him a xanax, but he refused it. She helped him get undressed and helped him into bed. He asked if she would lay with him and hold him for a bit, which of course she did, happily. They lay there in the bed, his head upon her breast, her arms around him until they both drifted off to sleep. They slept the night through, as Joanie had taken the xanax that Arkus had turned down. She woke at some point during the night and went to the bathroom. She was still dressed and even had her shoes on. She removed them, undressed and returned to bed, and was soon fast asleep.

 She woke before he did, but only by a few minutes. She went to the bathroom to relieve her bladder and was returning to the bed when he woke up. She smiled at him and came to the bedside. She was only in her panties. Her large nipples were erect and stood out in stark contrast to her small breast. He pulled her to him and kissed her, while fondling her breast. She returned his kiss and swung her leg over him and straddled him. He rubbed her round, sexy ass and pulled her to him. Tears began to flow down his cheeks and he turned his head away trying to regain control. She hugged his head to her, and started to cry herself. Arkus leaned back and Joanie laid down beside him, both crying. After a while she asked him if he really thought that Sandy was actually dead. He shook his head while larger tears spilled from his eyes. He had really loved Sandy and her death was breaking his heart. Joanie got up and got him a high dose sedative and some tea. Arkus took the pills without even thinking and downed the tea. She held him until he fell asleep. She dried his tears and wiped away her own, then kissed him on the forehead, dressed and went down stairs.

The news had traveled to everyone still in town and the Members started gathering at the Bar. A wreath with black ribbons adorned the doors, with the words "We Love you Sandy" on them. Everyone was upset about it and wanted to go to war with the mexicans, but Alexei said that it couldn't be done without Arkus having a say in it. Arkus awoke several hours later and washed his face and went down stairs. He was surprised to see everyone at the bar. Alexei had filled everyone in on what the Feds knew or thought they knew. Alexei handed Arkus some ice cold mead that had been dropped off by the SOA, after they had heard the news.

Everyone wanted to know if they were going to war or not. Arkus spoke and all sound stopped.
"We don't know anything right now, and the Feds only have a theory. We don't even know for sure if Sandra is dead or not. Or if she just ran away out of fright, because she couldn't handle the lifestyle. I am devastated by her leaving, whether or not it was of her own accord. For now, we wait and see! No one does **ANYTHING** that might cause trouble for the Club! Am I making myself clear?" He looked around and everyone agreed. He thanked them for being there and for their support. Joanie brought him another drink and lead him to a chair. In a way she was just a little bit happy that Sandra wasn't around, and she was ashamed of herself for feeling that way, but now she had a chance to be with Arkus.

As the weeks, then months passed, the FBI and other Agencies failed to turn up anything, and all leads dried up. At last Jack Kolchak returned to the bar to tell Arkus and Alexei that they were closing the investigations. However being the tenacious bastard that he was, he would never give up the chase. He told them that if they heard something to please pass it on to him first, they said that they would. Joanie and Arkus grew closer and were eventually married. Alexei had fallen madly in love with his little eighteen year old girlfriend, and they married as well. Sandra's secret grave remained just that until the day that Arkus passed away. Joanie passed shortly afterwards. Both were interred as per Arkus' last wishes in the secret mausoleum under the bar. All of Arkus' belongings were stored in the area adjacent to his grave, buried like a Demigod should be. Bodies were acquired and burned so that the Club could celebrate the passing of one of the founders and his Wylf. The ashes were spread over the Wolfsschanze. Only Alexei ever knew the truth. Sheriff Jack Owens and Special Agent Jack Kolchak eventually retired. Sandra Nonakris' disappearance was the case that had haunted both to their dying days, and remained, officially unsolved.

Το τέλος

8
INNER EARTH GODS

Entry 03 February 1929.

This is the journal of Professor of Archaeology and Mediaeval Metaphysics, Dyth Greffen-Feder, Ph.D. Miskatonic Univ. Arkham Massachusetts. Here in are inscribed my entries and reasons for undertaking my quest into the American Southwest Desert regions in search of information about the entities known separately as "Star People", "Snake People", and "Ant People", upon receiving a rather large and very thick book and maps that once belonged to one Wilbur Whateley, former student of Miskatonic Univ. Along with certain notes, drawings and artifacts related to my quest.

Among the artifacts was a small bronze charm with what looked like a branch of a tree on it, which was called an "Elder sign". All of these items were turned over to me by Dr. Henry Armitage after hearing of my studies concerning the American Southwest prehistoric cultures and the Anasazi. There have been suggested links between the Indigenous Anasazi and the Mesopotamian Annunaki. I was stuck by drawings of symbols and petroglyphs that seem to repeat all over the world among which were spirals, labyrinths, swastikas, "bird man" petroglyphs and "horned" men.

There are hundreds of drawings, some small, almost too small, within the the book of all these images. On six pagesof this book, are seventy three different forms of the swastika from all around the world. The petroglyphs as well, were unsettlingly similar even though the cultures that made them were separated by hundreds to thousands of years and miles. How could they all be so similar if they weren't in contact with each other? Was there any truth to the myths and legends? Some of which claim that these underworld gods live forever.

Entry 04 April 1929

I have informed the Administration of my intentions of heading out west, now that my courses were finished. Dr. Armitage has politely offered to take any duties of mine that might arise in the six months that I plan on being away. I have packed all of my archaeological tools, spare clothing, camping gear and several boxes of rounds for my Winchester carbine and Smith and Wesson revolver, both being .45 long colt in caliber, in my bison skin rucksack, donned my long coat and my wide brimmed hat and I am heading to the aeroport to catch a ride with a Postal flyer in his 1928 Stearman C3B aeroplane! I have never flown before and I am exceedingly excited! I hope that I can sleep tonight, tomorrow is the beginning of my quest.

Entry 05 April 1929

It's 0500 in the morning when I step out of my door at number 66 College Street. I turn left and cross West Street down to Boundary Street, turn right and up to Aylesbury Street. I walk the short distance and turn onto the Aylesbury Pike. The field where the Plane will land is but a short walk up. The sun is starting to peak over the horizon as I reach the field. I take out a biscuit that my Landlady, Mrs Annie Phillips had made for me, and eat it. It's not long after finishing my breakfast that I hear the planes engine humming louder as it nears. I can see it approach and my excitement builds as it lands. The Pilot, one Howard Lovecraft, greets me cordially enough and helps me don the flight suit and parachute. He tells me to wrap a silk scarf around my neck to keep it from getting chafed. I fasten the leather helmet and don the goggles, and we climb into the plane. He starts the engine and we are soon flying into the aether.

2nd Entry 05 April 1929

At 1036 we land in West Virginia to refuel and eat. I speak to Howard about flying and I can certainly understand his love for it. He was a

Pilot in the Great War and was quite proficient. We took some food with us and he dropped off a bag of mail for the local Postal Service and picked up one heading West. We stopped again in Memphis Tennessee with the same routine. I purchased an extra wool blanket form a store called A. Schwabs, close to where we landed. We were soon on our way again.

Entry 06 April 1929

Encountered a strange storm while over Texas or Oklahoma Territory. Compass was useless. Landed plane and weathered the storm. Starting out again today and try and find a landmark or town to land for location purposes. Flew Westward and came to the town of Amarillo, and landed outside of the Tri-State fairgrounds. Howard was able to procure food, water and petrol for the plane and we set off again and landing several hours later in Santa Fe New Mexico. I said good bye to Howard, whom I have come to like. I told him to check around in six months and I would very much enjoy flying back to Massachusetts in his aeroplane. I found a Hotel and procured a room. I ordered room service as I was very tired and happy to be sleeping in a bed once more. This would be the last comfortable lodgings for six months. After an early dinner, I checked my maps and papers. There was a rental truck for me near by, that had been rented for me by Miskatonic University. I readied everything for tomorrow, as I was just that much more anxious to arrive at Chaco canyon.

Entry 07 April 1929

I awoke early washed, shaved and made ready to leave the Hotel. Today is my birthday, though I have never celebrated them. I certainly felt like celebrating today because I was so close to one of the destinations I had read and dreamed about going to. I had a large breakfast and ordered some hard boiled eggs and fresh bread to take with me. I signed the truck out at the Petrol Station and checked my supplies. I had ample petrol with six extra cans secured in the bed of the truck, along with some dried food and lots of extra water, though there was a river close by where I was going to camp. I consulted my compass and map and headed out of town over terrain that was rough. There were no roads leading to where I was going, just trails. It was slow, rough going, but I arrived and pitched my camp at Una Vida where the first set of petroglyphs that I was going to study was located. As it was getting dark, I readied my equipment for tomorrow. I started a fire and prepared a simple meal of canned beans and some toasted bread.

Entry 08 April 1929

I was awakened at around two this morning to sounds of howling winds and whistles. I am sure it was just the wind as it was blowing through the canyon. As it was still early April, it was still chilly at night and I unrolled my extra wool blanket and added it to the others on my cot. I lay there and tried to go back to sleep. The wind was playing tricks on my ears, I would swear that I heard voices whispering. The light filtering through the canyon was also playing against my senses as I seemed to see strange lights as if the sky were a different colour, and there were strange sounds coming up through the earth. As if deep voices were muttering or gibbering in an unintelligible language. It seemed to me as if the one word that I could understand was "CTHULHU". It seems familiar to me somehow, but cannot place the memory of it. I eventually fell back asleep.

Entry 2, 08 April 1929

I slept fitfully as the wind played frightful tricks upon my hearing, and the moonlight played havoc with the light. When I woke and stepped from my tent, I noticed that the wind had blown the truck doors open. The interior of the truck was covered in dust. I warmed the rest of the beans from last night and toasted more bread and ate a quick meal and started towards the cliff sides. There were all the petroglyphs. I had several references to consult, the most disconcerting one was of course the Necronomicon transcripts. There was a scholarly drawn image with notes next to each, and scrawled in a spidery script was written someone else's interpretation of each one. Spirals, arches and circles were abundant, as well as what are obviously people in costumes and animals, there is even a crude swastika here. Very prevalent though are strange beings and symbols that have no explanations, except those offered in the Necronomicon notes. There is one that is most interesting. It appears to be a circle with tentacles coming out of it. There is a note as to where to find the the petroglyph. I can't wait to see it for myself. I seem to be forgetting something, something that I need to check, but can't seem to remember. It will come to me eventually.

Entry 3, 08 April 1929

Noticed several Natives off in the distance, but they seemed to hurry off in a direction away from the ruins. I took many photos of petroglyphs today to match with drawings in my notes. I can't shake eerie feeling of being watched, not by Natives but by "something" else. Probably just the heat and Natives. Matched up several drawing to photographs after developing the film in a makeshift dark room. Some of them are identified in Whateley's notes as "Azothoth", "Yig", and "Yog-Sothoth". I still seem to have the need to identify something that lurks at the back of my mind.

Entry 09 April, 1929

Natives seem to shun this place. I see many at a distance but none come close. Maybe I will ride out to meet them sometime. Venturing farther up the canyon today to take more pictures and explore the ruins. Slept fitfully last night. Heard strange sounds last night, and felt the earth tremble. Maybe aftershocks of an earthquake somewhere. Winds at night are very cold and strong. Had to repair my makeshift darkroom this morning.

Entry 02, 09 April 1929

Have returned to camp as my watch seemed to stop at a certain place in the ruins. I felt strange at one point almost as if I had become weightless and felt as if I might "float" away at any moment, and the sky seemed to "darken", and thought that I heard flutes piping madly at a great distance, and chanting. I am probably suffering from some type of heat exhaustion. Although it doesn't seem that hot yet. I have been drinking plenty of water to stay hydrated. After I rest in the shade of my tent's awning, I will pack up and move to another spot. Not much natural shade as the canyon runs almost due East to West.

Entry 03, 09 April 1929

I have moved my camp to the center point of the several sights that have ruins. I met Robert Howard, a Rancher from the RH Ranch near by, only a five mile trek. He says that is no distance at all in this part of the country where the nearest town can be thirty to forty miles away. He returned later with rope and canvas as well as poles to expand my tent capacity and to help me build a more stable darkroom. He brought food and some "jerky" that will last longer than uncured meat. We had dinner together, then he left before sundown. I am really thankful to him. He says that he will return in a few days and check in on me. The sun has set now and I am tired from my exertions today, and so I am retiring.

Entry 01, 10 April 1929

I was awakened around three a.m. This morning to the sounds of drums and flutes as well as chanting. No winds so it was very obvious. Must be Natives near by. I laid there and listened for some time until I drifted back to sleep. I awoke just before dawn and seemed to see lights, like lanterns in several of the ruins round about me. They may be the lights of Natives searching the ruins, or possibly Raiders looting the sites under cover of Darkness. I will definitely keep my pistol on my hip and my rifle within reach from here on out. I wonder if the fact that it was a new moon last night had anything to do with the drumming ceremony.

Entry 02, 10 April 1929

While exploring the ruins, I could detect no passage of humans here for sometime, whomever was here last evening, they left no signs of their being here. No obvious signs of searching for relics. Took many pictures today and have developed them. I found very few pottery shards and even found an arrowhead. Took pictures of them in situ, and left them there. I wanted to return to the place where I had the strange feelings, but time seemed to pass quickly as I explored and took pictures today. I enjoyed it immensely. Eating a simple meal of beans and tortillas. There is only a slight breeze tonight, but very cool.

Entry 01, 17 April 1929

Been an exciting few days, so much so, that I have forgotten to write in my journal. I have taken many pictures and developed them. Made copies and drove into town to get more supplies, and to send notes and pictures back to Dr. Armitage at Miskatonic University. I have purchased more photographic solutions and paper, as well as more food. Taking some wood, nails and a hammer back to build a more substantial shelter. Some of the winds have been very strong. While in town I also purchased a few sheets of corrugated steel for a better roof. I have paid the owner of a truck to deliver the building materials to my site. Even picked up some extra Military surplus rations and a small generator, as well as a small Military tent stove. Radioed the University to send me more funds for supplies, as I had given them access to my banks funds.

Entry 02, 17 April, 1929

I am awakened at midnight, according to the radium on my watch hands. There are strange lights in the sky outside my tent, as well as something immense, miles high, lumbering around. The moon is waxing, so it's not moonlight. I can again hear the mad flutes and the drums. The voices from deep underground seem to be saying, "Ph'nglui mglw'nafh Cthulhu R'lyeh wgah'nagl fhtagn". The desert heat, cold and loneliness must be getting to me.

Entry 01, 19 April, 1929

Returned to my site to find that my tent has been cut up, My things have been gone through, but nothing seems to be missing. Thank goodness that most of my notes and pictures were in my Bison rucksack. Expecting the delivery of my stores and supplies any time now. I will take this time to sort through my notes and try to arrange them according to drawings with photographs. High atop the imposing butte at the entrance of the canyon is the most interesting of Chaco's sites. There, a set of spiral petroglyphs pecked into a cliff face behind three giant slabs of rock functions as a solar marker. Obviouls the narrow beam of light intersects either of the spirals at certain times of the year. Most likely on the Equinoxes and Solstices.

Entry 02, 19 April, 1929

A Mr. Derleth delivered my lumber and corrugated steel. He stayed long enough to help me erect the walls, roof and door of my shack. Said that he would return tomorrow with some planking to fill in the flooring and to make walls. I now have a sturdy building that is more stable and more wind resistant than my tent, and thanks to the generator, I have electric lights for working at night. I have built myself a nice little cabin here and I have worn myself out.

Entry 01, 20 April 1929

Mr. Derleth arrived around eight this morning as did Mr. Howard. Together we finished the cabin. Mr. Derleth even brought me some green paint for the wood. I shot a large Bighorn sheep and we shared a wonderful meal. Both of my new friends left before dark as the terrain is hazardous enough in daylight, even more so in the dark.

My cabin door has a fine lock with a bolt for extra locking protection. I have made a shelf for my rifle and ammo. I have not shaven since my arrival here and now have a full beard, it is my first, and I do not like it but do not want to waste resources on shaving. Though there is a small river near by, the water is not as fresh as I would like it to be.

Entry 02, 20 April 1929

I was awakened to what sounded like scratching on the sides of my cabin. The winds were bad last night and seemed to howl and whistle on for hours. The cabin is much more wind proof and warmer than my tent. The wood burning stove helps immensely with the cold. I am enclosed within a framework of wood and steel and feel much safer from what ever is outside. On a whim, I have painted certain protective emblems from the Necronomicon, on the inside walls of my cabin. Tomorrow, I will paint them on the outside of the walls. As there are no windows in my cabin, I cannot see what the lighting is like outside, though the rumblings from deep down are still prevalent, they are now more muffled.

Entry 01, 21 April 1929

I have painted the symbols on the outside at first light. I am going to gather wood for my stove in my cabin. There were strange wavy lines that seemed to radiate outward from my cabin in the sandy dust. I know that the wind can make unusual patterns in the sand, and I guess that they are the results of wind acting upon the surface of the corrugated steel. I will return to the ruins where I felt the strange sensation of floating. I have packed some lunch and water and will head to the large kivas under the cliff face.

Entry 02, 21 April 1929

Entered the same kiva today, and as I neared it's center I seemed to hear the whistling and chanting again. I seemed to get lighter with each step nearer the center. The sunlight seemed to dim again to the point where I could see stars. I seemed to recognise Ursa Major directly overhead, but couldn't be sure. I could see the petroglyphs glowing on the walls of the canyon around me, and I lost all sense of time and direction. At one point I seemed to feel as if I was falling with excessive speed and force. I woke outside the kiva, indeed I was outside of the ruins all together. An old Native named Shilowa Yachunne, was there standing above me and chanting in some ancient tongue. When he saw me open my eyes. He put a cool cloth upon my forehead and offered me some water. It was obviously from the river and tasted of mud, He said that he saw me "fall from the sky". If my watch can be believed, I spent only a couple of hours there, but it was now near nightfall more than nine hours later! He helped me to my cabin and marveled at the symbols. He knew what they were and he knew that I had the "Elder sign" around my neck, and warned me not to remove it from my person. He helped me into my cabin and helped me to bed. He then locked the door and started to make us both a dinner of canned chili, and I reset the time on my watch. We ate and he laid down in a corner farthest from the door, and was soon asleep.

Entry 03, 21 April 1929

It's actually the next morning around 0230 in the morning. I was awakened by Shilowa chanting and shaking a rattle. Outside I could hear the sounds of what seemed to be angry hisses and whispers in an ancient tongue. The winds howled and the cabin shook, but remained unaffected by the winds. We sat there for some time until the winds died down and at last I once again fell asleep.

Entry 01, 22 April 1929

We woke this morning just after sunrise. Shilowa tells me this is the first night of the "Yig" moon and is a very dangerous time to be here. Outside there is sand piled up around the cabin and strange marks in the sand. Long thin footprints with six toes upon each foot. I took several photographs. Shilowa says they are ant people. I asked if he could show me some of them in the petroglyphs and he reluctantly agreed. I ask him about the kiva where I floated into the sky and he became visibly frightened. He mentioned something about a spirit called Yot'-shawgtah and closed his eyes and chanted a quick prayer. Then he said that the servants of the Spirit were called shott'gahs and could take on any form, but usually had no real form and sent out tentacles with eyes and mouths that formed randomly. They were so hideous that the mind could not truly grasp the horrible reality it had witnessed and would snap, usually with the person running out into the desert alone where they were never found again.

Entry 02, 22 April 1929

Shilowa and I have returned from our expedition to the rock faces. I came into the cabin to develop the photographs that I had taken. When I came out, Shilowa had disappeared. I followed his tracks and they lead to the cliff face behind the large ruins. All around them were the thin, six toed prints as well. The tracks lead right up to the cliff face and seem to go into the rock, as the cliff meets the earth right in the middle of the footprints. I felt a cold chill run down my spine and I shuddered in spite of myself. I took several photographs for further study. Likely a hidden door. I heard voices coming out of the cliff face and I turned and ran back to the cabin as fast as I could. I got the green paint and walked to the kiva and out to the center, where I opened the can of paint. The contents fell up, out of the can and I felt the familiar weightless feeling. I looked up and saw a face. It was a weird face to be sure. It was broad at the top and narrow at the bottom, with large black eyes, no nose and a slit for a mouth. The head was elongated and had antennae above the eyes where a forehead should be. It's skin colour was a uniform gray, like that of a dolphin. I turned and went back to my cabin, shaken by the impossible. It looked like the "ant-man" drawings that I had seen. Once back at the cabin, I locked the door and waited, for what, I could not tell. I set about developing the photos, and made copies to send back to the University. I took out the book, the Necronomicon and fragments and read them.

Entry 03, 22 April 1929

I have learned a terrible secret today, but cannot fully fathom the mysteries that lie there in. Shilowa mentioned a spirit named Yot'-shawgtah, and after reading certain passages, I have to believe that he is mentioning the Elder God Yog Sothoth! He who is the Gate and key to the Gate! The round image on the petroglyphs with the tentacles radiating out of it, that's Yog Sothoth! The Native legends tell of the

First, Second and Third worlds being destroyed by spirits from other worlds, (dimensions) and each time the "Ant-Men" saved certain ones for repopulating the Earth afterwards. The "gates are in certain areas where the stars align and the kiva and cliff face are where they align! The winds howl and moan tonight. Voices rise upon the winds and from below the earth. I hold the Elder sign out and the winds no longer touch the walls of my cabin. There is a buzzing in my head. Voices! The voices are talking to me CTHULHU FTAGN! IÄ! IÄ! CTHULHU F'TAGN!

Entry 01, 23 April 1929

I awoke this morning from terrible dreams. Shilowa is gone. I am alone. The sun is up and there is a gentle breeze outside. I fix myself a simple meal of beans and jerky and eat. I look outside and see nothing unusual. I try to remember what I was so frightened of last night. I take my camera and tools and head towards the kiva, as there are a few more pictures that I want to take.

I head down to the kiva, leaving most of my belongings back at the cabin. I walk the now familiar trail and head down into the ruins and work my way into the Great Kiva. As I near the center the sun darkens and it gets cooler. I am floating and my head is humming. I awaken later on the ground of the Great Kiva. I am naked except for the Elder Sign. It is dark and a full moon is rising in the East, huge and round. The Gray Ant-Men seem angry that I am wearing the Elder Signs. I can hear them in my head shouting. They are causing me terrible pains, trying to force me to take it off. There are thousands of them around the top of the kiva and around the walls, inside with me. They are shouting, pleading and threatening me, trying to get me to remove the Elder Sign, but I can't, I know that it's protecting me. The sky is so very black and the stars are so terribly bright. They burn into my eyes like the fire of thousands of suns. As the moon reaches directly over head, it changes. It becomes a huge glowing mass of tentacles and eyes and mouths. It is obscene, and it fills me with loathing for it. It takes all my might but I finally reach out and grab the closest "ant-man" by the throat and squeeze. I am able to crush it's throat with ease, but it's last act is to snatch the Elder sign from around my throat and take it with him into the void that yawns beneath him, and then closes just as rapidly. I am pulled screaming into that protoplasmic terror that is Yog-Sothoth. Through that terrible gate, where the stars are black and the spaces between the stars are filled with an oily iridescence. The stars are alive in this dimension, I can hear their voices, feel their malevolence reach out and rend my soul! We pass them, some I know, Betelgeuse, VY Canis Majoris, and NML Cygni. But still through this vacuous opalescence, we speed to the star UY Scuti, with other stars spinning and whistling, it's not a star at all, but the blind god Azothoth. The face of it! The damnedable face of it!

On the 24th of April, one Robert Howard finds the cabin of his friend abandoned. He searches the ruins near by, but can find no remains of his friend Dyth Greffen-Feder. He drives into town to file a missing person report with the local Sheriff. A manhunt is carried out and the Chaco Canyon area is searched, and after two days it is called off.

The disappearance of the Professor will remain a mystery. All of the belongings found at the cabin are boxed up and shipped to one Dr. Armitage, Miskatonic University, Arkham Massachusetts. The corrugated steel is removed from the cabin and the wooden structure burned to ashes.

Three years later during an Archaeological dig by Students and Professors of Rittner College's Archaeology and Anthropology Department, a body appears in the sky and falls to earth near the great kiva at Chaco Canyon. The appearance of the body is preceded by an blast of artic cold air, so powerful that the students and Professors near by, have to turn away and huddle together for warmth. Some of the students said that they heard voices, others claim to have heard wild piping, and one young man, an Artist, fell to the ground in some sort of fit. A strange, inhuman voice spoke from his mouth, in a language that none could identify.

A layer of irredescent ice formed around the walls of the kiva, too cold to touch, and that took well over an hour to melt. It did not melt like most ice, but became a violet vapor that trailed upward to the middle of the kiva, before disappating altogether. One of the students was dispatched in one of the vehicles to drive back to the Ranch of Mr. Howard to call the Sheriff. Mr. Howard accompanied the student back to the site. The Professors and students were waiting outside the kive, which was still very cold, and covered in the eerie, violet ice that was far colder than it should be.

Mr. Howard went alone into the kiva, and there found the body of his friend, Dyth Greffen-Feder. He covered his body with a woolen blanket, until the Sheriff arrived. The body was frozen solid and was incredibly cold. Mr. Howard hands were burned by the cold when he tried to move the body.

When the Sheriff arrived, he and Mr. Howard, identify the body as one Dr. Dyth Greffen-Feder, Professor of Mediaeval Metaphysics at Miskatonic University in Arkham, Massachusetts. He has not aged a day, nor can they find a cause of death, other than the extreme cold. The ice on the walls of ythe kiva had disappated by the time that the Sheriff arrived, and the Government was contacted about the strange ice, and Chemist and other Scientist were dispatched with the utmost alacrity from Labs and Universities near to the site.

While no one spoke of seeing him fall from the sky, there is no obvious damage to his body. However the look of sheer terror upon his face is quiet disconcerting. The Professors body was sealed in an insulated container and shipped back to Miskatonic University, where it was studied by Scientist and Staff for two weeks, when Dr. Armitage insisted that the Professors last wishes be honored and his body cremated.

The Professors body had been kept in a room on the fifth floor of the Main Office building. While the room had no ventilation, it remained as cold as a freezer the entire time that Professor Greffen-Feder's body was present. When the Attendants from the Crematorium arrived to receive his body, they were given heavy insulated leather gloves, so that they could move the body of the Professor into the pine box.

After the box was sealed up, it began to creak with the intense cold inside, and was loaded into the lorry for transport to the Crematorium. The Attendants had to roll the windows down and let in the Summer air to keep themselves warm on the long ride to the Crematorium.

At the Crematorium, the frost covered casket was loaded onto the rollers, to be slid into the furnace and cremated. A few moments after the doors of the furnace closed on the casket, a scream was heard from inside the furnace, the Attendants and Mortician were horrified, then strange voices, in an unrecognzable language. An irredescent, oily putresence poured forth from the furnace chamber, before the doors burst open and the flames engulfed the chamber around the furnace.

The Crematorium was half a mile outside the city, upon a low rise and could be clearly seen from most of the city, and so could the bright purple mushroom cloud, when the Crematorium exploded. Most of the inhabitants of the city of Arkham saw it, and how it went straight up into what appeared to be a black hole in the sky. The blast was deafening and windows on the outskirts of town nearest to the Crematorium, were shattered. At the same time, all around the world, the dreams and minds of sensitive people and Artist were filled with visions and sounds and words in a language that they had never heard before. Many swore that they could hear noises from deep under the Earth.

The official report about the explosion, was that some natural gasses had seeped up from underneath the Crematorium and had filled it with volitile fumes, which then ignited and destroyed the crematorium. The massive hole that was left at the site, was explained as a natural cavern where the volitile gasses had accumulated before finally seeping upward into the furnace. This ended the Official reports, but it was noted by others who kept track of such phenomenon, and added to the mystery that surrounds that area of the country.

ABOUT THE AUTHOR

Michael WhiteBear Sims is a Chaplain, Magickian, Storyteller, Writer, Creator, Maker, Genius and Author. Having had many jobs and life experiences to draw from, he has entertained many people both young and old with his stories and the things he makes. After suffering a devastating and disabling broken back, he has recovered with the help of his wife Patti of 30 years, his son Gunther, Daughter Kelsey, Daughter in law Corin and his precious cats. He learned to make jewelry while recovering from his disability. He has served the Community in which he lives all his life. He has saved many lives, most recently in May of 2019, and is certified in CPR, AED, Search and Rescue. He has served five years in the Tennessee State Guard and was part of the rescue mission at Union University when it was struck by a tornado. He is a life long History buff and Historical Reenactor. He has reenacted all times periods from Roman to the Vietnam War. He was in a movie about the War of Northern Aggression. He is now an Artilleryman and serves on a cannon crew. He has served in Honor Guards and Funeral Services. He is a Chaplain in the Tennessee Correctional System. He is a Pipe Carrier for his Tribe and a Tsikamagi Tsalagi, (Chickamaugan Cherokee).
He is very proud of his First Nations Ancestry as well as his Scots-Irish-Viking side as well.

Thank You for buying my book. I hope that you enjoyed it.

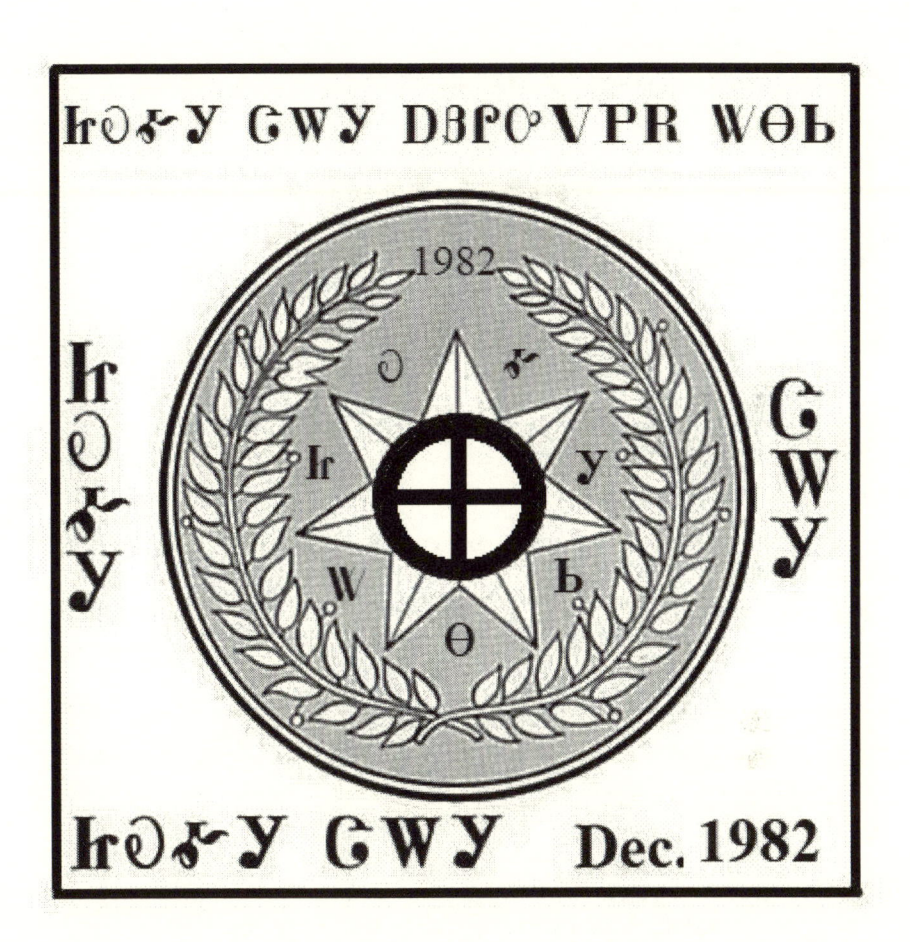

SGI !!!